G000045249

THE LONG WAY HOME

LAURA FARR

Copyright © 2022 by Laura Farr

All rights reserved.

No part of this book may be reproduced in any form or by any electronic or mechanical means, including information storage and retrieval systems, without written permission from the author, except for the use of brief quotations in a book review.

Editing by Karen Sanders at Karen Sanders Editing.

Proofread by Judy Zweifel at Judy's Proofreading

Cover by April Flowers Cover Design

The
long way
Home

PROLOGUE

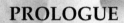

"*J*ust go, Zara!" I yell. "I'm surprised you've stayed this long. We both know you don't want to be here."

"Don't put all this on me," she screeches. My jaw clenches as the sound of her voice grates on my last nerve. "I never even wanted a fucking baby." My hands ball into fists at my sides, and I bite down on the inside of my mouth, anger coursing through me.

"Get out." My voice is low, and I can't look at her. My heart is breaking for the innocent little boy, asleep upstairs in his cot. He deserves so much more than the woman in front of me. I finally lift my eyes and watch as she picks up the bags she's already packed.

"I'm sorry it had to end like this." She looks at me, and I can't bring myself to answer her. She's not sorry. Jacob is only eighteen months old, but she checked out of our relationship and his life a long time ago. When I don't respond, she turns on her heel and walks out, the door slamming behind her. Despite knowing this moment has been coming for a while, I can't help but feel like a failure. Why weren't Jacob and I enough for her? She didn't even kiss him goodbye.

Zara and I had met almost three years ago in a bar. I'd been with the guys from work, and she was with her girlfriends. She was the life and soul of the bar, and I was instantly attracted to her. She was beautiful, with long blonde hair, stunning emerald green eyes, and a body I couldn't keep my hands off. She came home with me that night and we saw each other on and off for the next few weeks. It was nothing serious. I liked her, but she didn't seem the settling-down type. A couple of weeks later, she turned up on my doorstep, scared and pregnant. She wanted a termination, but after talking for hours, we decided to make a proper go of our relationship. I was as terrified as she was, but I thought we could go the distance. She moved into my place, and for a while, things were good. She stopped going out, and despite arguing occasionally, the nine months she was pregnant, our relationship was okay. It wasn't perfect, but what relation-ship is?

About six months after Jacob was born, everything changed. It was like a switch had been flipped, and she reverted to the Zara I knew when we first met. She was out every night drink-ing, sometimes not even bothering to come home. I tried to talk to her, tried to make her see what she had at home, but she wasn't interested. She'd struggled to adapt to motherhood, and

I knew she missed going out with her friends. I'd been the one who encouraged her to go out with them. Unfortunately, it turned into her being out with her friends more than she was home with us. I couldn't trust her to look after Jacob, and she spent most of her time in bed. Instead, I'd arranged childcare, dropping him off on my way into work. More often than not, when I'd arrive home with him in the evening, she'd be out. We rarely saw her.

Now she's gone. I'd known it was coming, and if I'm honest, I thought it would have happened sooner. I'd considered leaving more than once, but I naively thought staying together was better for Jacob. How wrong I was.

I'm not in love with Zara. I think I was at the beginning, but any feelings I had for her had slowly ebbed away as I watched her ignore our son time and time again. I won't mourn the loss of her, only the loss of what could have been. I've pretty much been a single dad to Jacob for the last nine months. I'm not afraid I can't look after him, just afraid of not being enough. What I do know is he doesn't need a mother like Zara in his life. He's the most amazing little boy, and I will never understand why she couldn't see that.

Jacob is the most important person in my life, and he will always know how much I love him. We don't need Zara.

CHAPTER 1

Jack
Six months later

"*M*um, I'm fine. I promise." I cradle the phone between my ear and my shoulder as I pick Jacob's toys up off the sitting room floor. Crossing the room, I toss them into his toy box.

"You sound exhausted. Why don't you let me and your dad take Jacob this weekend? You can have a break."

"I'm good, Mum. I like him with me." She sighs down the phone and I know she's worried about me. "Why don't you and Dad come over tomorrow? Maybe you could keep him occupied for an hour while I get on top of the laundry?"

"That's not exactly what I had in mind, Jack. Surely the laundry can wait?"

"I'm a single dad with a two-year-old," I tell her with a chuckle. "There's always laundry to do."

"I guess so," she replies. "We'll see you Saturday, then. We can take him to the petting zoo. Give Jacob a kiss from his nanny."

"Will do. Say hi to Dad for me." Ending the call, I throw my phone on the sofa and pick up the rest of the toys that are strewn across the floor. It's Friday, and my day off. Since Zara left, work has been amazing with letting me adjust my hours. I work out of the office Monday to Thursday, and I normally manage a couple of hours from home on a Friday when Jacob naps. So far, it works great. My parents live a little far away to help out with Jacob in the week. Instead, he's in nursery. It's hard work, but I love being Jacob's daddy. We haven't heard from Zara since she walked out six months ago, and that's fine with me. I like it being the two of us.

After tidying the sitting room, I creep upstairs and check in on Jacob. I put him down half an hour ago, but he was awake when I came downstairs and I want to check he's fallen asleep. Peeking around his door, I smile as I see him fast asleep, cuddled up to his favorite blue rabbit teddy. He's kicked his blankets off, so I cross the room and cover him up, kissing his head softly. He smells of baby powder and no-tears shampoo following his bath earlier, and I breathe in his smell, my heart swelling with love for him. How Zara can't want him, I'll never understand.

Half an hour later, I'm sitting on the sofa, a bottle of Bud in my hand. Liverpool and Arsenal are playing on the TV, but I'm too tired to concentrate on watching it. I drop my head back on the sofa and close my eyes. I've just nodded off when my phone rings. Groaning, I sit up and reach for it. Seeing Libby's name flashing across the screen, I smile.

"Hey, little sister. How are you?" I say, answering her call.

"I'm great thanks, Jack. How are you? How's that gorgeous nephew of mine?"

"He's good, Lib. Really good. How are you feeling? Not long left now?" Libby is almost eight months pregnant with her first child, and I couldn't be happier for her and her husband, Mason.

"Tired, but Mason's taking good care of me. You haven't sent me any pictures of Jacob in ages. I miss him."

"Lib, I sent you some last week," I tell her, chuckling.

"That was ages ago. He's changing so much. I don't want to miss anything."

"I'll take some and send you them in the morning. Okay?"

"Okay. Thanks." She pauses, and the line goes quiet. "So, I spoke to Mum." I roll my eyes and groan inwardly. "She's worried about you."

"I'm fine."

"Are you? Are you really?" I sigh heavily. "Jack? Talk to me."

"I'm just tired, Lib. Working and looking after Jacob is tough. I've just hit a bad patch. We'll be okay."

"God, I hate Zara. I can't believe she left you guys. Have you heard from her?"

"No, and I don't want to. We're good, just the two of us."

"Why don't you come out to the ranch? It's been ages since I saw you. I miss you."

"I miss you too, but I can't just fly halfway across the world to come see you. I have a job, bills to pay."

"You can take a holiday. Surely you have some leave? I know everyone would love to see you." I can hear the pleading in her voice, but there's no way I can make it happen. I wish I could. A break is exactly what I need right now, and I know Jacob would love it.

"I'd love to see everyone too, but I can't. I'm sorry, Lib. Maybe early next year."

"Okay." She sounds disappointed, and I feel bad, but I know there's no way I can make it happen. We chat for a while and she fills me in on life on the ranch, and what's been happening with everyone. Libby went to visit family on their ranch in Texas four years ago. Her best friend had just died, and she was lost. She went there to escape and ended up falling in love. She's been there ever since and married Mason just before I met Zara. I've never seen her happier, and while I miss her, she's where she belongs. I've visited her a couple of times, and she came home just after Jacob was born, but I wish I could see her more often. We talk for a few more minutes, and I promise again to send her some pictures of Jacob. We Face-Time often, and he loves his aunt Libby.

Ending the call, I decide to call it a night. Jacob had a rough night the night before with some back teeth coming through, and neither of us got much sleep. Hopefully tonight will be better and I can catch up a little. I turn off the TV, lock up, and head upstairs. Checking on Jacob, I'm relieved to see he's still fast asleep. I brush a kiss on his chubby cheek, then close his bedroom door behind me and head into the bathroom. After a quick shower, I crawl, exhausted, into bed.

Despite being tired, I'm still awake ten minutes later. My mind is full of the person who always seems to invade my thoughts when I lie in bed alone. Mia, Libby's best friend. Mia and Lib had been inseparable as kids, and Mia was always at our house. I'm two years older than Libby, and for a while, my sister and her friend were just annoying little girls. It wasn't until I was about sixteen or seventeen that my feelings toward Mia changed. She'd come over one day looking for Libby, who'd gone out. I ended up inviting her in, and we'd watched a film. Nothing happened, but I'd loved spending time with her, and it made me realize I'd liked her for quite a while. She was only fifteen, so I never said anything, figuring I'd have plenty of time to tell her how I felt when she got a little older.

I remember my dad calling me to say Libby and Mia had been involved in an accident. When he'd told me Mia hadn't made it, it felt like someone had ripped my heart out. It was only then I'd realized I'd been in love with her. It was too late though, and I never got the chance to tell her. I thought meeting Zara might have been a second chance at happiness, especially when I'd found out she was pregnant. Turns out I'd been wrong about that too.

I'm woken the next morning by Jacob's chattering filling the room through the baby monitor. Although it's early, there is no better way to be woken.

"Daddy, Daddy, Daddy," he shouts, and I chuckle as I sit up and swing my legs to the side of the bed.

"On the way, buddy," I shout as I make my way to his bedroom. Pushing the door open, I see him standing up in the cot, his face lit up in a smile as he sees me.

"Daddy!" he cries, holding his hands up in the air for me to pick him up. "Up, up, up!"

9

Laughing, I cross the room and scoop him up, pressing a kiss to his cheek.

"Morning, little man. Did you sleep well?" He nods, his small fingers finding my ears. Even when he was tiny, his little fingers would reach up and hold on to my ears. It's something he's always done, and something I know I'll miss when he's too big for me to pick him up.

"Let's get you cleaned up and fed." Placing him on the changing table, I make quick work of changing his nappy. I decide to leave him in his sleepsuit and get him dressed after breakfast. Feeding time is always messy and I've enough laundry to do.

I carry him downstairs and place him in his high chair while I flick on the coffee machine. "Do you want juice, Jacob?" I ask as I open the fridge.

"Yes!" he shouts, banging his hands on the tray of the high chair. Laughing, I fill his juice cup and pass it to him. "Tank you, Daddy," he says as he takes the cup from me and begins to gulp down the juice. I smile at his mispronunciation of thank you. His speech is really coming on, and I try to talk to him as much as I can.

"Nanny and Pops are coming over today," I tell him as I make his porridge. "You can play trucks with Pops."

"Pops, play trucks," he cries as he puts his juice down and claps his hands. To say he loves cars and trucks is an understatement. Nearly every one of his toys has wheels, and he plays for hours, lining them up and racing them along the wooden floor of the sitting room. I love watching him play. Even at two, his imagination is amazing.

After finishing up with breakfast, I take Jacob back upstairs and get him dressed. Leaving him to play in his bedroom, I wash up before getting dressed myself. We've got an hour before my parents arrive and the weather's good, so we head to the park on his three-wheel bike. He can't pedal just yet, so I use the parent handle to push him along. He squeals with excitement when he sees the swings.

"Swings, Daddy. Push me."

"Come on, then," I tell him, lifting him off his bike and onto the swing. "Hold on tight." I push him gently, watching his little legs dangling from the seat.

"Higher, Daddy," he cries. Smiling, I push him a little higher before coming around to the front of the swing so I can see his face. Grabbing my phone from my pocket, I take a few pictures and send them to Libby. After a few more minutes on the swing, he wants to go on the slide. I lift him from the seat and follow him to the small climbing frame. Standing behind him, I watch as he climbs the ladder, crossing the walkway to the slide.

"Catch, Daddy." I stand at the end of the slide and crouch down, my arms open wide.

"One, two, three, go!" I shout. His face is flushed with excitement, and he belly laughs as he shoots down the slide into my waiting arms. "Again," he cries, running back around to the steps. We do this another handful of times before going on the roundabout and back on the swings again.

"Time to head back now, Jacob. Nanny and Pops will be coming soon."

"No, stay!" he shouts, stamping his little feet on the ground.

"Jacob," I warn, kneeling down in front of him. "We've had fun at the park, but now it's time to go home. Okay?" Since he turned two a couple of months ago, he's been testing the boundaries and voicing his opinion more. This is normally followed by a tantrum when he doesn't get his own way. I'm hopeful I've avoided one today as he nods, his bottom lip wobbling. Pulling him into my arms, I give him a cuddle, not wanting to see him cry. "We'll come back another day," I promise. I tickle his side, and he giggles. I think I've averted a meltdown.

It's about a ten-minute walk back home, and when we get there, my parents are waiting on the driveway. After a round of hellos, we go inside, Jacob pulling my dad into the sitting room to play with his trucks. My mum follows me into the kitchen and leans against the counter as I turn on the coffee machine. The gurgling of the machine fills the silence, and I busy myself, tidying up the breakfast dishes. I know she's worried about me, and after last night's phone call, she likely has more to say.

"Did Libby call last night?" she asks flippantly. Turning from loading the dishwasher, I raise my eyebrows.

"Yes. But I'm guessing you already know that?"

Her face flushes pink and she shrugs. "I'm concerned about you. I'm your mum. You might be twenty-five, but I still worry about you."

I put the last dish into the dishwasher, then turn and pull her into a hug. "I'm okay, Mum. Sure, I'm tired and fall asleep most nights before nine, but I love every minute of being Jacob's dad."

She pulls out of the hug and her hand cups my face. "And you are the most amazing dad to that little boy. I am so proud of you." She smiles at me and I smile back. "He's lucky to have you. I just think you need a break."

"You're giving me a break this morning," I tell her with a wink.

"I mean a proper break, Jack. One that's longer than an hour, and where you aren't doing laundry."

"Lib asked me to go to the ranch." I've no idea why I've shared that with her, it's not like I can go. I'm guessing if she knows Lib called me though, she probably knows she asked me to go.

"What did you tell her?" I turn away from her and pour three cups of coffee. Turning to hand one to her, I shrug.

"I told her no. Don't get me wrong, I want to go. Jacob would love it. I just can't take time off right now."

"If it's about the money—"

"It's not about the money," I tell her, cutting her off. "I'm an accountant, Mum. I make good money and good money choices. I just need more time to plan with work for time off. I told Lib maybe early next year, once the baby's born."

"If you're sure, honey. Your dad and I will help out whenever you want. If you want a night out with the guys, we'll have Jacob overnight anytime."

"I know, Mum, and thanks. I appreciate it." I haven't seen the guys in a while. Maybe a night out will do me good. "I'll message them, see when's good." She smiles, and I think my agreeing to let them have Jacob while I go out has somewhat pacified her for now.

"I'll go and see what your dad and Jacob are up to." She goes up on her tiptoes and kisses me on the cheek. "Take your time with the laundry."

Two hours later and the last of the laundry is in the machine, I've also had time to clean the bathroom and vacuum upstairs, which is an added bonus. I can still hear my parents in the sitting room with Jacob, laughter and squeals of delight filling the air.

"How about some lunch, my treat?" I ask as I walk into the sitting room. I can't help but smile as I look around. Almost every one of Jacob's toys is out, and he's currently driving a digger over my dad, who's lying in the middle of the floor. Clearly playing with the trucks won out over the petting zoo.

"Daddy!" Jacob cries as he sees me come in. "Look, digger!" He holds it in the air. My dad takes that as his cue to get up, moving to sit next to my mum on the sofa.

"Hey, buddy. It looks like you're having great fun with Pops." He nods and walks over to me, holding his hands up. Scooping him up I kiss his cheek. "You hungry?" He nods again and snuggles into my neck. "Let's go eat."

After lunch at the local pub, my parents say their goodbyes, my mum promising to call in the week. When we get home, I put Jacob down for a nap and tidy up the sitting room before finishing off the laundry. The chores seem never-ending, but I do manage thirty minutes or so to myself before Jacob wakes, which is a novelty.

The rest of the weekend flies by, and as I climb into bed on Sunday night, I groan as I think of my week ahead. Despite Jacob waking early every morning, it always seems to be a mad rush to get him dressed, fed, and off to nursery. I have to be at work for 8:30 a.m., and I need to drop Jacob off by 7:45 a.m., or else I'll be late. Mornings are chaotic, but I have somewhat of a routine to follow. I can only hope everything goes to plan and Jacob doesn't decide to fill his nappy just as we're about to leave the house.

CHAPTER 2

Jack

 breathe a sigh of relief as I make it to work just before 8:30 a.m. Despite Jacob throwing his breakfast all over the kitchen this morning, I'd managed to leave on time and get him to nursery. As I step off the lift, I see my assistant, Liz, is already at her desk, and I give her a small wave as I push open the door to my office. Liz follows me in a few seconds later, a coffee in her hand.

"Good morning, Mr. Davis. How was your weekend?"

I smile as I take the coffee from her outstretched hand. Despite Liz working as my assistant for almost a year, she insists on calling me Mr. Davis, even though I've told her numerous times to call me Jack.

"Thank you, Liz. My weekend was good. How about

yours?"

"Busy. I had John clearing the attic. He's gone off to work for a rest." Liz and her husband are downsizing and have spent the past few weeks packing and getting rid of things they no longer need.

"Well, if you're as organized at home as you are here, then I'm sure you'll have things sorted in no time."

She chuckles before turning and heading for the door. "Oh, I almost forgot. Mr. Copeland called a meeting this morning. Nine a.m. in the conference room."

"Mr. Copeland?" I ask in surprise. She nods before going back to her desk. Mr. Copeland is the owner of the company and very rarely calls or even attends meetings. I can't help but wonder what the meeting is about.

After finishing university with a degree in finance, I'd taken a year out and traveled around the USA, taking a job with an accounting company in Liverpool when I'd returned. It's a fairly small company, but we have some pretty big clients. I've done okay for myself, climbing the ladder from within. It isn't my dream job. At twenty-five, I still haven't figured out what is, but it's stable and paid well. Something I need as a single father.

I sort through a few emails whilst I wait for the 9 a.m. meeting. At five to nine, I make my way through the open-plan desks to the conference room. There are ten accountants at the company, and as I take a seat around the table, I see almost all of them are here.

"Any idea what's going on?" my colleague Alan asks. I shake my head.

"No idea. Maybe we're getting a raise."

"Hmphhh. Don't count on it," Jessica, another of my

colleagues mutters from the side of me. I turn to ask her what she means but think better of it as Mr. Copeland enters the room, a woman in a suit accompanying him.

"Thank you all for being here today. I'm sorry for the short notice." He pulls out a chair and sits down. His shoulders are tight, and his face is almost gray. An uneasy feeling settles in the pit of my stomach, and I can't help thinking this isn't going to be a meeting about a pay rise. He fills a glass of water from the pitcher on the table and swallows down a mouthful. My eyes flick to the woman he came in with, who is now standing off to the side, her eyes on some papers in her hands.

"There's no easy way to say this, so I'll just say it. The company is in trouble. I'm looking for at least four of you to consider voluntary redundancy. If that doesn't happen, we're looking at compulsory redundancies." A gasp goes up around the room, and I sit back heavily in my chair. Four redundancies. That's almost half of the staff.

"I know this will come as a huge shock to all of you, and I haven't come to this decision lightly. There really is no other option. For anyone interested in the voluntary redundancy, there will be an enhanced package available. My PA is emailing out the details to you all now. Take some time to think about it. My door is always open." He stands and pushes his chair under the large table. "Karen from HR is here to answer any questions you may have." He nods across the room to Karen and then leaves.

"Well, shit! I wasn't expecting that," Alan says from beside me. "I'm not volunteering." My gut reaction is to agree with him, but images of the ranch in Texas flood my mind, along with Libby's invitation to go. I can't take redundancy though. I need a stable job. "Guess I'll just wait and see if I'm forced into it. I can't imagine Copeland's going to get many that want to volunteer," Alan adds as he stands up and heads out of the conference room. I watch his retreating back and frown.

He's right, I could end up without a job anyway if the redundancies end up being compulsory. Maybe it would be better to take the enhanced package now rather than wait and walk away with less. I need to check what they're offering.

Back in my office, the email from Copeland's PA has arrived. What they're offering seems more than fair, and I'm seriously considering volunteering. I could spend a couple of months on the ranch, be there when Libby has the baby. I'm only renting the house Jacob and I live in, and I only need to give a month's notice on it. I've always been careful with my money, and I've got some savings. Maybe this could work. The last six months have been hard. A change of scenery could be just what Jacob and I need. For the first time in months, excitement bubbles in my stomach at the thought of doing something different. I'm the first to admit I'm stuck in a bit of a rut.

My fingers fly over the keyboard of my laptop as I email Mr. Copeland, accepting the offer of redundancy. With the package they're offering and the money I have saved, I'll be okay financially for a while.

I still can't believe I'm really doing this, and I pause as my finger hovers over the send button. I was always impulsive before Jacob came along; I could be when there was only me to worry about. Now, every decision I make centers around him and how it will affect our lives. As I press the send button, my gut tells me I've made the right choice. I've barely had time to process my decision when a knock sounds on my door.

"Come in," I call out, my eyes fixed on the door. I'm surprised to see Mr. Copeland when it opens. "Mr. Copeland, come in." Standing up, I wait as he closes the door behind him.

"Jack, I've just had your email." He pauses and I gesture to the chair on the other side of my desk.

"Please, take a seat."

He nods and pulls out the chair. "Got to say, son, I was a little surprised. I'm not sure I want to lose you."

I'm taken aback at his comment. I wasn't aware he thought that much of me. Don't get me wrong, I'm good at my job, but I don't think I'm any better than anyone else here.

"I thought you needed to lose four accountants?"

"I do, but I was hoping to keep my best one. Do you want to leave?"

"Well, I wasn't planning on leaving when I got up this morning," I say with a chuckle. "But if I'm honest, I think it was the push I needed."

I don't know Mr. Copeland that well, but he is aware of my situation with Jacob. He was the one who signed off my change of hours when Zara left. "Things have been hard since my relationship broke down. I think Jacob and I could both do with a change of scenery."

He nods. "I can understand that. What are your plans?"

"My aunt and uncle have a ranch in Texas. My sister lives there with her husband. I haven't seen her since Jacob was born. With the redundancy package you're offering, visiting her is something I can do without having to worry about money. I'll find something else when I get back. I might even look for something closer to my parents."

"It seems like you have it all worked out. I'll be sorry to see you go. You're good at what you do though, Jack. You won't have any problem finding something when you're back." He stands up and holds out his hand.

"Thank you, sir," I say as I stand and shake his outstretched hand. It seems I do have everything worked out, in my head at least.

"You know the redundancy is effective immediately?" he asks as he goes to open my office door.

"I do. I read the email." Coming around my desk, I gesture through the glass of my office to where Liz is sitting. "What happens to my assistant? I don't want my leaving to put her out of a job."

"We still need admin. Her job is safe." I breathe a sigh of relief as I watch him leave. Turning back to my desk, I power off my laptop and pack up the few belongings I have, including a framed photograph of Jacob that sits on my desk. I say a quick round of goodbyes. I'm not one for big emotional scenes. Most people are shocked I'm leaving, and I can't say I blame them. I'm a little shocked myself. I promise to keep in touch with a few of my close colleagues, knowing I might need the contacts when I get back from Texas.

As I drive home, I glance at the time on the dashboard of my car. I've been in work for less than two hours. Despite having no idea I'd be in this position when I woke up this morning, I can't help but feel excited for the adventure Jacob and I are about to embark on. I just need to break the news to my parents. I might even encourage them to come out to the ranch too. We can have the whole Davis family together for a bit. Libby is going to freak when I tell her. I can't wait.

CHAPTER 3

Jack

Ten days later and I close the door behind me to the house I've lived in for the past three years. Notice has been given to my landlord, and any furniture that didn't come with the rental has been put into storage. Our bags are packed and the flight to Texas leaves in a few hours. Explaining my plans to my parents was harder than I thought. While they'd encouraged me to visit Libby for a holiday, knowing I was going there with an open-ended ticket was a different story. Despite them being happy Libby had settled with Mason in Marble Falls, especially after her breakdown when Mia died, I know they miss her. Now I'm taking their only grandson away from them. It isn't forever though, and I assured them of that.

My parents insisted on driving us to the airport, even

though the flight's in the middle of the night. I'm a little apprehensive about flying with a toddler, especially on my own. I chose a night flight thinking Jacob will sleep for most of it. I hope I'm right. He's excited when we pull up at the airport, and my dad parks the car so they can come into the terminal with us. Once I've checked in, the goodbyes I've been dreading have to happen. My dad's holding Jacob, so I pull my mum in for a hug. She holds on to me tightly, and I know she doesn't want to let go. When she does pull back, there are tears in her eyes.

"It's not forever, Mum. We'll be back." She nods and gives me a sad smile. Turning to Jacob, she takes him in her arms.

"I'm going to miss you and your daddy. Will you look after him for me?" she asks. Jacob nods and yawns. We kept him awake in the car, wanting him to be ready to sleep when we boarded, so he's tired.

My dad pulls me into a one-armed hug and claps me on the back. "Take care, son, and have fun."

"Thanks, Dad. Give Nanny a kiss, Jacob."

He puckers his lips and kisses my mum on her cheek. She holds him against her until he begins to squirm and she passes him to me. My dad ruffles his hair before kissing him on the cheek.

"Be good for Daddy, Jacob," he says, tickling his side. "We'll see you really soon, okay?" Jacob drops his head on my shoulder and nods. After I'd told them I was going to be spending time at the ranch, they'd decided to come over for three weeks, just before Libby is due to have the baby. It's still a few weeks away, but it's something for them to look forward to. After another round of hugs, I leave my parents and head through security. My dad has his arm around my mum, and I can tell she's crying. I'm sure she's thinking the last time one of her children went to stay at the ranch, they decided not to come back. That isn't going to happen for Jacob and me. This is just a break away.

An hour later and our flight is called. Jacob has loved watching the planes take off out of the departure lounge window, and any sign of him being tired is long gone. I hope once we're on board and the excitement has worn off, he'll fall asleep. I send a quick message to Mason, telling him I'm about to board. Although I'd been excited for Libby to know we were coming, the more I thought about it, the more I wanted to surprise her. Mason and the rest of the family are keeping it a secret from Lib, and Mason is meeting us at the airport in Austin. I can't wait to see her face when we turn up at the ranch.

Despite my apprehension at flying alone with Jacob, it had been fine. He hadn't fallen straight to sleep, instead waiting until after our in-flight meal had been served. Fortunately, the seat next to us had been empty and I'd been able to lay him across the two seats. He'd slept until the seat belt sign for landing had come on and I'd had to move him. I'd also managed a few hours and was feeling good when we landed.

Once we have our luggage, I place Jacob on the trolley that carries the suitcases and call Mason.

"Hey, Jack," he says as he answers the call.

"Hi, Mason. We've landed and have our luggage. We're just coming through now."

"I'm waiting for you both in arrivals."

"Great, see you in a few." I end the call and slip the phone in my pocket.

"Let's go and find Uncle Mason," I say to Jacob, tickling his sides. He giggles and pushes my hand away. Walking into arrivals, I spot Mason straight away, raising my hand in a wave. He tips his hat and heads over to us.

"Great to see you, Jack," Mason says, pulling me into a one-armed hug.

"You too. Thanks for coming and meeting us."

"Hi, little man," he says to Jacob. "You've gotten so big." Jacob looks at Mason, then up to me. He looks unsure, so I pick him up.

"This is Uncle Mason, Jacob." We FaceTime with Libby all the time, but Mason isn't always there. He might not recognize him.

"Do you want to try my hat on?"

Jacob looks again at me, and I nod in encouragement. Mason takes off his hat and places it gently on Jacob's head. "Wow, you look like a real cowboy," Mason says, smiling at him. Jacob giggles and reaches his hand up to touch the hat.

"Shall we go and see Aunt Libby?" I ask him.

"Yes!" he cries, bouncing in my arms.

"Come on, then, buddy," I say with a chuckle.

Mason takes the trolley, and we follow him out of the arrivals hall. Even though it's early morning, it's already warm, and the July sun hits me as we walk outside. I look up at the sky, seeing there isn't a cloud in sight.

"I'd forgotten how hot summers are here," I say to Mason as we walk across the road to where his truck is parked.

"A bit different to home, then?"

"Yeah, just a bit. We've had rubbish weather so far this year."

"Well, you won't be short on sun here, that's for sure."

As we reach where he's parked, I put Jacob back in the trolley as I fix the car seat we brought with us into the back of the truck. Mason puts our luggage into the flatbed section of the truck as I strap Jacob into his seat. Once we're all in the car, I turn to Mason.

"Is Libby still in the dark about us coming?"

"Yep. She has no idea. She was leaving to meet Savannah in the stables when I left. She thinks I've come out for a part for one of the ranch trucks."

"I can't wait to see her face when she sees Jacob. I know how much she misses him."

"She misses you both. She's going to freak!"

I laugh as he pulls out of the parking space and away from the airport.

It's about an hour's drive to my aunt and uncle's place, and Mason fills me in on how everyone's doing. My cousins, Savannah and Brody, both live on the ranch with their partners, Josh and Quinn. Savannah and Josh have the most adorable little girl called Hope, and I'm hoping Jacob and Hope become firm friends while we're here. When I spoke to Aunt Claire earlier in the week, she'd invited us to stay in the ranch house with them. Since Savannah and Brody moved out, there's plenty of room, and I think she misses having a full house.

"We're almost there. I'm just going to pull over and message Sav, let her know to keep Libby away from the driveway." Mason pulls to the side of the road and types out a message on his phone before pulling back on to the road. A few minutes later and we're heading up the oak-lined driveway that leads to the ranch house. Suddenly, the driveway opens up and the house comes into view. It's an impressive sight and I'd forgotten just how beautiful this place is. The large wraparound porch has been painted white since I was last here, and the steps up to the front door have colorful flowerpots on them. The porch swing still sits to the left of the door, and as I climb out of the truck, the door opens, and Aunt Claire comes flying down the steps.

"You're here!" she cries, throwing her arms around my neck and hugging me tightly. "Where's that beautiful little boy of yours?" she asks, stepping out of the embrace.

"Great to see you, Aunt Claire. Thanks for having us to stay." She waves her hand and shakes her head.

"No need to thank me. We love having you here." I chuckle as she tries to look through the tinted windows to get a glimpse of Jacob. "He is in there, isn't he?" she asks, peering through the glass.

"He is," I assure her. "Let me get him." Opening the door, I unfasten his straps and lift him from the car. His face nuzzles into my neck, and I know he's feeling shy. "Jacob, this is Aunt Claire. Do you want to say hi?" He shakes his head, his face still buried in my neck.

"When your daddy was little, he used to love playing with cars. Do you like cars, Jacob?" she asks, the palm of her hand coming to rest on his back. He's still for a few minutes before nodding his head and slowly looking round at her. His eyes drop to her open hand where a toy pickup truck sits. "This is for you." His eyes widen before he looks to me for reassurance.

"Go ahead, Jacob. Take it," I tell him, smiling encouragingly. His little fingers clasp around the truck as he takes it from her hand. "What do you say?"

"Tank you."

She smiles and ruffles his hair. "You're very welcome. Hope is going to love playing with you. We're a little light on children around the ranch."

"Not for long though, with Lib due soon," I say, putting Jacob down so he can drive his car on the ground. "Talking of Lib, where is she?"

"She's in the stables with Aria, the horse trainer. Savannah's standing guard outside. It's been killing me to keep your visit a secret. Why don't you go and find her?" She gestures with her head to the stables, which stand a little distance from the house.

"I'll come with you," Mason says from behind me. "In case you send her into early labor." He chuckles when a look of horror crosses my face. "I'm joking, Jack. I just want to see her face." He slaps me on the back before scooping Jacob up and guiding me toward the stables. Despite Jacob only having met Mason an hour ago, he's happy for him to carry him. Mason told him he was a cowboy during the journey from the airport, and now he thinks he's Woody from *Toy Story*.

As we reach the stables, I see Savannah bouncing up and down outside the doors. "I can't believe you're really here," she whisper-shouts as we get nearer. She throws her arms around my neck as I reach her, and I kiss her on the cheek.

"Great to see you, Sav. How's Josh and Hope?"

"They're great. I actually need to run and pick Hope up from her friend's house. She had a sleepover last night. I really wish I could stay and see Lib's face when she sees you. She's inside with Aria." She turns to Mason, who's holding Jacob, and squeals. "Oh my God, is this Jacob? I can't believe how big he's gotten. Hi." Jacob buries his head in Mason's shoulder, and I let out a chuckle.

"He's a little shy."

"Wait 'til he meets Hope. She'll bring him round." She ruffles his hair before going up on her tiptoes and kissing my cheek. "I've really got to run. I'll catch up with you later though. Have fun." With a wave, she rushes off toward the ranch house.

I push on the stable door, and it opens silently. I can see Libby at the other end of the building, tending to one of the horses. She hasn't seen us yet, and I grin at Jacob before taking him from Mason. We're almost halfway toward her when she looks up and sees us. The brush she's holding falls to the floor as her hand covers her mouth.

"Oh my God! What are you doing here?"

I place Jacob on the ground, and he runs to her, throwing his arms around her legs. She scoops him up and showers kisses all over his face.

"Be careful, Lib. He's heavy." She ignores me and continues to kiss him.

"I can't believe you're here. How are you here?" She lowers Jacob to the ground and bursts into tears. I walk toward her and pull her into a hug as she cries.

"Why are you crying?" I ask, stroking her hair.

"They're happy tears, I promise."

"Trust me, a commercial for cereal can make her cry at the moment," Mason says from behind me.

"It's the hormones!" Libby exclaims as she pulls out of my arms and wipes her face. "How are you here? How long are you staying for? Mason, did you know they were coming?" I can't help but laugh at her succession of questions.

"I swore everyone to secrecy, so don't get mad at Mason," I tell her, still laughing.

"Everyone!" she exclaims. "Who else knows?" She shakes her head. "I don't care. You're here and that's all that matters." She hugs me again and squats down as best she can with her swollen belly in front of Jacob. "I can't believe how big you've gotten."

"Mason, cowboy," Jacob says, pointing at Mason.

"That's right. Mason is a cowboy." She smiles as she stands up.

"In answer to your other question, I'm not sure how long we're here for. A couple of months, maybe. We have an open-ended ticket." I see the confusion in her eyes and I quickly explain about my job and how I've given notice on my rented house. "I didn't realize how much I needed a break until all this happened. And now I get to be here when my niece or nephew is born." She bursts into tears again and Mason chuckles.

"Told you, she can cry at anything. Come here, sweetheart." He wraps his arms around her, and she sobs against his shirt.

"I guess as you're already crying, now would be a good time to tell you Mum and Dad are coming over in a few weeks too. They're going to stay 'til the baby comes." A fresh wave of tears washes over her, and she pulls out of Mason's arms and throws herself at me.

"I've missed you all so much," she says through her sobs. "Thank you for coming."

"We've missed you too, Lib." I really had missed her,

although I'm not sure I really appreciated how much until this very minute.

"Libby! What's wrong?" a voice shouts from the other end of the stables. "Is it the baby?" As Libby takes a step away from me, I look toward where the voice came from and my mouth goes dry. Heading toward us is the most beautiful woman I've ever seen. Her long blonde hair is swept away from her face and tied up with a hair tie, loose strands framing her face. My eyes sweep down her body, the cutoff shorts she's wearing showing off every curve of her toned and tanned legs. As my eyes track upwards, I see her face is a picture of concern, her steel blue eyes full of worry. Her focus is fixed on Lib, and as she takes her hand, I can't take my eyes off her.

"Aria, I'm fine. My brother and nephew surprised me with a visit." Relief floods Aria's face as her eyes drop to Jacob.

"Well, aren't you the cutest," she says to Jacob, who grins at her seemingly as mesmerized by her as I am.

"This is Jacob," Libby tells her. "And this is his daddy, my brother, Jack." She gestures to me and I watch as her eyes leave Jacob and find mine. My heart pounds in my chest and my palms begin to sweat. It's an irrational reaction to someone I've never even spoken to, but I'm powerless to stop how I'm feeling. Her eyes widen as she looks at me for the first time, and I hold my hand out to her.

"Nice to meet you, Aria." Her name feels good on my lips, and I could have been standing in the middle of Wembley Stadium with a full-capacity crowd and I wouldn't have known. Everyone and everything ceases to exist in that moment as I wait to feel her hand in mine. Our eyes remain locked on each other as she slowly raises her arm.

"Good to meet you too, Jack." She places her hand in mine, and a shot of electricity shoots up my arm. I know she feels it too as her eyes drop to our joined hands before she pulls her hand away.

"Aria, you'll come over for dinner later, won't you?" Libby asks. Turning around, I see her pressed up against Mason, his arms wrapped tightly around her. She has a huge smile on her face as she looks from me to Aria.

"Oh, no! I wouldn't want to intrude on your family time. I'm sure you have a lot to catch up on." Her eyes flick quickly to mine before going back to Lib.

"You're more than welcome. Mason's cooking."

"I am?" he asks in surprise.

Lib digs her elbow into his side. "Yes! You are," she mutters, a smile plastered on her face.

"Right, yes, of course. I'm cooking. The more the merrier." I know Lib is playing matchmaker, but I don't care. I find myself holding my breath as I wait for Aria to answer. Despite just meeting her, I want to know everything about her.

"Erm… well, if you're sure, then I'd love to," Aria says. "I'd better get back to work." I know I'm grinning like an idiot, but I can't seem to stop myself. She smiles at me before turning and heading back to the horse she was grooming before we arrived.

"Well, that was interesting," Libby says with a chuckle. "I can't wait to see what happens later."

"Is she, er, dating anyone?" I ask as I scoop up Jacob, my eyes still fixed on her retreating back.

"No, she's very much single," Libby replies. I nod as I follow Mason and Libby out of the stables. Maybe coming to the ranch is going to be one of the best decisions I've made.

CHAPTER 4

Aria

"Holy fuck," I mutter as I walk away. I want to turn around and steal another glance at Jack, but I know he's watching me. I can feel his eyes on my back. His beautiful, chocolate brown eyes. I've never been someone who believed in love at first sight, but I definitely believed in lust at first sight, especially after meeting Jack.

I'd heard Libby talk about her brother and Jacob on more than one occasion, and I could tell by the way she spoke of them she loved them both. I could see why. Jacob was adorable and the double of his dad. Libby had been so upset when she'd found out Jacob's mom had walked out. How anyone could do that to that gorgeous little boy was beyond me. My dad had walked out on me and my mom, and to this day I can't forgive him for it.

Standing in front of the ranch's newest horse, I stroke her nose as she nuzzles against my hand. "Hey, Marble. Wanna take a ride?"

She doesn't answer, of course, but I could do with clearing my head, and a ride always does that for me. I've been the horse trainer at the ranch for almost twelve months. I was only ever supposed to stay a few weeks to break in a particularly difficult horse Savannah had brought. A few weeks turned into twelve months, and they are still finding work for me. I love my job though, and I've fallen in love with the ranch too.

I saddle up Marble and lead her from the stables into the blazing July sun. I love summers in Texas, the heat of the sun on my skin never getting old. Summers as a kid were always cold. I'd grown up in Vermont, my mom choosing to leave there after my dad walked out on us. At twelve, I hadn't wanted to leave my friends and my life behind. My mom needed a fresh start though, and she had friends in Marble Falls, so it made sense. It didn't take me long to fall in love with Texas and its unending summer sun.

Mounting Marble, I glance over to the ranch house. I can't help but wonder if Jack and Jacob will be staying there while they're visiting. Claire, Libby's aunt, had offered me a room in the ranch house when Savannah had first asked me to help with one of her horses. My mom was moving to Austin, and I'd been looking for somewhere to rent. At the time, I only thought I'd stay for a couple of weeks. As the weeks turned into months, I'd offered on numerous occasions to find something more permanent, but Claire wouldn't hear of it. She said she missed having someone other than her and her husband, Ryan, in the house. I'd stayed, and I'm still there.

I'm just about to head off on Marble when I see Jack descending the porch steps. I feel my cheeks flush as he glances at me, a smile erupting on his face.

"Aria," he calls as he jogs toward me. "You off for a ride?" I can't help but notice how gorgeous he is. His dark hair looks like he's run his hand through it about a million times, and his chocolate brown eyes almost sparkle as he looks up at me, waiting for me to answer.

"Yep. Marble is one of the ranch's newest horses. I'm just making sure she's ready for guests." He nods and offers his hand to Marble. She sniffs him and he strokes her nose.

"She's beautiful." He's talking about the horse, but his eyes are fixed on mine. "I'd love to get out on one of the horses while I'm here. See some of the ranch."

"I can take you out sometime…" I trail off, wondering if he meant a ride with one of his cousins. He's here to see his family, after all. "Unless you want to go with Savannah or Brody, of course?"

"No! I'd love for you to take me out. I'd just need to organize for Lib or Claire to look after Jacob."

"Sure. I'm here most days. Just come find me when you're ready." He nods and pats Marble on the neck.

"I'd better get back. I only came out to get our bags from Mason's truck. We're staying at the house with Claire and Ryan." He glances back toward the house, but makes no attempt to move away. I guess that answers my earlier question of where they'll be staying.

"Has Jacob ever been on a horse?" I ask as he continues to

pat Marble's neck. He shakes his head. "I have the perfect horse for his first time, if he wants to try it?"

"You don't think he's too young?" he asks, a frown appearing on his flawless face.

"Not at all. I'd walk with him, make sure he didn't fall."

He nods, and a smile pulls on his lips. "He really will think he's a cowboy once he gets on a horse."

Before I can respond, we're interrupted by a voice calling him from the porch.

"Daddy! Daddy!"

"I'm coming, buddy," Jack shouts to Jacob as he takes a step back from Marble.

"I've got to go. I'll see you later, at Libby's?" I nod and smile as he walks backwards toward the house. "Enjoy your ride." He raises his hand in a wave before turning and jogging toward where Libby is standing on the porch with Jacob. When he reaches them, he picks up Jacob, showering his face with kisses. Even from here, I can hear Jacob's laughter. My stomach somersaults as I watch Jack's outpouring of love for his son. There's nothing sexier than a guy who isn't afraid to show his feelings.

Tearing my gaze away from them, I guide Marble through the guest accommodations. Once we've passed the beautiful wooden cabins, the land opens up, and I kick my legs against Marble, encouraging her into a gallop. As my body rises and falls with her movement, I throw my head back, loving the feel of the warm breeze rushing across my face. I didn't start riding until we moved to Texas, and then only occasionally. Riding is expensive, and I knew my mom couldn't afford lessons. It was only in high school when I got a job helping out at a riding school I was able to ride more often. The owner of the stables was kind, letting me ride once my jobs were done. I used to go there all the time, even when I wasn't scheduled to work. I spent hours observing the staff as they broke in new horses. I knew then I wanted to make working with horses my career.

Guiding Marble to a stop, I dismount and let her graze. As I sit in the shade of a tree, my mind wanders back to Jack. I've never been so affected by someone I barely know and who I've only spoken to for five minutes. I have to admit, I'm a little uncomfortable with my instant attraction to him. It's not like we can really start anything, he's only visiting, but I'm looking forward to dinner at Libby and Mason's tonight. I can't wait to spend some more time with Jack and his adorable little boy.

A couple of hours later and I'm in my room, getting ready for dinner. When I'd gotten back to the stables an hour or so ago, everyone had disappeared. I'd finished what I needed to do with the horses and came back to the ranch house to shower. There is a bathroom off my bedroom, and I stand under the hot spray of the water, nervous excitement swirling in my stomach at the thought of getting to see Jack again. Outfit choices swirl through my mind as I dry my hair, and now as I look through my closet, I know exactly what to wear.

Reaching for my black skinny jeans, I pull them on before grabbing my sky blue cami. The cami is silk, and I love how it feels against my skin. Thin spaghetti straps sit on my shoulders and I gently tuck the material into my jeans. Slipping on some heeled pumps, I take one last look at my reflection in the mirror before picking up my purse and heading downstairs and out of the house.

CHAPTER 5

Jack

"So, how long have you been in the cottage?" I ask as I flop down on the sofa.

"About six months. When we found out about the baby, we knew our old place wouldn't be big enough. Savannah and Josh had a house built on some land by the river and were moving out. It all kind of fell into place," Libby replies as her hand rests on her swollen belly. "If we have any more children, then we'll need to move, or maybe we could extend. For now though, it's perfect."

"There will definitely be more babies, Lib," Mason shouts from the kitchen, and Libby rolls her eyes.

"How about we have this one first, then we'll see. Last time I checked, it wasn't you who's got to do the pushing!"

"Would if I could, sweetheart." He pokes his head around the kitchen door and grins stupidly at my sister. Her face softens as she grins back at him.

Happiness radiates off them, and for the first time, I feel jealous. I don't begrudge my sister her happiness. God, after everything she went through, she more than deserves it. I just wonder sometimes if I'll ever experience what they have. Life as a single dad leaves no time for dating, and honestly, up until right now, I haven't been interested. Jacob has always been enough. But maybe there's more than falling asleep on the sofa alone every night. My mind drifts to Aria, and I know that's crazy. We've only just met, but something is pulling me toward her, something I can't explain.

Standing from the sofa, I walk toward the small window that looks out over the front garden. "Does Aria live nearby? What time did you tell her to come?" I ask as I peer through the glass. Libby giggles from behind me and I turn around. "What? What's funny?"

"She doesn't have too far to come. Maybe five hundred meters."

I frown and turn back to look out the window.

"Five hundred meters? What do you mean?" She laughs again and kisses Jacob, who's sitting beside her, on the cheek.

"I think Daddy might have a little crush on someone," she whispers to him. Thankfully, he has no idea what she's talking about and continues to play with the cars he has in his hand.

"Lib, what do you mean? Where does she live?" I ask, exasperated.

"She lives next to you."

"Next to me? Will you stop talking in riddles and just tell me?"

She must hear the tone of my voice and grins. "You like her, don't you?"

Sighing, I run my hand through my hair. "I barely know her… but, yeah. I like her."

"She has a room at the ranch house. She was only ever meant to stay a couple of weeks. Sav had a horse she was struggling with and Aria offered to help. That was almost a year ago. Her room is Sav's old one."

"Next door to mine…" I trail off wondering how I'm ever going to get any sleep knowing she's going to be in the room next to me.

"I asked her to come for six. So, any minute now." Before I can respond, there's a knock on the door. "That'll be her now. Why don't you get the door? It takes me too long to get up."

Nodding, I move the short distance to the door and swing it open. My breath catches in my throat as I see her standing on the porch. Her long hair is loose and falls in waves over her shoulders, and the blue of her top makes her eyes pop. Her jeans accentuate the curves of her body, and I hold on tightly to the door, forcing myself not to reach out and touch her.

"Hi, Jack," she says after a few minutes as we stand staring at each other. "Can I, erm… can I come in?"

"Shit! Yes, of course. Come in." Dragging myself from my lust-filled haze, I step to the side, holding the door open for her.

"Thanks," she whispers as she passes me, the scent of strawberries invading my senses. Closing the door, I turn to see her hugging Libby, who's still sitting on the sofa. "How you feeling, Lib?"

"I'm good, Aria. You want a drink?"

"I'll get it," I say, heading across the room to the kitchen. "What would you like?"

"Wine, please. If you have it?"

I glance at Libby, who nods.

"There's red and white in the kitchen," she says.

"White, please, Jack."

"Sure, I'll be right back. Lib, you want anything?"

"I'm good, thanks."

I head into the kitchen where Mason is preparing dinner. "Hey, man. Point me in the direction of the wine?" I ask as I grab a wineglass off the countertop.

"Just in there." He gestures to a cupboard and I open it, pulling out a bottle. Finding a corkscrew, I open the wine and pour Aria a glass. "There's beer in the fridge. Help yourself." Opening the fridge, I take out two bottles and open them, handing one to Mason.

"Cheers, man," Mason says as he takes the bottle from me and swallows down a mouthful. I stand awkwardly in the kitchen, Aria's wine in one hand and my beer in the other. After a few minutes, Mason turns from the stove.

"You okay?" he asks, his eyebrows raised in question.

"Yeah, just psyching myself up to go back out there."

"Jack, I don't know you all that well, but you don't strike me as someone who normally gets nervous around women. What's going on?" Taking a deep breath, I groan.

"Before Zara, I wasn't. Now…" I sigh. "Now, I've no idea if I'm good enough. I wasn't for her."

"She really did a number on you, didn't she?" I shrug, but I know he's right. Zara leaving affected me more than I've ever admitted. "Aria's a great girl, and nothing like Zara. You should go for it." He slaps me on the shoulder. "You've got this. Get out there."

"Should I start something when I know I'm not staying?"

"You're here, she's here. Live in the moment, man." I nod before taking a deep breath and heading to the kitchen door. I can't let my past stop me from moving forward. Zara's issues were her own; it wasn't anything Jacob and I did. We were just in the firing line.

"Thanks, Mason." His back is to me as he concentrates on the pan on the stove, and he raises his hand in acknowledgement.

As I make my way back to the sitting room, I stop in my tracks as I see Aria on the floor with Jacob. He's given her one of his cars, which is a surprise. He loves his cars and rarely lets anyone have one. Only my dad and I have ever had that privilege. Now, it seems Aria has it too. They're currently racing them around the rug they're lying on, Jacob's laughter ringing out as she chases him with her toy car. Libby catches my eye, and I can't help but smile at her.

"Having fun?" I ask as I sit on the carpet next to them. Aria turns and grins at me, my heart stuttering as her eyes fix on mine.

"We are, aren't we, Jacob?" She drags her eyes from mine and reaches out to tickle Jacob, who squeals with laughter. Aria sits up as I hold out her glass of wine.

"Thanks," she whispers as she takes it from me, her fingers brushing mine. Heat tracks up my arm, and I want nothing more than to pull her onto my lap and kiss her. Instead, I take a pull of my beer, needing to do something with my mouth when I can't do what I really want. Jacob rubs his eyes and yawns.

"Tired, little man?" I ask, knowing the time difference must be playing havoc with his body clock.

"Milk, Daddy?" he asks, his thumb finding his mouth.

"Sure, buddy. I'll get it for you now." I start to stand when Libby eases herself off the sofa.

"I'll get it, Jack. I need the practice," she says as she heads to the kitchen.

"Thanks, Lib," I call to her. "It's in the fridge."

"Got it," she calls back.

I turn back to Aria, and she's stroking Jacob's hair as he lies on the floor, his thumb still in his mouth. A sadness washes over me as I realize Aria is doing something his own mother never did. Shaking off my melancholy, I force a smile.

"How was your ride today?" I hadn't been able to stop myself jogging over when I'd seen her earlier. It had been nice to talk to her alone, even if it had only been for a few minutes.

"It was great. I think Marble is ready for the guests."

"Do you think maybe we could fit that ride in on the weekend?"

"Erm… sure. Do you have a sitter for this little one?"

"I do. He has a playdate with Hope on Saturday afternoon. I'll be child-free."

"Great. It's a date, then." I grin like an idiot and watch as her eyes widen and her cheeks flush pink. "I mean not a date, date, just a ride, the two of us." She groans and covers her eyes with her hand. "God, I'm such an idiot," she mumbles, her cheeks getting even pinker. I reach for her hand and pull it away from her face.

"I think it's cute." Her hand is still encased in mine and my eyes drop to her lips. God, I want to kiss her. I can't though, not with Lib and Mason in the next room, not to mention Jacob on the floor next to us.

"Here it is," Libby cries as she appears from the kitchen with Jacob's bottle in her hand. She catches sight of us on the floor and pauses. "Oh, I'm sorry. Am I interrupting something?" Aria pulls her hand away and shakes her head.

"No, no. We're just talking," she says quickly before taking a mouthful of her wine. Seeing how uncomfortable she is, I change the subject. "How's dinner coming along?" Libby looks between us before handing me Jacob's milk.

"Good. It's almost done."

I nod and stand up. "Your milk is ready, Jacob." I pick him up and settle him in the corner of the sofa before handing him his bottle. "I think he'll be asleep before dinner is ready." Expecting him to immediately start drinking his milk, I'm surprised when he wriggles off the sofa, bottle in hand. Walking over to Aria, he turns and backs up, sitting right in her lap. My heart explodes in my chest as she wraps her arms around him, placing a kiss on his silky blond hair. I think Jacob might be as captivated by Aria as I am, and I think we might both be in trouble.

CHAPTER 6

Aria

Sitting on the sofa at Libby and Mason's, I'm stuffed after eating the lasagna Mason served. It was delicious, and I'd even helped myself to seconds. I've also had three glasses of wine, which is maybe why I'm feeling so relaxed. I've had a great night, and the cutest little boy is asleep beside me. It wasn't something I'd been expecting, but I'd loved it when Jacob had decided to sit with me and drink his milk. I think Jack was a little surprised too.

The evening flies by and is filled with laughter and conversation. Libby and Jack tell me all about their childhood in England, and Jack talks about his job, and what brought him and Jacob to the ranch. I tell Jack a little about how I got into horse training, and it feels like I've known him forever.

"I guess I better get this little guy home and into bed," Jack says as he stands up.

"I'll walk back with you. Let Libby get some rest."

"I'm okay," Libby says on a yawn, and I laugh.

"You're growing a person, Lib. You need to sleep." I'm sure she doesn't need reminding of this, but I can see she's tired.

"If you insist. I am pretty whacked."

"Thanks for dinner, you guys. I've had a great night. Maybe Jack and I could repay the favor next time Claire and Ryan go out? You up for that, Jack?"

"Definitely. I'm a wiz in the kitchen," Jack says with a grin. Libby bursts out laughing, and Jacob stirs on the sofa. She puts her finger to her lips and shushes us, even though she's the one making the noise.

"Since when were you a wiz in the kitchen?" she whispers.

"Okay, I'm not," he admits, his hands going up in defeat. "But I can do a mean toasted cheese."

"I think between us we can manage something a little more elaborate than toasted cheese," I assure them.

Jack leans into me and places his mouth by my ear. His breath is hot on my skin and his dark stubble tickles my ear. He says something, but I have no idea what. All I can think about is how his mouth is almost on me, and how good it feels to have him so close. He steps back slightly and our eyes lock. I know my cheeks must be flushed, and a smile pulls on his lips as he realizes how affected I am by him. Libby clears her throat and I step away from Jack, the lust haze lifted.

After a round of goodbyes, we're finally on our way back to the house. Jacob is fast asleep on Jack's shoulder, and we walk the short distance from the cottage in comfortable silence. As we climb the porch steps, I hold the door open for him.

"Do you want a drink in the den after I've put Jacob down?" he asks as I close the door behind us. "I think Claire and Ryan are still out."

"Erm… okay. I'll just get changed. Do you need any help?"

"Nah, I'll be okay. Meet you back down here in ten?" I nod before following him upstairs. Jacob is still fast asleep, but I'm guessing he might wake up if Jack has to change his diaper. He already has on cute little dinosaur pajamas, so at least he doesn't have to get him changed.

"Isn't he in your room?" I whisper as Jack walks past the room I know he's staying in. He shakes his head.

"Uncle Ryan set Hope's old cot up in one of the other rooms when they knew we were coming. He sleeps in his own room at home and is in a good routine. I didn't want him to get used to sleeping with me." He comes to a stop outside the room opposite mine.

"That makes sense. Here, let me get the door." I reach around him and swing the door open. "Do you want the night-light on?" I ask, seeing a unicorn-shaped light on the dresser.

"Please. That'll give me just enough light to get him ready for bed." I walk into the room and turn the night-light on at the wall. A dull light illuminates the room just enough to allow him to walk in without tripping over anything. He comes to stand next to me, a sleeping Jacob still in his arms.

"I'll see you downstairs, then?"

He nods and my eyes drop to Jacob. He looks so peaceful. His head is on Jack's shoulder, his long eyelashes resting on his chubby cheeks. Reaching out my hand, I stroke his face. "Goodnight, sweetheart." Without thinking, I place my hand on Jack's arm and go up on my tiptoes to kiss Jacob on the cheek. Surprise flashes across Jack's face, and I realize maybe I shouldn't have done that. Embarrassed, I drop my hand.

"I'll leave you to it," I mumble as I walk backwards. I'm sure he thinks I'm crazy. When I reach the door, I lift my eyes to see Jack watching me, a smile pulling on his lips. Relief courses through me and I give him a small smile back, slipping out of the room before I make a bigger idiot of myself.

After changing into some yoga pants, I go downstairs and into the kitchen. Deciding to stick to wine, not wanting to mix drinks and get sick, I reach for an open bottle in the fridge. I guess Jack will want a beer, so I grab him a bottle before heading into the den. I've drunk most of my drink by the time I hear the den door open.

"Hey, I'm sorry. I thought you might have given up on me and gone to bed. Jacob woke up as I was putting him down. It took me a while to get him off again." He sits on the sofa next to me and I pass him his beer from the table.

"No worries. Is he settled now?"

He nods before taking a pull of his beer. "Fast asleep."

A silence descends over us, the background noise from the television the only sound in the room.

"Tonight was fun, right?" he asks as he takes another pull of his beer.

"Yeah, it really was," I agree.

"Well, you've definitely come away from tonight with one admirer, that's for sure." He chuckles and bumps his shoulder with mine.

My cheeks flush and my stomach flips. "I have?" I ask quietly, my fingers playing with the stem of my wineglass.

"Yeah. Jacob adores you." My heart sinks when I realize he's not talking about himself. Of course he's not, why would he? We only met a few hours ago. "I've never seen him so comfortable with someone he's only just met. You must be pretty special." Despite my initial reaction to his comment, my heart warms thinking Jacob likes me.

"I'm not sure about special. I think I won him over with my car playing skills." I chuckle as I turn to look at him. "What can I say, I'm a big kid at heart."

"I think you're pretty special." His voice is low and I barely hear him over the noise of the television. "You definitely won me over."

"I did?" I mutter, my eyes finding his.

"Yeah, the second I saw you."

"Oh…" I reply, not knowing what to say. He puts his half-empty bottle of beer on the table in front of us and reaches for my glass, setting it down next to his.

"Do you think I could kiss you now? I might go mad if I have to wait a minute longer."

My eyes widen in surprise. No one has ever asked if they can kiss me before. I don't know if it's his British accent or whether it's just because it's him, but I've never heard anything sexier.

"Well, I wouldn't want you to go mad because of me," I whisper, my eyes already dropping to his lips. Despite only meeting a few hours ago, I've thought a lot about how it would feel to kiss him. My heart pounds in my chest as he turns to face me on the sofa, his hand snaking into my hair. His palm cups my face and his thumb gently strokes my cheek. As he lowers his mouth toward mine, I close my eyes. When I don't feel his lips a few seconds later, I open one eye, only to see him staring at me.

"What's wrong?" I ask, self-conscious I have lasagna from earlier around my mouth.

He shakes his head. "Nothing. I just wanted to remember this moment."

His lips crash against mine before I have a chance to say anything, and I find myself tugging on his t-shirt in a desperate attempt to get as close to him as possible. His tongue swipes across my bottom lip, and I open to him. It's the most perfect kiss I've ever received, and my whole body feels alive. My fingers leave his t-shirt as my hands trace up his toned chest and over his shoulders, my fingers finding the hair at the nape of his neck. In one swift movement, he's laid me on the sofa, his body over the top of me. His weight presses me into the cushions, and I can feel his erection against my thigh. I shamelessly raise my hips to try and find some relief for the growing ache that's building between my legs. When I grind against him, he moans into my mouth, and that turns me on even more.

"God, Aria," he says against my lips as he pulls out of the kiss and rests his forehead on mine. "We've got to stop." His breathing is labored, and I'm panting too. "If we don't, I'm going to take you right here on this sofa."

His words make the ache between my legs even stronger and I tilt my head, capturing his lips with mine. I pepper kisses around his jaw and my lips come to a stop by his ear. "You know that turns me on even more, right?" I whisper, nibbling gently on his ear.

"You're killing me," he groans. "I should have chosen the cabin."

Lifting my head, I see the pained expression on his face. "What cabin?"

He sits up and pulls me up with him. His arm goes around my shoulder and he holds me tight against his chest. "When I knew I was coming, Aunt Claire offered me a room in the ranch house or a cabin that wasn't in use. I chose the house. I'm thinking I made the wrong choice."

I chuckle.

He leans down and kisses me again. "Tell me about you. Lib and I have talked all night about us. I want to know about you."

"There isn't much to know. If I tell you quickly, can we get back to making out?"

He laughs, and if possible, pulls me even closer to him.

"Oh, there will be plenty of making out, don't worry."

We spend the next hour talking. I tell him all about moving to Texas when my parents split up, and discovering my love for horses, which is ultimately what brought me here. I tell him about my mom and how she's finally found happiness again with a guy she met online. She wouldn't date when I was growing up, instead preferring to remain single and focus on me. I often wonder if that's something she regrets. It's lonely being a single parent. If she'd met someone earlier, would she have gone on to have more children? I would have loved a brother or sister. I realize I've gone quiet as I think about my mom, and I feel Jack tighten his hold on me.

"You okay?" he asks softly. Moving out of his embrace, I sit up so I can see his face.

"Do you want more kids?"

Surprise flashes in his eyes. "Yes. Eventually. Why do you ask?"

"Sorry. That must seem like a strange question considering we've only just met." I realize what I've said a second after I've said it. "Not that I'm suggesting I should be the person you could have more kids with." I drop my head into my hands and groan. He laughs and pulls my hands away from my face.

"Then what are you asking for?"

"My mom never dated when I was younger. She said she didn't want a string of men coming in and out of our lives. I wonder if she ever regretted not meeting anyone. Whether she regretted not having more kids."

"Did you have a happy childhood?"

"The happiest."

"Then I'm guessing she has no regrets. You should talk to her."

I nod and cuddle back into his chest. "Why does it feel like I've known you forever?" I whisper, my fingers tracing circles on his forearm.

"You feel it too?" he asks. I nod and tilt my head to look at him. My lips find his again and I'm soon lost in him. This gorgeous man and his adorable son have burst into my life, and I can't help but wonder if things will ever be the same again. This is only a short visit for them. Am I going to lose my heart to someone who isn't planning on sticking around?

CHAPTER 7

Jack

Opening my eyes, I stretch my arms above my head, smiling as I think of last night. It had been late when I'd finally climbed into bed. Aria and I had talked for hours. I've never felt such a connection with someone so quickly, and I'm pretty sure she feels it too. Despite my obvious attraction to her, I'm painfully aware my stay in Marble Falls isn't a permanent one. My head is telling me not to get involved, my heart is saying the opposite. I'm pretty sure I know which one will win out.

Glancing at the clock on the side table, I jump out of bed as I see it's after nine. Jacob's sleep is a little all over the place with the time difference, but he's never slept in this late before. Not thinking to put any clothes on, I run down the landing in just my boxers, throwing open the door to Jacob's room.

"Daddy!" Jacob shouts, and I'm shocked to see Aria on the floor playing with him. Her head flicks around to me, her eyes heating as she looks me up and down. Jacob wanders over to me and puts his arms in the air. "Up, Daddy," he says, and I pull my eyes off Aria, scooping Jacob into my arms.

"How long have you been awake, little man?" I ask him, my eyes flicking to Aria.

"I heard him chatting to himself about half an hour ago. I thought you might be jet-lagged and need to sleep in." She sounds unsure, and bites down on her bottom lip, my eyes drawn to her mouth. "I changed his diaper."

I don't say anything, speechless she would think to do that for me. She must take my silence as something else and moves uncomfortably from one foot to the other.

"I'm sorry. I should have woken you." She goes to move past me, and I reach out my hand, my fingers entwining with hers.

"Aria, wait." She stops, her eyes on the floor. "I don't know what to say. Thank you." She looks at me and I smile. "I can't remember the last time I lay in."

She smiles back before looking at Jacob. "We had fun, didn't we, Jacob?" She ruffles his hair, and he nods. "I better get to work."

"Let me make you breakfast as a thank-you?" I say, not wanting her to leave.

"I thought you couldn't cook?" she asks, raising her eyebrows.

"Erm... you like toast, right?"

She bursts out laughing. "How about you get dressed and I'll make *you* breakfast?"

"What about work?" I ask, not wanting her to be late.

She shrugs. "I'm sure my bosses won't mind me cooking their nephew breakfast." Releasing her hand from mine, I slide my fingers around her neck and drop my mouth to hers, kissing her softly.

"Thank you." Jacob squirms in my arms, and I drop my hand from Aria's neck. Putting Jacob down, I watch as he goes back to his toys on the floor. "I guess I should jump in the shower."

Her eyes track over my chest, and I want nothing more than to push her against the wall and have her wrap her legs around me. Flicking my eyes to Jacob, I see he's occupied with his cars, so I grab her hand, tugging her into the hallway.

"What are you—"

I cut her off as I push her against the wall, my mouth covering hers. As I push my tongue into her mouth, her hands wind around my neck and she moans against my lips. My cock hardens in my boxers, and I push against her, letting her know the effect she's having on me. She gasps as she feels my erection, her hands tugging on the hair at the base of my neck.

"Jack," she moans as my lips leave hers and pepper kisses around her jaw and down her neck.

"Daddy!" Jacob shouts, and I rest my forehead on hers, both of us panting. She pushes me gently away, and I adjust my hard cock.

"You should shower. I'll take Jacob downstairs."

"You don't have to do that."

"I want to." She won't look at me and I frown, wondering

what's going on in her head. Before I can question her, Jacob flies out of the bedroom.

"How about we get some breakfast, cowboy?" Aria says. He nods, and she picks him up.

"I won't be long," I say, and she finally looks across at me.

"No rush. I'll see you downstairs." I watch as they walk away before I head back to my room. Aria seems a little conflicted this morning, and I wonder if I've come on too strong. I hope not.

I turn the shower on and strip out of my boxers, my cock jutting out in front of me. I palm my erection, desperate for a release. It has been well over a year since I've been with a woman, and after kissing Aria, my body craves some physical contact. I've become very well acquainted with my right hand over the past twelve months, but it's no substitute for a warm, soft body. Thrusting into my hand, I close my eyes and picture Aria, my body pressing her against the wall. Her legs go around me, and I lift her up, my cock lining up with her hot, wet pussy. My hand pumps faster, and I feel the familiar pull in my stomach as my impending orgasm builds. I imagine taking one of her nipples into my mouth, my tongue rolling around her pebbled bud as I sink my cock inside her. Her walls grip me, and I can almost hear her moaning in my ear as I pound inside her. I'm rock hard and my hand works double time as I imagine Aria coming undone on my cock. Her soft moaning filling my senses. I thrust once more into my hand before my whole body shudders and I come harder than I have in a long time. Ropes of cum shoot across the bathroom as her name falls from my lips, and I lean on the vanity unit as I come down from my orgasm.

Fifteen minutes later, I'm showered, dressed, and heading downstairs. Walking into the kitchen, I see Jacob in Hope's old high chair, a piece of toast in front of him. Aria is at the stove, making what smells like pancakes.

"Something smells good," I say as I stand next to Jacob, leaning down to kiss his cheek.

"That was quick," Aria says, turning from the stove to look at me. "Pancakes aren't quite done yet. I fed Jacob first. He's had oatmeal and now he's having some toast."

"You're spoiling us," I say as I walk up behind her. She stiffens as I get close, and I frown, taking a step back. "Everything okay?"

"Maybe we should talk later." She turns and her eyes flick to Jacob.

"Sure," I reply, moving away from her and turning on the coffee machine. I can't help but feel a little deflated. I was certain we'd shared a connection last night, but maybe it had been one-sided. The kiss earlier certainly hadn't felt one-sided, but I guess I could be reading more into it than is actually there. I haven't done this in a while and I'm out of practice. Glancing across at Aria, I see her staring at me, and she gives me a small smile, leaving me more confused than ever.

Things feel a little strained as we eat breakfast and make small talk about the ranch and, embarrassingly, the weather. I've no idea what's changed from last night to this morning, but I intend to find out.

CHAPTER 8

Aria

Walking away from the ranch house, I leave Jack and Jacob finishing their breakfast, an uneasy feeling settling in the pit of my stomach. Last night with Jack had been incredible. There's no doubt we have a connection, but I know I've hurt him this morning. Something I'd never intentionally want to do. I can't deny my attraction to him though. My body comes alive when he touches me, and I'd wanted nothing more than to jump in his arms when he'd kissed me earlier. However, there is a niggling doubt in the back of my mind that I just can't push down. He isn't staying, and I know if I get too close, I'll end up heartbroken when he leaves.

"Hey, Aria. Did you have fun last night?" Libby calls out as she walks up from the cottage.

"I did. Thanks again for dinner," I tell her as she reaches me.

She waves off my thanks and links her arm with mine. Together we walk toward the stables. "So, you and Jack seemed close last night." She looks sideways at me, and I can't help but sigh.

"Did we?"

She frowns, pulling me to a stop. "What's happened?"

"Nothing. Well, not nothing, but…" I trail off, feeling my face flush.

"You like him?" she asks gently, and I nod. "So, what's wrong? I know for sure he likes you too."

I shrug. "I don't know if I can keep it casual with him. I think it might just be best not to start anything."

"Why does it have to be casual?"

"He's here on vacation, Lib. How can it be anything other than casual?"

"This sounds familiar," she says, a smile playing on her lips.

"What?" I ask, confused.

"Aria, this is just how Mason and I met, and look at us now." She holds up her left hand, flashing me her wedding ring before patting her swollen stomach.

"What happened with you and Mason was totally different." I know the story of how she came to stay here when her friend died in an accident. "You didn't have a child you had to provide for. He can't just decide to stay. His whole life is back in the UK."

"I guess, but if it's meant to be, then it's meant to be."

"I wish I had your optimism."

"If you like him, just see how it goes. Who's to say it will work out anyway?"

"Geez, thanks for the vote of confidence," I say with a giggle. "I like him though, Lib. I know it might be a bit weird me talking to you about him since he's your brother, but I've never felt a connection with someone like I do with him."

"Please don't write anything off with him before you've even tried. Promise me."

I sigh, but nod my head. "Okay, I promise, but I'll blame you if I end up heartbroken and alone." Her eyes widen and I laugh. "I'm kidding, Lib."

She looks relieved, and we carry on walking toward the stables. I might have made a promise to Libby, but I'm not going to make myself vulnerable. I've made that mistake before. Whatever this is with Jack can't go anywhere, but that doesn't mean I can't have fun while he's here. As long as I go into it knowing it's fun and nothing more, my heart could stay intact. I hope.

Despite being employed as a horse trainer, I turned my hand to most things around the ranch, helping out wherever I could. Today, I'm mucking out. Libby is too pregnant to help, even though she insists she isn't. The horses have already been moved to the exercise area, and I pick up the pitchfork and head into one of the stalls.

"How are you feeling today? Any twinges?"

She shakes her head. "I'm good. Just a bit of backache."

"Why don't you sit down? You don't need to help out today."

"I want to."

"I know you do, but you're going to have to slow down

soon, Lib. I'm surprised that cowboy of yours even lets you out of his sight," I joke.

"I don't normally," Mason says as he appears behind us. "She snuck out on me this morning."

"I did not sneak out on you," Libby says, and I turn to see Mason pull her into his arms.

"You should listen to Aria though, Lib. Hell, you won't listen to me!" He kisses her and I smile before carrying on with what I was doing.

"I'm fine! You're all fussing."

"God, woman! You drive me crazy."

"Cowboy!" the sweetest voice shouts, and I look over my shoulder, smiling as Jacob runs toward Mason. Jack follows him, his eyes meeting mine. Tearing my gaze off him, I watch as Mason lifts Jacob into the air, spinning him around.

"He saw you coming in here from the porch swing. He wanted to see the cowboy," Jack explains with a chuckle.

"Seems someone's made quite the impression," Libby says as she presses a kiss on Mason's cheek.

"Hat," Jacob says, and Mason takes his hat off, placing it gently on Jacob's head. It's huge and completely covers his eyes.

"He needs a cowboy hat of his own. The store in town has them," I say.

"Why don't we go for lunch in Marble Falls? We can stop and get him one," Libby suggests.

"Sure, sweetheart. You up for that, Jack?" Mason asks.

Jack nods, his eyes flicking to me.

"I can hold down the fort here while you're all out," I say.

"You're coming too, silly!" Libby exclaims.

"Down," Jacob says before I can respond. He wriggles in

Mason's arms and he lowers him to the ground, plucking his hat off Jacob's head. "Ria," he says as he toddles toward me. "Play?" My heart melts as he tries to say my name, and I drop to my knees next to him.

"I can't play, buddy. I've got to work. Maybe later, okay?" He nods and throws his arms around my neck. Completely taken aback, my eyes go to Jack, who smiles at me. I can't help smiling back as my arms go around Jacob's tiny body, holding him tight.

"You'll come for lunch, won't you, Aria?" Jack asks. I look across to Libby, who nods.

"Yeah, I'll come." I release Jacob, who runs to Jack. "I'd better get finished here if I'm sneaking off in work time."

"Let me help you." He moves to pick up another pitchfork, but I step in front of him.

"No chance! Go and have fun with Jacob. Do you want to see the horses, little man?"

"Yeah!" he cries, bouncing up and down by Jack's side.

Laughing, I point to the door at the back of the stables. "They're out in the exercise area." He runs through the stables and out the door, Mason and Libby following him.

"I'm sorry if I came on a bit strong earlier," he says quietly. "I didn't mean to make you feel uncomfortable."

"No! You didn't." My stomach drops as I realize he thinks he's done something wrong. "God, I'm sorry I made you think that. I just…" I trail off and sigh.

"What?" he prompts, taking a step toward me.

"Whatever this is between us, Jack, it has to be casual. Just some fun while you're here."

His eyes flash with disappointment. "So, friends with benefits?" I nod. "Okay. If that's what you want?"

"It has to be that way. I can't fall for you and then have you leave." He pulls me to him, enveloping me in his arms.

"I won't hurt you, I promise," he whispers in my ear, and I shiver as his hot breath hits my skin. I don't tell him it's probably already too late for that, and when he walks away, I'll be broken. I just have to keep my feelings for him under control and not get too close. I can do that, right?

CHAPTER 9

Jack

"Whatever this is between us, Jack, it has to be casual. Just some fun while you're here." I try to hide the disappointment I know must be evident on my face.

"So, friends with benefits?" She nods and my heart hurts a little. "Okay. If that's what you want?" I tell her, knowing I'll take whatever she's willing to offer, even if that's only friendship.

"It has to be that way. I can't fall for you and then have you leave," she whispers.

I pull her to me, wrapping her in my arms. She's protecting herself from getting hurt. I can understand that.

"I won't hurt you, I promise," I whisper in her ear, and she shivers as my breath hits her skin.

"So, we can keep things casual?" she asks, and I nod.

"Casual includes kissing, right?" My hand reaches up to stroke her face, and she leans into my touch.

"Oh, definitely." Her voice is breathless, and I lean down, pressing my lips against hers. Her hands reach up and loop around my neck as her tongue pushes into my mouth. I open up to her, deepening the kiss, and she moans. It's like a direct line to my cock, which is now straining against my jean shorts. There's nothing casual for me about this kiss. It's all consuming and like nothing I've ever experienced. I can't tell her though. She's already running scared, and I don't want to push her away. Pulling out of the kiss, I take a step back, her arms falling from around my neck.

"Are you sure you don't want some help?"

She shakes her head. "No, go and spend some time with your sister. Have you seen Brody or Josh yet?"

"No. But I think they're heading over later."

She smiles at me and I want to kiss her again, but after what she's just said, I don't. Instead, I walk backwards toward the exercise area.

"I'll see you later?" She nods and I turn and head outside.

Once outside, I look over to see Mason holding Jacob while he strokes one of the horses.

"Look, Daddy!" he cries when he sees me, and I smile, making my way over to them. I'd always loved visiting the ranch, but it's only being here with Jacob I realize how amazing it would be to grow up in a place like this.

"Everything okay?" Libby asks as I come to stand with them.

"I think so." She frowns at me and I shrug. I've no idea how things are going to go with Aria. I want more than a holiday romance, but she's right, there's an ocean between us and anything more seems impossible.

A few hours later and we're all in Mason's truck heading to Marble Falls. It's a tight squeeze with the five of us. Libby's riding up front with Mason, which leaves me, Aria, and Jacob in the back. Aria has insisted on sitting in the middle seat by Jacob, and I feel bad she's squashed against his car seat. My eyes drop to her bare leg that's pressed tightly against mine. I'm so close to her I can smell the strawberry shampoo from her freshly washed hair. My fingers itch to touch her, but I hold back, keeping my hands to myself.

"Are you sure you have enough room?" I whisper in her ear, seeing Jacob has fallen asleep.

She turns her head, her lips millimeters from mine. "I'm good," she mutters.

Her gaze is fixed on me, and I'm unable to look away. There's a heat in her stare, and I know my eyes mirror hers. Libby clears her throat from the front of the truck, and I'm pulled from my trance.

"We're here," Libby says, and I'm surprised to see we're parked in the center of town. I hadn't even realized we'd stopped moving. Climbing out, I watch as Aria scoots across the back seat. I hold my hand out and she takes it as she jumps down from the truck. Reluctantly, I drop her hand and make my way around to the other side, opening Jacob's door. He's still fast asleep, and I lean in, unbuckling his harness.

"Will he stay asleep?" Aria asks from behind me.

"He's not been asleep long, so I doubt it." Plucking him gently from his seat, I lift him out and hold him against my chest, his head resting on my shoulder. Not surprisingly, he stirs, and I smile as Aria places her hand softly on his back before closing the truck door.

Following Libby and Mason along the street, we come to a stop outside River City Grille. I've been here a few times when I've visited the ranch before, and the food is great. As we enter, the host asks us if we'd like to sit outside. The restaurant borders the Colorado River, and the views are amazing.

"Will Jacob be okay outside?" Libby asks, and I nod.

"Yeah, he'll be fine," I assure her.

"In that case, let's sit outside." The server grabs a handful of menus and we follow her outside to a decked area, right on the water. Showing us to our table, she takes a drink order before returning a few minutes later with a high chair for Jacob. He's still tired, so I keep him on my knee until he's woken up a bit.

After we've all chosen off the menu, Jacob is a little more awake and wants to go and see if he can find any fish in the river.

"I'll take him," Aria offers as she stands and holds out her hand.

"Come on, let's see what we can find," she says to him, and I smile as I watch Jacob's chubby hand nestled in Aria's. The decked area is raised up out of the water, but a small walkway leads down to the water's edge and they slowly make their way toward it. Aria picks Jacob up when the path narrows before they disappear from view.

"He's really taken to her, hasn't he?" Mason says, and I nod before taking a pull of my beer.

"Yeah. It normally takes him a while to warm up to people,

but Aria's definitely won him over." Libby and Mason share a look, and I roll my eyes, knowing exactly what they're thinking. She's won me over too.

"We'll have to plan a night out, the eight of us, before this baby decides to make an appearance," Libby suggests as her hand rubs her swollen stomach.

"Eight of us?" I ask.

"Yeah. Me and Mase, you and Aria, Brody and Quinn, Sav and Josh. Aunt Claire would love to watch Hope and Jacob, I'm sure."

"Well, we'd better organize something soon, then. That bump isn't getting any smaller." Libby gasps and hits me on the chest. "I'm going to go and find my son, that way you can't hit me anymore." I chuckle.

"I think that's a wise idea," she warns, her voice full of humor.

Laughing, I make my way down the walkway in search of Jacob and Aria. I spot them throwing pebbles into the water. Aria scoops Jacob up and holds him in the air so he can get his pebble to go farther. He squeals with delight as his stone hits the water, making a splash. She moves him to her hip and passes him another pebble. My heart swells as I watch them, and I want nothing more than to pull them both into my arms. Walking up behind Aria, I slip my hands on her waist, squeezing gently.

"Looks like you're having fun," I whisper in her ear. She stiffens for a second, relaxing when she realizes it's me. Her head drops back onto my chest, and I wind my arms around her.

"Watch, Daddy," Jacob cries when he sees me, throwing his stone into the water.

"That was a big splash," I tell him. "Are you hungry?" He nods, and I let go of Aria, taking him from her. "Shall we go and have some lunch?" He nods again and we start to make our way back to the restaurant. Taking Aria's hand, my mouth drops to her ear.

"Is this okay?" I lift our joined hands and she nods, giving me a small smile. As much as I respect Aria wanting to keep things casual, I need to touch her.

"How about a movie and takeout tomorrow? I would offer to take you out, but I don't want to leave Jacob just yet."

"I'd like that."

"It's a date, then," I tease, repeating her words from last night. Her cheeks flush pink and I chuckle, squeezing her hand. I'm looking forward to spending some time, just the two of us.

After eating far too much at lunch, we all head to Blair's Western Wear in search of a cowboy hat for Jacob. He's beyond excited when we get to the shop, and he looks adorable in the tiny hat.

"Why don't you get one too?" Aria says, placing one on my head. She stands behind me while I look in the full-length mirror. "You look hot," she whispers, her arms snaking around my waist as her head rests on my back. My hand comes over hers on my stomach and our fingers entwine.

"Daddy, cowboy!" Jacob shouts as he runs over to us. I feel Aria try to pull her hand from mine, but I keep a tight hold on her as I scoop Jacob up.

"Let me get a picture," Libby cries as she looks up, seeing us both with a hat on. "Aria, you need a hat!"

"Oh, no. I don't need to be in the picture," Aria insists, shaking her head.

"Of course you do. Here…" Libby reaches down a hat and places it on her head. "There, now smile." Libby takes a picture, and I can see Aria looks uncomfortable, so I squeeze her hand gently before dropping it, giving her the choice to move away. Before she can, Jacob spots her hat and squeals.

"Ria, cowboy!" he says excitedly, and she bursts out laughing.

"I think you mean cowgirl, buddy." She chuckles. He reaches his arms out to her and she looks at me, surprise on her face. I nod, and she takes him, putting him on her hip.

"Should we get Daddy a hat too, Jacob?" she asks him, and he nods, dropping his head on her shoulder. He must be tired after only having a short nap in Mason's truck earlier. Seeing them together makes my heart swell. I reach into my pocket and take out my phone, quickly taking a picture of both of them. Aria sees me and gives me a small smile as her hand goes to Jacob's back.

"We should get him home so he can have a nap. Do you want me to have him?" I ask, removing his hat as his eyes begin to close.

"I've got him," she says quietly.

After paying for both hats, the five of us head back to Mason's truck. Jacob isn't the only one who's tired as Libby yawns.

"Nap time for you too, Lib?" I joke.

"Yeah. I didn't get much sleep last night; someone was using my bladder as a football." Her hand rubs her stomach as she yawns again.

"Make the most of whatever sleep you can get now. The sleep deprivation after they're born is a killer."

"Worth it though, I'd imagine?" Aria asks, her eyes dropping to Jacob.

"Every second." My heart breaks for him that his own mother never thought he was worth it. Aria has known him less than forty-eight hours and already has a better relationship with him than he had with Zara. He deserves so much more.

CHAPTER 10

Aria

Tonight is my date with Jack. We might only be watching a movie in his room, but I much prefer that to a night in a restaurant. I haven't seen much of him since getting back from Marble Falls yesterday. One of the ranch hands was sick, and I'd offered to pick up his workload. I'm finally done for the day though, and I head back to the house to shower and change.

"Hi, Aria," Claire says as I walk into the kitchen and grab a bottle of water from the fridge. "Thanks for all your help the past couple of days. We couldn't have managed without you." I wave off her thanks.

"No need to thank me. I'm happy to help out."

"Any plans for tonight?"

"Oh, erm… I'm having a movie night with Jack. We're ordering takeout." I feel my cheeks flush and she raises her eyebrows. "I'd better go and get ready."

"Have fun." I give her a wave as I head into the entryway and upstairs. When I reach Jack's room, I knock lightly on the door.

"Come in," he shouts. Pushing open the door, I walk in to find a chaotic scene. Jacob's toys are strewn all over the floor, and Jack is chasing a naked Jacob around the room. He stops when he sees me and grins.

"Hey, Aria. You're early, right? Or am I running late?"

"I was just stopping by to check we're still on for tonight. It looks like you're having fun," I say, a smile pulling on my lips.

"I'm trying to get this one into the bath," he says. "He thinks it's funny to have me chase him." My eyes go past him to Jacob, who's now stopped running and is playing with one of his toys.

"Need some help?"

"Oh, you don't have to. I know you've had a busy day with Taylor being sick."

"I don't mind." He walks over and slips his arms around my waist, pulling me against his chest.

"Thank you," he whispers. I smile as he stares at me. Dropping his head, he kisses me softly. "And we are definitely on for tonight."

We finally manage to coax Jacob into the tub, and I sit on the vanity as he splashes Jack, who's sitting on the floor. Once he's washed and there's more water on the floor than in the tub, Jack lifts him out and wraps him in a towel. He lets out a yawn and his thumb goes into his mouth.

"He's worn out. It must be all the country air," he says, kissing him on the head. I follow them out of the bathroom and begin to pick up Jacob's toys as Jack dries and dresses him in his pajamas. When I'm done, I make for the door.

"I'm just going to shower, and I'll be right back."

"Make yourself at home if I'm not here when you come back. I'll be putting Jacob down."

I nod and smile. "Sleep tight, Jacob."

"Bye, Ria," he mutters sleepily. I give him a wave and make my way along the hallway to my room.

I shower in record time and quickly dry my hair. I debate what to wear, but settle on jeans and a tank. I want to look nice, but be comfortable too. I put on some mascara and lip gloss, and take one last look in the mirror before heading back to Jack's room. Taking a deep breath, I knock lightly on the wood, nervous excitement swirling in my stomach. I'm met with silence, and I glance up the hallway, knowing Jack must still be getting Jacob to sleep. I open the door and walk in, before crossing the room and sitting on the bed.

I have no idea what to do while I wait for him, so I reach for the TV remote and search through what movies we can watch. I lie on the bed as I flick through the channels, stopping when *Dirty Dancing* flashes onto the screen. I love this movie. I know Jack won't, but I can watch a little while I wait for him. My eyes feel heavy, and I fight to keep them open, vowing to myself that I'll only close them just for a second.

When I open my eyes, the room is dark, the only glow of light coming from the TV. I sit up and groan inwardly when I realize I must have fallen asleep.

"Hey, you," Jack says from the side of me.

"How long have I been asleep? I'm so sorry I ruined our date."

"You didn't ruin our date. You've only been asleep for about an hour."

"An hour!"

"It's fine, Aria. You've had a busy couple of days." He leans down and presses a kiss to my lips.

"You should have woken me. Have you eaten?"

"No. I was waiting for you. We can order now." He reaches back to the nightstand and holds up a bottle of wine. "Do you want a glass?"

"Yes, please. I really am sorry. I'm so embarrassed." I push myself backward against the headboard and draw my knees up to my chest.

"Stop apologizing. You looked so peaceful when I came in. I couldn't bring myself to wake you." He pours me a glass of wine and holds it out. Taking it from him, I take a sip.

"Did Jacob fall asleep okay?"

He nods. "He fell asleep drinking his milk. He was exhausted." He hands me a Chinese takeout menu. "What do you want?"

I take the menu from him and flick through it. "Chow mein, please."

"Great choice." He dials the number on the front and places my order and his, giving over the ranch's address. "It'll be here in twenty minutes," he says, putting his phone back on the nightstand. I nod and we fall into a comfortable silence as we watch the end of *Dirty Dancing*.

"Hey," I say after a few minutes. "Have you been watching

Dirty Dancing while I've been asleep?" It might be dark in the room, but I can see the pink flush cross his cheeks.

"Erm…"

I laugh. "I'll take that as a yes."

"Lib used to watch it on a loop when we were kids. She loved it. I haven't seen it for years."

"It's a classic!"

"It is." He chuckles. "What do you want to watch now?" I look across at the TV to see the credits rolling.

"I don't mind. You choose."

"How about a comedy? *Bad Neighbors?*"

"Sounds good."

The movie starts, and I take a mouthful of wine before placing my glass on the nightstand.

"What did you and Jacob do today?" I ask as I stretch out my legs and roll onto my side so I'm facing him. He does the same, putting his face level with mine.

"We went to Lake Marble Falls with Lib. It was great to spend some time with her."

"That sounds fun."

"We were going to hire a boat and go on the lake, but I thought taking a two-year-old and a heavily pregnant woman out on the water maybe wasn't such a good idea."

He laughs and his chocolate brown eyes shine. My eyes drop to his mouth, and I've never wanted to kiss anyone more. When I look back into his eyes, they're full of heat, and I wonder if he's thinking the same. I don't have to wonder for long when he suddenly moves, bringing his body across me. His weight presses me into the mattress as his mouth drops to mine. The kiss starts off gentle, but soon becomes more urgent, and I reach my arms around his neck, pushing my tongue into his mouth. Our tongues dance together, and he moans as I arch up into him. He's hard already, and I roll my hips, eliciting another moan from him. His hand finds its way under my tank and my skin tingles in every spot he touches. His fingers dance up my stomach before brushing the underside of my breast, and I gasp into his mouth as his thumb sweeps over my pebbled nipple. His lips leave mine and he peppers kisses around my jaw and down my neck. I'm panting and so turned on I can barely think straight. Suddenly, a knock on the door makes us both jump.

"Takeout," a voice calls. Jack brings his forehead to mine and chuckles, his breathing as labored as mine.

"Hang on," he shouts. He plants a kiss on my nose before sitting up and climbing off the bed. He adjusts himself before he crosses the room to the door. Sitting up, I quickly pull my tank down and run my fingers through my hair. I catch a glimpse of Claire on the other side of the door, and she flashes me a smile before handing the food to Jack.

"Enjoy," she calls over her shoulder as she walks away. Jack closes the door and comes back to the bed.

"Do you think she knew what we were doing?" I ask, embarrassment washing over me.

"I think she had a pretty good idea." He sits down on the bed and kisses me softly. "Let's eat." I scoot backwards and sit up, reaching for my food. We've missed the start of the movie, but it's easy to pick up and we eat in comfortable silence. When we've finished, Jack tosses everything onto the floor and pulls me down to lie with him, my head resting on his chest.

"What are your plans for the rest of the week?" I ask, as his arms wrap around me.

"Not much. I thought I might take Jacob down to the river and let him have a splash in the water, and I saw a park in Marble Falls today that I think he'll love." He looks down at me. "We still have our ride planned for Saturday, right?" I nod, and he smiles. "And then Saturday night I'm out with Mason, Brody, and Josh."

"Boys' night?"

"Yeah, it's been a while. I'm looking forward to it."

"I guess you don't get much time to yourself?"

"Try none, but I'm not complaining. I love being Jacob's dad." I want to ask about Jacob's mom, but I don't. I barely know him and it's nothing to do with me. I know from Lib she walked out on them, so I'm guessing he gets no help from her. I can't help thinking what an idiot she must be to have left them both.

We don't see much of the rest of the movie, spending most of the night making out. It never goes beyond that though, despite my body craving him. When the credits roll on the movie and the room is plunged into darkness, I sigh.

"I guess I should go. I have to be up at six," I say, adjusting my tank. My lips are swollen from his kisses, and my hair is tangled from where his fingers have been. Reaching up, I try to smooth down my hair. "I've had a great time. I'm sorry I fell asleep."

"Stop apologizing," he says, his hands tickling my sides. I squeal as he tickles me, and I try to push his hands away.

"Okay, okay. I'll stop," I gasp, out of breath from laughing. He stops tickling me and brings his mouth to mine in another scorching kiss. I'm panting again by the time he pulls away.

"I'll walk you to your room," he whispers in my ear.

"It's next door."

"It's a date. I have to walk you home." He stands up and holds out his hand to me. I take it, and he pulls me off the bed. We walk hand in hand to my room. We're there in twenty seconds, and I laugh.

"At least you don't have a long walk back."

He smiles before gently pushing me against my closed door and kissing me again. He pulls away before it gets too heated, and as much as I don't want the night to end, I'm grateful he stopped. If he carried on kissing me, I'm not sure I'd have let him go back to his room.

"I'll see you tomorrow?" he asks.

"Maybe. I have a full-day riding excursion. I'll be home for dinner though."

He nods. "Have a good day."

"You too."

"Sleep tight."

"Night." I reach behind me, feeling for the door handle. Finding it, I push on the door and walk backwards, my eyes fixed on him. I close the door slowly and drop my head onto the wood. My plan of keeping my feelings for him under control and not getting too close seem to be failing already.

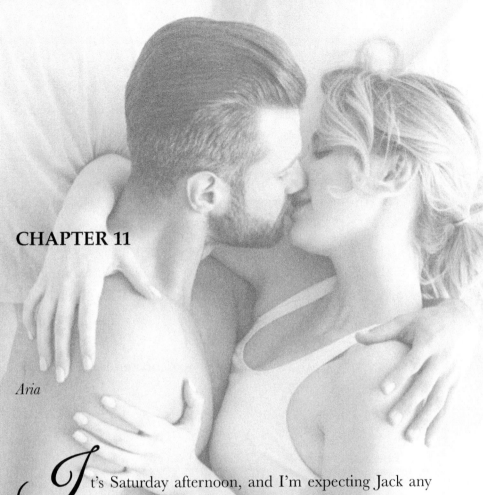

CHAPTER 11

Aria

It's Saturday afternoon, and I'm expecting Jack any minute for our ride. Titan's waiting in the exercise area, and I'm in the stables getting Marble ready to go. Nervous excitement swirls in my stomach at the thought of seeing him again. Since our movie night a couple of days ago, I've hardly seen him. We are still a ranch hand down, and in the height of the holiday season with all of the accommodations booked out, we're swamped.

"Hey," Jack calls from the stable door. "I'm just taking Jacob up to Savannah's and I'll be back."

"Why don't we ride up with him? He can sit with me on Marble. It'll save you going up there and then coming back down again." Savannah and Josh have a house down by the

79

river. I'd planned on taking him down that way anyway, so it makes sense. I see the indecision on his face, and I walk toward him. "He'll be safe. I promise."

He kisses me gently. "Okay, I trust you." He looks down at Jacob, and I kneel in front of him.

"Do you want to go on a horse, cowboy?" His face lights up in a smile and he jumps up and down.

"Yes, yes, yes," he chants, and I laugh.

"I think that might be a yes. Titan is saddled up in the exercise area for you. I'll just walk Marble out." They both follow me out, and I mount Marble, reaching down for Jacob. Jack hands him to me, and I place him just in front of the saddle. Wrapping my arms around him, I pick up the reins, his little hands going over mine.

"Smile," Jack says, and I turn to see him holding up his phone.

"Look at Daddy, Jacob." I tickle his side, and he giggles just as Jack takes the picture. He pushes his phone back in his pocket, and mounts Titan. He looks a little nervous, and I kick my heels gently, encouraging Marble to move. Trotting over, I stop next to him.

"You okay?"

"Yeah, it's just been a while."

"It's like riding a bike. You never forget."

We set off at a gentle pace, and after a few minutes, Jack looks like he's spent his whole life around horses. It really is something you never forget. I hold on tightly to Jacob, seeing Jack looking over at him every few minutes. Jacob seems to be enjoying it, and he strokes Marble's mane as we ride. At this pace, it's about a ten-minute ride to Savannah's place. Jack's quiet, and I know he's apprehensive about Jacob riding.

"Everything okay?" I ask, glancing over at him.

He nods. "He's normally such a fidget. I was sure he wasn't going to sit still."

"He's doing great," I assure him. "And we're almost there, look." I point ahead as Savannah and Josh's house comes into view. It's a large two-story building with a wraparound porch. Claire and Ryan had gifted them the plot of land not long after Hope was born, and Josh had built the house with his dad, designing it exactly as he and Savannah had wanted. It's beautiful inside, and the views of the Colorado River out back are stunning.

"Wow," Jack says in awe.

"Haven't you been here yet?"

"No. We've spent most of our time with Lib since we arrived."

"Wait 'til you see inside," I tell him as we come to a stop just outside their white-picket-fenced front yard. I wait for Jack to dismount Titan, and I pass Jacob down to him before climbing off Marble. Tying both horses to the hitching rail Savannah had installed so she could ride Marley out here, we head up the porch steps.

Knocking on the door, I glance down to Jacob, who has his head buried in Jack's leg.

"Is he okay?" I whisper, gesturing down to Jacob.

"He's a little shy. I hope he's going to let me leave him."

"We can always stay for a bit until he's settled."

Before Jack can answer, the door swings open, and Josh stands there with an excited Hope in his arms.

"Hey, Josh. Good to see you," Jack says, shaking his hand.

"Good to see you too, man. You too, Aria. Come on in. Hope's been waiting for you." I wave to Hope, and she smiles back. I see a lot of her around the ranch. She's definitely following in Savannah's footsteps when it comes to loving the horses. She's already a confident rider, and I know Sav and Josh are thinking of buying her a horse of her own.

Following Josh and Hope into the house, we're led into the living room, where Hope has all her toys out. Fortunately for Jacob, they aren't all dolls, and I see him looking at a wooden road that's been set out with a few cars on it.

"Grab a seat. I'll fetch Sav. She's just upstairs." Josh puts Hope down, and she looks a little shy too as she climbs on the sofa and stares at Jacob, who's climbing onto Jack's lap. Kneeling on the floor, I start to pick up one of the cars from the wooden road.

"This looks fun," I say to Hope. "Do you want to play?" She nods and slides off the sofa. I think this might be the quietest I've ever seen her, but I know she can be shy around people she doesn't know. Pushing the cars around the wooden track, I turn to see Jacob watching us.

"Do you want to play, Jacob?" He looks unsure but eventually nods, climbing off Jack's lap and coming straight to sit on mine. I hand him my car and he leans forward, driving it along the road, his eyes occasionally flicking to Hope.

"Hey, guys," Savannah says from the doorway. "I see you rode here. Jacob, did you go on a horse?" she asks him, and he looks up at me before nodding shyly. "Wow, you're like a real cowboy." He smiles, and my heart melts as he turns around and wraps his arms around my neck, hugging me tightly. Despite needing to keep things casual with Jack, I'm already head over heels in love with his little boy. How could I not be?

"You've made quite the impression on little Jacob, Aria," she says, a smile pulling on her lips.

"I don't know what I did to deserve it," I tell her honestly as I hug him back. "I think it's my epic car playing skills."

"Is that why his daddy likes you too?" She wriggles her eyebrows and my cheeks flush pink.

"You still have no filter, then, Sav," Jack says with a chuckle as he stands up and pulls her into a hug.

"Where would be the fun in that?"

"Causing trouble?" Josh says from behind her as Jack steps out of the hug.

"Always!" She goes up on her tiptoes to kiss him. He wraps his arms around her and it's clear to see how in love they are.

"This place is amazing, you guys," Jack says as Josh puts Savannah down.

"Let me show you outside," Savannah says, taking his arm. "Josh insisted on putting in a pool. I should have told you to bring Jacob's swim trunks."

Josh comes to sit on the floor with Jacob and Hope, and I watch them play for a few minutes before following Sav and Jack outside. The back yard is massive, edged by the same white picket fence that lined the front yard. The low fence allows unspoiled views of the Colorado River, which sits a few hundred yards from the bottom of the yard. Beyond the swimming pool is a decked area with a built-in barbeque and a comfy-looking rattan sofa.

"Beautiful, isn't it?" I say, sidling up to Jack. He nods, slipping his arm around my waist. Butterflies erupt in my stomach at being this close, and I lean into him.

"It is. Puts my rented house back home to shame," he says with a chuckle.

"Anytime you want to cool off, feel free to use the pool. I know you Brits don't manage all that well in the Texas heat," Savannah says, holding back a laugh.

"I'd argue with you, but you're right. Liverpool doesn't see heat like this very often. I'll likely be taking you up on your offer! Although, by the look of those clouds, there's some rain coming." Looking past me, he frowns. "Where's Jacob?"

Grinning, I take his hand. "Come and see," I say, pulling him back inside the house. Coming to a stop in the doorway of the living room, he looks across to see Jacob and Hope playing. Their heads are pressed together as Hope chatters away, Jacob joining in occasionally.

"I think we're good to go for that ride," he says with a grin.

After a round of goodbyes, he takes my hand, and we head to where the horses are tied up. Nervous excitement bubbles through me at the thought of being alone with him, and I suddenly can't wait.

CHAPTER 12

Jack

I'm apprehensive as we ride away from Savannah's. I haven't seen much of Aria since our movie night. She's been so busy with work, and as much as I want to be alone with her, I know this "friends with benefits" thing she wants is going to be hard. I'm already attracted to her, and I'm willing to bet the more time I spend with her, the further I'll fall. After a few minutes of riding in silence, I look over.

"Where are we heading, then?"

"I thought we'd head to the river. I know a quiet place." I nod. "I think a lot has changed since you were last here. Did you know Brody has a house on the ranch now, and they've started holding small weddings in the barn where Lib and Mason had their wedding reception?"

"Lib told me about Brody's place. I didn't know about the barn though."

"They've only done a handful of weddings. It was Quinn's idea. She wants to bring more events to the ranch and offer out the accommodations to guests."

"Sounds like a great idea. I love how everyone is involved with the ranch."

"I love it here. It's like one big family. Even the staff who aren't family are made to feel like they are." She smiles. "It was just me and Mom growing up, so I really love that big family feel."

"I can see why Aunt Claire and Libby came to visit and never went home. The ranch seems to pull you in somehow."

"I know," she agrees, laughing. "That's why I'm still here twelve months later."

"You think you'll stay, then?"

She shrugs. "As long as they need and want me. I've been thinking of finding my own place though. I've been at the ranch house too long, and it feels a little like I'm taking advantage."

"What about your mom? Can you move in with her?" She shakes her head.

"She lives in Austin with her boyfriend. She moved there just after I got the job on the ranch. That's why I needed some-where to stay when I first got here."

"You know, I'm sure Claire and Ryan don't think you're taking advantage."

"Maybe not, but I can't stay in their home forever." We've reached the river, and it's a great spot. It's secluded and surrounded by large trees. The water laps gently onto a pebbled shore, and the only sounds are from the birds overhead. It's beautiful. She jumps down off Marble. I follow her and we let the horses graze. She walks to the edge of the river and picks up a stone, skimming it across the water.

"What about Libby and Mason's old cabin? I'm guessing that's been empty since they moved into the cottage," I say, coming to stand next to her.

"Yeah, that's a thought. It would be a lot easier to live on the ranch. I'll speak to Claire and Ryan about it." She reaches over and kisses my cheek. "Thank you."

Turning to face her, I pull her into my arms. "I take my thanks in kisses," I tell her quietly, my eyes dropping to her lips. Her arms go up and around my neck, and I capture her lips. She bites down on my bottom lip and I open up, her tongue duelling with mine. As the kiss becomes more heated, spots of rain begin to fall on my cheek, and the storm that was building hits. Within seconds, it's raining heavily, and Aria laughs as she pulls out of the kiss, both of us soaked.

"Well, I didn't imagine this would happen on our ride. Where's the sun gone?"

She steps back and tilts her head to look at the darkening sky. My eyes drop to her white top, which has gone see-through in the rain. Her lace bra leaves nothing to the imagination, and I can see her dark, pebbled nipples against the thin material. My cock hardens, straining against my shorts, and my hands itch to touch her.

"Fuck!" I growl. Her eyes flick to mine, and she must see the heat in them as she bites down on her bottom lip. Unable to stop myself, I take a step toward her, crashing my lips against hers. Her arms go around my neck, and I lift her up, her legs sliding around me. Walking with her in my arms, I press her back against the trunk of a large tree, hearing her gasp as my cock presses between her legs. Her hips roll against mine and my mouth leaves her lips as I pepper kisses around her jaw and down her neck.

"Oh God, Jack," she moans as I bring my hand up, pinching her nipple through the material of her top. Moving her away from the trunk, I lay her on a patch of dry grass under the canopy of the tree. My lips never leave her skin, and I can feel her trembling in my arms.

"Are you cold?" I ask against the skin of her neck.

"No," she breathes out. "Just the opposite."

I smile as I realize she's trembling because of me. She pushes gently on my chest and I roll off her, frowning slightly.

"You okay?"

She shakes her head. "I need to touch you."

I inhale sharply as her fingers snake under the wet material of my t-shirt, her hands warm on my skin. She tugs the shirt over my head, tossing it to the side.

Her fingers trace over my chest, her nails digging into my back as her lips meet mine again. My cock is pulsing against my shorts and I'm desperate to sink inside her. It's been far too long, and my body is humming with desire. I feel her fingers reach for the button on my shorts and she slips her hand inside. I'm not wearing any underwear, and I moan when her fingers slide around my erection.

"Aria," I whisper against her lips as her hand pumps my shaft. It's been months since someone touched me, and if I don't stop her, this will be over before it's even started. My breathing hitches, and despite knowing I should stop her, it feels too good.

"Wait," I mutter a few minutes later, gently pulling her hand off me.

"Is something wrong?" Her voice is small, and her eyes look anywhere but at me.

Lifting her chin, I wait until she looks at me. "No, Aria. Nothing's wrong. It's just... it's just been a while and if you carry on..."

"How long?"

I sigh. "About eighteen months." My cheeks flush with heat at my admission.

"Eighteen months, wow. I better make this good."

My eyes widen at her words, and she sits up, pulling her top over her head, leaving her in just her bra. My fingers reach around her back, undoing the clasp. The material falls from her body and I can't take my eyes off her. She's perfect. Needing to see more of her, I undo her shorts, tugging them down her legs.

"Holy fuck, you're not wearing any underwear," I exclaim, and she giggles.

"Neither are you."

"Yeah, but it's so much hotter when *you* don't wear any!"

"I'll have to remember that. Touch me, Jack. Please," she begs, and I don't have to be asked twice.

Starting at her foot, my mouth brushes kisses up her leg, and by the time I reach the inside of her thigh, she's panting. My head comes between her legs, and I lick through her folds. Her back arches off the ground. Her hands tangle in my hair and she pulls gently, moaning as my tongue circles her clit. Her breathing becomes ragged, and I can feel her legs shaking on either side of me. I slide two fingers inside her wet heat, and her body hugs my fingers. She gasps as I thrust them in and out of her. My tongue continues its assault on her clit, and I can feel her walls fluttering around my fingers, telling me she's close.

"I'm going to come, Jack," she pants, her legs holding my head in place. Increasing the pressure on her clit, I feel her whole body shudder, her name falling from my lips as she comes. I slowly kiss up her body, and her breathing is still labored when I reach her lips. I drop my forehead on hers.

"Can I make love to you?" I ask quietly, my lips grazing hers.

"No one's ever asked me that," she whispers, and I sit up.

"You're a virgin?"

She laughs. "God, no! I've had sex, just no one's asked me before. It must be a British thing." She cocks her head. "Unless it's a Jack thing? Whatever it is, it's sexy as hell."

"Is that a yes?" I ask her, my voice tinged with humor.

"Sex in the rain with a hot British guy? I'd say that's a hell yes!" Chuckling, I stand up, pushing down my shorts. My cock springs free, hitting my stomach, and her eyes widen.

"Shit!" I exclaim, running my hand through my hair. "I don't have a condom. I'm sorry." Biting down on her lip, she sits up, taking my hand.

"I'm on birth control… and I'm clean." Dropping to my knees, I tuck a stray piece of hair behind her ear.

"Are you sure? I'm clean too."

She nods. "I want you," she whispers.

"God, Aria, I want you too." I carefully push her onto her back, my body coming over hers. My mouth goes to her neck, my teeth nipping her skin. Her hands brush up my arms and over my shoulders, goose bumps erupting on my skin where she's touching me. My head drops to her perfect tits, and I suck one of her already pebbled nipples into my mouth. My tongue swirls around it, and I bite down gently as she gasps, arching her back. Releasing her nipple with a pop, I reach for my cock, positioning it against her entrance.

"Please," she begs, rolling her hips when I don't move. Sliding inside her, I groan as her body pulls me in. She feels wet and warm, and I close my eyes, dropping my forehead onto hers.

"You feel so good, Aria. I want to stay buried inside you forever." My voice is low and full of emotion. If she hears it, she doesn't let on.

"Please move, Jack." Her hands run up and down my back, and I slowly pull out, slamming back into her. She cries out, her nails digging into my skin. She kisses me, snaking her tongue into my mouth as I continue to move in and out of her. Her pussy grips my cock like a vise, and I know I'm not going to last long. I reach between us, circling my thumb over her clit, my mouth finding her nipple again. My thrusts become more urgent as my orgasm builds, and I increase the pressure on her clit.

"Jack, I'm close," she cries, her body moving with mine.

"Come for me, Aria," I whisper in her ear as I lift my head from her tit. My words push her over the edge, and she cries out, her walls pulsing around my cock as she comes. Her orgasm triggers my own, and I come hard, my body shuddering with pleasure. Breathless, I drop my head into her neck, kissing her skin as her fingers stroke through my hair.

Rolling to the side, I pull her into my arms, her head resting on my chest. She's quiet, but I guess I am too. My fingers stroke up and down her arm and she holds on tightly to me. After a few minutes of silence, I look down at her.

"You okay?"

Her eyes meet mine and she nods. "You?"

I nod back, flashing her a smile. "That was something else, Aria." I'd been with my fair share of women, but it had never felt like that with anyone. It was like I couldn't get enough of her, and as amazing as the sex had been, I was equally as happy holding her. I was fucked. Big-time.

CHAPTER 13

Aria

Pressing my body tightly against Jack, I sigh inwardly. Why couldn't sleeping with him have been crap? Why does he have to make my heart stutter and my body come alive with his touch? Before I slept with him, I knew saying goodbye was going to be hard. Now, I know it's going to be impossible.

"Are you sure you're okay? You've gone very quiet," Jack asks, and I can hear the concern in his voice.

Turning in his arms, I lean up on his chest. "I'm good," I assure him, brushing my lips across his. "That was incredible, Jack." He holds my gaze and smiles. "It's never felt…" I shake my head and trail off, not knowing how to finish what I was going to say without taking us out of the casual zone.

"Me too, Aria," he whispers, and I know he feels it too.

"You should know I don't usually do this."

"Do what?"

"Sleep with a guy I've just met. In fact, I've never slept with someone I'm not in a relationship with. You just make me a little crazy." He chuckles and kisses my head.

"You make me a little crazy too, Aria." He gives me a small smile and I look up to the sky.

"I think the rain has stopped," I say, changing the subject. His fingers reach up and stroke my cheek. "I guess I can't keep you here naked all afternoon, as much as I'd like to."

"I guess not."

Sitting up, I reach for my bra, but it's still damp from the rain. "This is still wet. I think I'll leave it off."

"No!" Jack exclaims, and I swing my head around to look at him. "Put it on, please. I won't be able to concentrate enough to ride Titan knowing you don't have any underwear on at all." He has a pained look on his face, and I burst out laughing when I realize he isn't joking.

"Fine, I'll put it on." He exhales sharply. "If I catch pneumonia though, I'm blaming you." I wink at him, and he laughs.

"Aria, it's like a million degrees, even when it's been raining. I don't think you're going to catch pneumonia."

"You never know!" I quickly get dressed, his eyes all over me as I do, and I feel myself getting turned on. "I'll be wanting to get naked again if you keep looking at me like that," I warn him, bending down to kiss him.

"I wouldn't say no to that."

"As appealing as that sounds, we have to get back. Aren't you going out tonight? Boys' night?"

He nods. "Spoilsport. But, yeah. We should get back. I need to feed and bathe Jacob before I go out."

I'm the one staring now as he stands and pulls on his shorts, followed by his t-shirt, which pulls tight across his chest.

The dark clouds have cleared, and the sun is hot on my already heated skin as we slowly ride back. We talk the whole way, and I feel like I've known him forever. I don't want the ride to end, but I know it has to when we arrive back at Savannah and Josh's place. Tying up the horses again, I can hear squealing, and Jack smiles.

"Sounds like they're having fun," he says. "We may as well head straight round the back." I nod and follow him around the side of the house and through the gate that leads to the backyard. Josh, Hope, and Jacob are all in the pool, and Josh is pushing Jacob and Hope on a pool float. Shrieking, they fall off and into the water. Both are wearing floaties and pop up to the surface, their floaties keeping them afloat. Savannah is lying on one of the loungers around the pool, and she waves as she sees us.

"Hey, you're back. Did you have fun?" she shouts across the pool. I flick my eyes to Jack, who winks at me.

"Yeah, we did," I shout back, my cheeks flushing with heat. Thankfully, she's far enough away not to notice.

"Come and sit down." She gestures to the lounger next to her. "I found some of Hope's old swim diapers. I hope it was okay to let Jacob in the pool?" she asks Jack.

"Of course. It looks like he's loving it! I'm going to have trouble getting him back to the house," Jack says on a laugh as he sits down sideways on the lounger. "He hasn't even noticed I'm here yet."

Sitting next to him, I watch as Josh chases an excited Hope and Jacob through the water.

"What are your plans tonight, Aria?" Savannah asks, looking over her sunglasses at me.

"Probably just a movie and bed." I shrug. "Nothing exciting."

"Come over here. Quinn is coming after she's dropped the guys off. I'm ordering pizza."

"Okay. If you're sure?"

"Of course I'm sure," she says, waving her arm.

"What about Lib? Is she coming too?"

She shakes her head. "I asked her, but she's exhausted. She said she has a date with a bubble bath and her Kindle."

"Sounds like Lib," I tell her, chuckling. I watch Jack stand and make his way to the edge of the pool as Jacob notices we're back.

Savannah sits up and leans across to me. "You do know you have grass in your hair, right?" She smirks at me as I feel heat travel up my neck and over my cheeks. Reaching over, she plucks a few strands of grass from my hair, tossing them behind her. "I want to know all the details tonight!" Before I can respond, Jack comes to stand in front of me with a wet Jacob wrapped in a towel.

"Can you take him, babe, while I fetch his clothes from inside?" My heart stutters when he calls me babe, and I hold out my arms.

"Come here, little man." My eyes flick to Savannah, who raises her eyebrows and grins.

"All the details," she mouths, and I roll my eyes, a smile tugging on my lips.

Pulling Jacob against me, he snuggles into my chest, his head dropping onto my shoulder. "I think he'll sleep well tonight. You've worn him out," I tell Josh as he climbs out of the pool with Hope.

"I think I will too! I'm knackered!" He leans over Savannah, kissing her on the lips. She's taken her sunglasses off and her eyes track all over Josh. I think they're more in love now than ever, if that's even possible. I'm a little jealous watching them. I know I can't have anything remotely similar with Jack, and that makes me sad.

Jack returns a few minutes later with Jacob's clothes and a clean diaper. "I think he's fallen asleep," I whisper, dropping a kiss on his damp hair. "I can walk him back to the house and come back for Marble?"

"You don't need to do that. I'll carry him," Jack says, and I nod as he tosses the clothes on the lounger and reaches for Jacob. "I'd better get this little guy home. Thanks for watching him this afternoon." Once Jack has Jacob in his arms, I grab the clothes and diaper from next to me and stand up.

"Anytime. Hope's loved having someone to play with," Savannah assures him. "He's had something to eat too." Jack smiles gratefully at her.

"I'll catch you in a bit, man," Josh says to Jack as he scoops Hope up. "Brody and Josh are meeting us at the ranch house at eight. Quinn is giving us a ride to the Brass Hall." Jack nods and waves as Josh carries Hope inside.

"Come over whenever you're ready, Aria. Have a good night, Jack."

Jack waves over his shoulder and we make our way out of

the side gate, coming around to where Marble and Titan are tied up.

"Are you riding back?" he asks.

"I think I'll walk them back. It'll be easier." He nods and watches as I untie both horses. Walking slowly back to the house, we're both quiet and it feels a little awkward. When I can't take the silence any longer, I make small talk. "The Brass Hall won't know what's hit it when all you guys turn up tonight."

"What do you mean?" he asks, confusion lacing his voice.

"Four hot cowboys? The women will be falling over themselves." I laugh, but it's a cover for how bad I feel at the thought of anyone hitting on him. It's not like we're dating; he's free to do what he wants.

"I'm pretty sure there will only be three cowboys, babe. Three very attached cowboys."

I shrug. "Maybe. Once they hear your British accent though, you'll be fighting them off."

He bursts out laughing. "I doubt it."

We've arrived back at the entrance to the stables, and Colt, one of the ranch hands, takes both reins off me, leading Marble and Titan inside. With Jack's spare arm, he pulls me to his side, his hand snaking around me. "Plus, there's this girl I'm casually seeing so… I'm good." He leans his head down to me and brushes his lips against mine. I can't help but do a little imaginary dance knowing he's not going out to pick anyone up, not that I thought he would go looking. He's gorgeous though, and his accent only adds to his appeal. Jacob stirs, and he squeezes my waist before dropping his arm.

"Hey, sleepyhead," he says quietly as Jacob lifts his head. "Did you have fun with Hope?"

He nods and yawns before looking around. "Horses?" Jacob asks as he realizes we're outside the stables.

"We can see them tomorrow, buddy," Jack promises as he reaches for my hand.

"Now!" Jacob shouts, squirming to get out of Jack's arms.

"It's dinnertime, and you need to go in the bath," Jack explains as he drops my hand to contain a wriggling Jacob. "I'll bring you to see them tomorrow."

"No!" he shouts.

Jack sighs and looks across at me apologetically. "Jacob, we can't see the horses now."

He promptly bursts into tears, and my heart squeezes.

"How about tomorrow, if it's okay with Daddy, you can ride one of the horses on your own?" I suggest, my hand resting on his back. My eyes flick to Jack as I realize maybe I should have run it past him first. He's smiling, so I think I've gotten away with it.

"Ride now!" Jacob cries excitedly, and I grimace, hoping I haven't made his meltdown worse.

"We can't now, they're sleeping," I lie. I glance across at Jack and shrug, not having a clue what else to say to Jacob to stop his tears.

"Okay," Jacob says, and as quickly as the meltdown started, it's over. "Down, Daddy," he shouts, and Jack lowers him to the ground. He removes the towel wrapped around him and runs toward the house in just his swim diaper.

"That was over fast," I say with a chuckle.

"The terrible twos! Literally the week he turned two, the

tantrums started." He laughs and shakes his head. "They almost always stop as soon as they've started. Thankfully. he's easily distracted."

"I meant what I said about that ride tomorrow, if you're not busy."

"I'm not busy. I might be hungover, but definitely not busy."

"Hungover? Planning a big night, then?"

He laughs. "Not really, but it's been a while since I went out drinking."

"Well, if Savannah has her way, I'll likely be hungover too. Josh brought her some cocktail-making books, and every time we have a girls' night, it's a different cocktail. I needed help walking home last time."

Sliding his arm around my waist, he pulls me into his side. "Hmm, I can't wait to see drunk Aria," he whispers, kissing the skin below my ear. I shiver as his stubble tickles my neck, and heat pools in my stomach.

"How is it you have me wet with just one kiss?" I mutter as I tilt my head to the side to give his mouth better access.

"Fuck, Aria. I think I should cancel guys' night and make love to you all night instead."

My eyes widen, and I can't help but think friends with bene-fits don't make love. That's the second time he's called it that. Maybe I need to take a step back.

"Don't you dare. You deserve a night out." I step away from him, trying not to notice the small frown that develops on his face as I move away. I go on ahead, scooping up Jacob and carrying him up the porch steps. Jack follows, and I pass him Jacob as we reach the entryway. "Have a good time tonight." I go up on my tiptoes and brush my lips across his cheek. "Bye, little man," I say to Jacob, who's dropped his head on Jack's shoulder.

"I'll see you tomorrow, then?" Jack asks, and I nod. "Have fun with the girls."

I smile before turning and heading upstairs. I can feel his eyes on me as I walk away from him, and I know I'm giving him mixed signals. I'm just trying to save my heart. Trying to save both our hearts. I don't think I'm succeeding.

CHAPTER 14

Jack

I can't help sighing as I stand in the entryway and watch Aria walk away from me. I know she has feelings for me. I can see it in her eyes, and I can feel it in her kisses, but she's holding back. I get it, she doesn't want to get hurt, and despite promising not to hurt her, I'm beginning to question whether I can keep that promise. Why couldn't I have met her back home? Why does she have to live thousands of miles away? Maybe this "friends with benefits" thing is a bad idea. Maybe sticking to friends with *no* benefits is the answer. I just don't know if I can stay away from her.

"Come on, Jacob. Let's get you in the bath." He squeals with excitement, and I carry him upstairs to my bedroom.

Setting him on the floor, I find him some cars to play with while I head into the bathroom and run the water. When it's ready, he refuses to put down the car he's playing with, and not having the energy to argue, I give in, letting him bring it into the bath with him. He drives it around the edge, making car noises as I quickly wash him. When he's clean, I sit on the floor and play with him for a while. As hard and exhausting as it is being a single dad, it's so rewarding. I might have to deal with all the hard times alone, but I also get all the good times to myself as well. All the cuddles, all the laughter, all the fun.

After I've dried Jacob and put him in his pajamas, he's pretty much asleep on my knee. Carrying him across the hall-way, I kiss him on the head before placing him in his cot. "Love you, little man," I whisper as I turn on the night-light and close the blind.

"Love you, Daddy," he whispers around his thumb, and my heart swells with love for him. Backing slowly out of the room, his breathing has evened out and he's asleep by the time I reach the door. Closing the door behind me, my mind flicks back to Aria. I know I'm not going to be able to enjoy myself tonight unless I speak to her. Walking the short distance to her room, I knock lightly on her door.

"Aria, it's me," I call out. I'm met with silence, so I slowly open her door, finding the room empty. The bathroom door is closed, but I swear I can hear her singing in there. Crossing the room, I push gently on the door, chuckling as I listen to her singing badly to a song I don't recognize. Despite her singing, she must hear me laughing as she pokes her head around the shower curtain.

"Shit, Jack, you scared me. What are you doing?" she asks, wiping the water off her face. She must be halfway through washing her hair as she's covered in lathered shampoo.

"Sorry, I didn't mean to scare you. I just wanted to talk. I'll come back." I turn to walk away when she calls out.

"Where's Jacob?"

"Asleep," I tell her as I turn back around.

She bites down on her bottom lip, and I can see the conflict in her eyes.

"Want to join me?"

I hesitate. Of course, I want to join her, but I came in here to talk. I'm too selfish though. I want her.

"Yes," I say, stripping out of my clothes. I pull the curtain back and climb into the tub, my eyes roaming every inch of her perfect body. I slip my arms around her waist and tug her to me. She gasps as my rapidly hardening erection presses against her. Lowering my head, I capture her lips with mine, and her tongue pushes into my mouth. Her nipples pebble against my bare chest and I turn slightly, pushing her gently against the wall. She gasps again as the cold tiles hit her skin, and I drop my lips from hers, kissing around her jaw and down her neck. My lips continue over her collarbone, my hand cupping her breast as my tongue comes to circle her nipple. My kisses continue over her flat stomach, and I kneel in front of her, lifting one of her legs onto my shoulder.

"Jack," she mumbles, her cheeks flushing pink as she realizes how open she is to me. She closes her eyes as I run my fingers through her folds.

"So ready for me," I whisper as I drop my head, my tongue

circling her clit. I feel her fingers snake into my hair as she holds my head. My tongue continues to lap against her as I push two fingers inside her wet heat.

"Ohhhh," she moans as I thrust my fingers inside her, her walls gripping them tightly. She tugs on my hair as I suck her clit into my mouth, feeling her legs begin to shake. Knowing she's close, I add another finger and bite down gently on her clit, my tongue lapping at her over and over again. Suddenly, her whole body shudders as she comes, and I have to hold her up as my mouth and fingers tease out every last bit of her pleasure. Her breathing is labored as I gently remove my fingers and lower her leg. Her head is resting back on the tiles, and her eyes are still closed. Kissing my way back up her body, I find her lips, and she kisses me hungrily.

"I need you," she moans, her hand reaching down for my rock-hard cock. She pumps my erection with her small hand, and I gasp, dropping my head.

"Fuck, Aria," I mutter into her neck. Wrapping my arms around her legs, I lift her up, her legs winding around me. Using the wall as support, I reach down and remove her hand, guiding my cock toward her entrance. Pushing into her, I drop my head back as her heat envelops me. She feels so good, and I try not to think about how perfectly we fit together. I pull out slowly before slamming back into her. She cries out in pleasure, and I capture her cries with my mouth.

"You feel so good," she moans against my lips, her hands tugging on the hair at the base of my neck. I continue to pound into her, the familiar feeling settling into the pit of my stomach. I'm going to come soon.

"Are you close?" I ask, my voice breathless.

"God, yes. Don't stop." I reach my hand between our bodies, circling my finger around her clit. "Oh, yes!" she cries, her nails scratching down my back. "I'm coming, Jack." Her pussy contracts around my cock, and she whimpers. Her body convulses against me as she comes, and I carry on pounding into her, her orgasm seeming to last forever. Her pleasure triggers my own, and I come hard, my body trembling with the power of my orgasm. I've never felt anything close to this with anyone else, as wave after wave of pleasure engulfs me.

We're both out of breath as I pull out of her, lowering her legs so she can stand. Slipping my arm around her neck, I pull her mouth to mine. "It gets better and better, Aria," I mumble against her lips, before kissing her softly. "Can I finish washing you?" She looks down at me and nods.

"Okay," she whispers.

"Turn around."

Her eyes hold mine for a few seconds before she turns, her back to my chest. Reaching for the shower gel, I lather it between my fingers, dragging my soapy hands up her back and over her shoulders. I step closer to her as my hands go over her collarbone. She drops her head back on my chest, moaning as my hands soap her tits, my fingers tugging and pinching her nipples. My cock begins to harden again, and I inhale sharply as she pushes her ass back against me. Turning her in my arms, I kiss her lips before dropping to my knees. My hands work up her calves and over her knees, my fingers kneading the soft skin on her thighs. I lift my eyes up to see her staring at me. Her breathing is ragged, and I know when my hands reach between her legs, she's going to be wet again.

"You okay?" I ask, as she continues to stare at me. She nods, and I hold her gaze as I slide my hand between her legs. She gasps as I find her swollen clit, my thumb circling it. She bites down on her lip, her hands threading into my hair. She whimpers as I remove my hand and stand up. Reaching for the showerhead, I swill the soap from her body, her eyes still fixed on me.

"Turn back around," I whisper. She does as I ask, and I slip my arm around her waist, pulling her back against my front. Flicking the showerhead to massage, I direct the spray between her legs. She cries out as the jet of water hits her clit, and her legs shake. I tighten my hold on her as she moans.

"Fuck! Jack! Fuck!" she gasps as my other hand cups one of her tits, my fingers flicking and twisting her nipple. She pushes her hips forward, her breathing labored. "Oh, God!" she moans. "I'm going to come." Her head falls back onto my chest as her body shudders with her release, moans escaping her lips. Removing the showerhead, I hold on to her until her orgasm subsides and she goes limp in my arms.

"How many orgasms have you given me today?" she whispers, her head still dropped back onto my chest. "I've lost count."

I kiss her neck and squeeze her gently. "I love watching you fall apart."

She turns in my arms and kisses me. "Now it's your turn," she says against my lips.

Her mouth peppers hot kisses around my jaw and down my neck. Dropping to her knees, she wraps her hand around my cock, pumping my shaft.

"That feels so good, Aria," I moan, my head falling back against the tiles. I inhale sharply as she takes me in her mouth, her tongue swirling around the head of my cock. Her head bobs up and down as she sucks and licks my length, and my hands tangle in her wet hair. My legs shake and I'm panting as she takes me to the back of her throat. I thrust against her mouth and moan as I feel my orgasm build. Her hand still grips the base of my cock as her tongue continues to swirl around my erection.

"I'm going to come," I warn, giving her the chance to stop. She doesn't and I tug on her hair as I come harder than I ever have. Her hand continues to work me over, dragging the last of my orgasm from my body, and I lift her up to me, kissing her hard. "That was incredible, Aria." She smiles and I pull her into me.

"We should get ready."

"I think I should wash myself or we'll never get out of here."

She smiles and reaches up on her tiptoes to kiss me.

"Spoilsport." She rinses the shampoo out of her hair and climbs out of the shower, leaving me to wash up. "Hey, what was it you wanted to talk about?" she asks from the other side of the shower curtain.

"Erm, I just wanted to check you were okay, after earlier."

"Earlier?" she asks, poking her head around the shower curtain.

"Yeah, after what happened by the river. You just seemed a little quiet."

She stares at me and I wonder if I've read her wrong.

"I'm good, Jack. What happened at the river was good." She smiles, but it doesn't reach her eyes, and that one smile tells me I didn't read her wrong. I don't push it though; she clearly doesn't want to talk. It's obviously her way of dealing with this, and that's fine. For me this is way more than friends with bene- fits, and the selfish side of me wants her to feel the same. I've just no idea what this means for my stay at the ranch.

CHAPTER 15

Aria

Iraise my hand in a wave as I walk backwards and away from the ranch house. Quinn has just arrived with Brody, and Josh and Mason arrived a few minutes before. Jack kissed me on the porch like I was the air he needed to breathe, and I swear if everyone hadn't turned up, we'd be having sex again. My body had never come alive as much as it does when I'm around him. There's no way I can deny the sexual attraction between us. Maybe that's all this is, and I'm confusing lust for something else? That must be it. I haven't known him long enough to feel anything more. Right?

Shaking away my crazy thoughts, I walk through the stables on the way to Savannah's to check on the horses. Seeing they're all settled for the night, I take my time walking across the ranch.

It's a beautiful night, and I'm looking forward to some girly fun with Savannah and Quinn.

When I reach Savannah's house, she pulls me into a hug before leading me into the kitchen and handing me a Sex on the Beach cocktail. I smile to myself, thinking I was right about ending up with a hangover tomorrow. "Mmm, this is good," I tell her as I take a sip of the yellowy orange drink.

"It's my favorite. I tried a mojito last week, but I think I added too much rum." She pulls a face and I laugh. "Still drank it though!"

"Why am I not surprised," I say with a giggle.

"Let's take these outside." She raises her glass in the air and I nod, following her through the bi-folding doors that lead to the decked area in the backyard. Flopping down on the sofa, she puts her feet up on the small glass table. "Quinn is bringing pizza back with her from Papa Murphy's."

"Yum! I love that place," I say, sitting next to her.

"Me too." She takes a mouthful of her drink, her eyes sliding to me. "So, come on, then, spill. What's going on with you and Jack?"

"That didn't take long," I say with a sigh as I place my drink on the table. "I think I'm getting in way over my head, Sav."

She frowns and turns to me. "What do you mean?"

"We're supposed to be doing this friends-with-benefits thing—"

"Jack suggested that?" she interrupts, surprise evident in her tone.

"No, I suggested it."

She pulls a face and shakes her head. "Why the hell would you do that?"

"Self-preservation," I say quietly. "If I let him in, what do I do when he goes home?"

"Seems to me you've already let him in."

Sighing, I drop my head back on the sofa. "Why did I have to fall for someone I can't have?" It's a question, but not one I expect an answer to.

"But you *can* have him, Aria. You've just got to have a little faith that things will work out how they should."

"I know exactly how this ends. I fall in love, he leaves, and I end up alone and heartbroken."

"You don't know that's going to happen. What if he decides to stay?"

I groan. "You sound like Lib."

"That's because we are both very wise," she says, sticking her tongue out and pulling a face. I can't help but laugh. "Seriously though, you seem great together. Watching you earlier, it's like you've known each other forever."

"It feels so right," I admit, and I'm mortified to feel a single tear slip down my cheek. I never cry. Sav notices and reaches her arm around me.

"You *really* like him, don't you?" I nod. "Have you talked to him?"

I shake my head. "And say what? I've only known him a couple of days. All these feelings are crazy. Maybe we should just stay friends and forget the benefits."

"Can you just be his friend, though? How would you feel if you saw him with someone else?"

"Devastated," I admit.

"Then there's your answer. You need to talk to him." She

sits up and takes a mouthful of her drink. "Tell me about the benefits!"

"What?" I ask on a laugh.

"The sex! Tell me about the sex! I want *all* the details."

"Wait!" a voice shouts from inside, and we both look toward the house to see Quinn grabbing a soda from the refrigerator. "It seems I've arrived just in time for the juicy part," she says as she makes her way toward us, soda and pizza in her hands. I laugh as she places the pizza box on the small table and sits next to me. "Carry on," she says, waving her hand.

"I'm not going into details. All I'm going to say is wow!" I flip open the pizza box and pick up a slice.

"What? That's it?" Savannah cries. "We need more than that! You had grass in your hair earlier, spill."

"We had sex down by the river, that's all I'm going to say. He's your cousin, Savannah. Surely you don't want all the details?"

"He's not my cousin," Quinn exclaims. "Tell me!"

I laugh and shake my head. "It's the best I've ever had, okay? Can we change the subject now!"

"Get a few more cocktails inside her. She'll tell us more then," Savannah says, plucking my almost empty glass from the table and wriggling her eyebrows at me. "I'll get you another one."

"I'll never be that drunk," I call after her as she heads inside.

"We'll see," she shouts over her shoulder.

"She's not going to give up, is she?" I ask Quinn, and she laughs.

"Nope. Afraid not."

I groan and drop my head back on the sofa. "Are you picking the guys up later?" I ask, hoping to change the subject before Savannah comes back.

"Yeah, they all have work tomorrow. All except Jack, so it won't be a late night."

I nod. "How are the wedding plans coming along?" Brody had proposed to Quinn a couple of months ago, and they're planning a fall wedding.

"Really good. I have my dress, as you know, and the flowers and cake are ordered. It's all coming together." After Brody proposed, Quinn had asked me to be one of her bridesmaids, along with Savannah, Libby, and Hope. We'd all gone shopping in Austin a few weeks ago, and she'd chosen the most beautiful wedding dress. We're waiting on getting our bridesmaid dresses until after Lib has the baby. That just means another girly shopping trip, and I can't wait. I've gotten close to Savannah, Libby, and Quinn during my time at the ranch. They've made me feel like part of the family, and I love them all.

"I'm excited for you, Quinn. I've seen some of the weddings you've organized. It's going to be beautiful."

"Thanks, Aria."

"How is the new business going? I was telling Jack about it earlier—"

"Telling Jack what?" Savannah interrupts as she hands me another cocktail. "And was it before or after the hot sex in the rain?"

I roll my eyes. "We've moved on from that conversation, Sav. Sorry." I chuckle as I take a mouthful of cocktail. Coughing, I put my hand over my mouth. "Fuck! Why is this one so much stronger than the last?"

"I *really* want the details."

"Urgh," I groan, putting the ridiculously strong drink down on the table. "I was asking Quinn about the wedding and the events business. You remember your brother's getting married, right?"

She holds her hands up in defeat. "Okay, I'll drop it. And of course I remember my brother is getting married. One of my best friends is going to be my sister. How could I forget that?"

"I can't believe you'll all be married soon," I say wistfully. Savannah and Josh had married on the ranch at the beginning of the year. Josh proposed right before Christmas, and they'd planned the wedding with Quinn's help in a matter of weeks. Only close family and friends had been invited. It was small, but beautiful. Just how I'd want my wedding to be, not that I've thought about it much. There'd been no one in my life I'd come close to being that serious about. In fact, other than a relationship with a guy I'd met in college that ended badly, I haven't dated much at all. I can't help but think if I'd met Jack in another lifetime, he could have been that someone. I haven't met him in another lifetime though, and it looks like we are only destined to be together for a short time.

"Who'd have thought we'd all be so grown up and responsible?" Savannah says with a smile. "Do you want kids, Aria?" she asks.

"Sure, someday."

"You seem pretty taken with Jacob."

"He's adorable." I don't admit that I'm already getting attached to him. "What about you, Quinn?" I ask, steering the conversation away from me. "Are babies in the cards for you and Brody?"

Her face flushes pink and she sips on her soda. Savannah must see it too, as she catches my eye and grins.

"Quinn Montgomery, do you have something you need to tell us?" Savannah asks, bouncing in her seat. She shakes her head and drops her eyes. "Oh my God! I'm going to be an aunty, aren't I?" A small smile pulls on her lips and Savannah squeals.

"We weren't going to say anything yet," Quinn admits. "It's still early." Savannah jumps off the sofa and throws her arms around Quinn.

"Congratulations! How far along are you? Were you trying? Do Mom and Dad know?" Savannah's words tumble out, and I can't help but laugh. I reach my hand over and squeeze Quinn's.

"I'm really happy for you, Quinn," I tell her, she smiles at me and turns to Savannah.

"No one knows except Brody, and now you two. We only found out last night. I think I'm around six weeks, and yes, we were trying," Quinn says, answering all of Savannah's questions.

"How did Brody take the news?" she asks excitedly.

Quinn laughs. "He was a little surprised. We both were. We've only been trying for a few weeks. I don't think either of us thought it would happen so quickly. He's happy though."

"Mom is going to be so excited. When do you think you'll tell them?"

"We have a doctor's appointment next week, so we were going to wait until then. Can you keep it a secret?"

"Of course!" Savannah exclaims, and I can't help but smile. There is no way Savannah will be able to keep it a secret.

Quinn's eyes flick to mine, and the look on her face tells me she knows that too.

After we've eaten the pizza, the night is filled with talk of weddings, babies, and for me, drinking far too many of Savannah's ridiculously strong cocktails. We've moved inside and Savannah's put a movie on, not that anyone is watching it. We're more than happy chatting, but it's good for background noise.

"I should go and get the guys. I said I'd be there around eleven," Quinn says on a yawn, making no attempt to get up off the sofa. Sliding my phone from my shorts, I see it's just after eleven. She looks tired, and I feel bad she has to go out this late to pick them up.

"You look tired. I could have driven if I hadn't had so much to drink." She waves her hand dismissively.

"I'm good, I'll go in a minute."

"I've drunk too much too. Maybe the guys could call a cab?" Savannah suggests.

"I'm fine, really," Quinn mumbles, her eyes closed.

"Yeah, you look wide awake," I joke. Just then the door to the living room opens and Josh walks in.

"Hey, babe. Quinn was just going to come get you all. Is everything okay?"

He nods and crosses the room, dropping a kiss on her lips. "Mase was worried about Lib and wanted to come home, so we all came back in a cab."

"Is Libby okay?" she asks, concern on her face.

"Yeah, we've just come from there. She wasn't answering her phone, but she'd just fallen asleep."

"Where are Brody and Jack?" she asks. "I think Quinn might need carrying home," she says with a chuckle.

"Just in the kitchen. They're grabbing a beer." My stomach flips knowing Jack is here.

"I should head home," I say, standing up. "Thanks for a great night, Sav. You too, Quinn."

"Why don't you stay for another drink now that the guys are here?" Savannah says, raising her eyebrows.

Before I can answer, Brody and Jack walk in. Jack's laughing at something Brody's said, and God, he looks hot. The sleeves of his white shirt have been rolled up, showing off his forearms, and it looks as though he's been running his hand through his hair all night. There's dark stubble on his perfect jaw, and my cheeks flush with heat as I remember how it feels to have it brush against my thigh when his mouth is between my legs.

Shaking away my inappropriate thoughts, I drag my eyes off him before he catches me staring. "I really should go. I've got an early start tomorrow. Are we still going to look at that horse in Llano?" Savannah was looking at a filly for Hope and had asked me to go with her to check the horse over.

"Not until the afternoon, and I can get Colt or Taylor to see to the horses in the morning. Stay, please." My eyes flick to Jack, who's staring at me. He smiles when my gaze meets his and my heart stutters in my chest.

"Okay," I whisper, my eyes never leaving his. I'm in way over my head with Jack, but I just can't stay away. At least I know I'll have Sav, Quinn, and Lib here to pick up the pieces of my shattered heart when he leaves. He's here now, though, and as much as I argue with myself, I just want to be with him.

CHAPTER 16

Jack

"I can't get a hold of Lib. I'm going to head home," Mason says, concern lacing his voice. "I'm sure she's just asleep, but I need to check she's okay."

"I'm ready to call it a night," Brody says. "What about you two?" he asks, looking between me and Josh.

"Sure. I'm ready to head home to my girls," Josh says, drinking down what's left of his Bud.

"I'm good to go too," I tell him, wanting to know myself Lib is okay. I'm secretly hoping if we leave early, I'll get to see Aria again. They'd all wanted to know what was happening with us after seeing me kiss her goodbye on the porch steps. I told them what Aria wanted, that we're fucking and nothing

119

more. It's so much more than that though, and I know she can't deny it forever.

As the cab pulls away from the ranch house, we all head with Mason to their cottage. I can see the relief on his face when he finds Libby fast asleep on the couch. I slap him on the shoulder and drop a kiss on Libby's head before watching him scoop her up and carry her to bed. Watching them together makes me want Aria in my arms.

"Do you think Aria will still be at yours?" I ask Josh as we head toward his place.

He nods. "Yep. Savannah was making Sex on the Beach cocktails when I left. I'm expecting them to be very drunk."

"Is she really just your fuck buddy?" Brody asks from the side of me. "Because, believe me, I've been there. You think it's good at the time, but it's really not."

I sigh. "It's already so much more for me, but she says that's all she wants." I drag my hand through my hair. "I can't blame her. I'm not staying. We can't have any sort of future."

"What's keeping you in the UK?" Brody asks, and my head flies around to look at him. He shrugs. "I know for a fact it isn't Jacob's mom."

"Dude!" Josh hisses from the other side of me. "Just like your sister. No fucking filter."

I laugh. "It's fine, Josh. He's right. It isn't Zara, she couldn't give a fuck about either of us." A wave of sadness crashes over me when I voice that aloud. I know it's true, and I don't care that she doesn't give a fuck about me. Any feelings I had for her are long gone, but Jacob, how can she not love him? I still can't understand it. I don't think I ever will.

"How can I take him away from my parents? They already miss Libby so much. I don't think I could do that to them."

"I think they'd want you to be happy," Brody says.

"Maybe, but at what expense?" Neither Brody nor Josh answer as we reach the house, seemingly neither knowing what to say.

"I need a beer," I say, breaking the unease hanging in the air.

"Help yourself, I'm going to say hi to Sav," Josh says, waving his hand in the direction of the kitchen.

"God, he's still as pussy whipped as he ever was!" Brody exclaims, opening the fridge and grabbing out three bottles of beer. He hands me one and I open it, taking a pull. Heading out of the kitchen, I follow Brody to the sitting room.

"Seems all three of you are," I say on a chuckle as we walk into the sitting room.

"I really should go. I've got an early start tomorrow. Are we still going to look at that horse in Llano?" Aria says as we walk in. My heart drops as I hear her saying she's leaving.

"Not until the afternoon, and I can get Colt or Taylor to see to the horses in the morning. Stay, please," Savannah says, and I look across to Aria. She turns her head, and I smile as her eyes fix on mine.

"Okay," she whispers. Crossing the room, I slide my arm around her waist and pull her against me.

"Hey, baby. Did you have a good night?" She nods, reaching up and pressing her lips against mine.

"Did you?"

"Yeah, it was good to get out and unwind for a bit. Did you get plied with Sav's cocktails?" She laughs.

"Yeah, just one or two!"

"What's going on with Sav and Brody?" I ask as Savannah throws her arms around Brody.

She laughs. "She's bad at keeping secrets, that's what," she says cryptically.

"She told you, didn't she?" Brody says to Savannah as he pulls out of her embrace. There's a smile on his face and Savannah nods.

"She didn't want to. I kind of guessed. We got to talking about who wanted kids and I could tell by her face." Savannah's practically bouncing on the spot, a huge grin on her face.

"What's going on?" I whisper in Aria's ear, and she shivers as my breath hits her skin.

"I think you're about to find out."

"I'm so happy for you, Brode. I can't wait to be an aunty."

"Quinn's pregnant?" Josh says, and Brody nods. "That's great news!"

"We only found out last night. We were going to wait to tell everyone until after the doctor's appointment next week. Seems Savannah worked it out," he says on a laugh.

"Congratulations, man," I tell him, leaving Aria's side and pulling him into a hug. Glancing at Quinn on the sofa, I see she's fast asleep. "Seems the exhaustion is kicking in already." I remember the first few weeks after Zara found out she was pregnant with Jacob. She could pretty much fall asleep standing up and rarely made it past 9 p.m.

"I'd better get her home," Brody says as he scoops a sleeping Quinn into his arms.

"Have you been drinking?" Savannah asks, a frown on her face.

"I've only had one beer. I'm good, and the truck's just outside. See you all tomorrow," he says as he carries her out of the sitting room.

"Another drink, Aria?" Savannah asks.

"Can I just get a soda? I think I've had enough alcohol for tonight."

"Lightweight!" she exclaims as she leaves the sitting room, pulling Josh along with her.

"Seems we're alone," I whisper, leaning over and snaking my hand into her hair, pulling her mouth to mine. Kissing her, I swipe my tongue across her bottom lip, and she opens up to me. I feel her wind her arms around my neck as her tongue duels with mine. She tastes of orange juice, alcohol, and Aria, and I can't get enough of her. Pulling out of the kiss, I rest my forehead on hers as I catch my breath.

"Stay with me tonight?" I whisper. "I want to wake up with you in my arms." I feel her sigh, and I close my eyes as I wait for her to say no.

"Okay," she says, so quietly I wonder if I've heard her wrong. I lift my head and search her eyes with mine.

"Was that a yes?" I ask, and she nods. Smiling, I drop my lips back to hers and I'm soon lost in her again. Hearing someone clear their throat, I reluctantly stop kissing her. She drops her head on my chest, seemingly embarrassed to be caught making out. I chuckle as I wrap my arms around her and glance up to see Josh and Savannah standing in the doorway.

"We interrupting?" Josh asks with a wink.

"Actually, yes—" I begin.

"No, of course not," Aria rushes out, interrupting me. "We were just…" She trails off, and Savannah laughs.

"Going at it in our living room?" she jokes.

"You're doing it all wrong if that's how you're having sex," Aria says, her voice deadpan, and I burst out laughing. "Maybe Josh needs some tips?"

"No tips needed thanks, Aria," he says, pulling Savannah against him. "We're good."

"This is the strangest conversation I've ever had. I think we need to change the subject," Savannah says, holding out Aria's soda. She chuckles and leaves my side to take the can from Savannah.

"Did I hear you say you were heading out to look at a horse tomorrow?" I ask, attempting to steer away from the awkward conversation.

"Yeah," Sav says. "We're looking at getting a filly for Hope. She loves to take care of the horses and she's getting more confident riding. I think it's time. The one I've seen is three, and the perfect age to be broken in. I need Aria's expert opinion."

"Does Hope know?" I ask.

"God, no!" Josh exclaims. "She'd be asking constantly when the horse is arriving. We made the mistake of telling her about Libby being pregnant, and she asks every day if today is the day the baby arrives! It's been a long eight months."

"What are your plans for tomorrow?" Savannah asks me.

"I was thinking I might take Libby for lunch if she feels up to it. I heard Mason say he was checking the perimeter fences all day, so I figured she'd be on her own."

"That'll be nice," Aria says as she sits next to me on the sofa and presses her body against mine. She yawns and I wrap my arm around her.

"Shall we head back, baby?" I ask her, seeing she's tired.

"Yeah, I think all the Sex on the Beach has made me tired." My eyes widen and Savannah snorts with laughter. "Hang on," she says, sitting up. "That came out wrong." Her cheeks have flushed pink and she looks beautiful. "Urgh, you know what I mean," she says, waving her hand, and I laugh.

Standing up, I hold out my hand and pull her up off the sofa. I watch her as she goes to Savannah and pulls her into a hug. Savannah whispers something in her ear, and Aria shakes her head before looking across at me, and I can't help but wonder what was said. After a round of goodbyes, we head back to the ranch house, hand in hand. The house is in darkness as we come to the porch steps. Claire and Ryan must already be in bed. We enter the house silently and climb the stairs, Aria's hand still entwined with mine.

"I just want to check on Jacob," I whisper as we reach my bedroom door. "I won't be long."

"Can I come too?" she asks shyly. I nod and smile, tugging her down the hallway with me. I slowly push open Jacob's door. The unicorn night-light gives off just enough of a glow to cross the room without falling over anything. Dropping Aria's hand, I peer into his cot, seeing he's fast asleep. His thumb is in his mouth and his other hand holds on tightly to his blue rabbit toy. Leaning over the side, I press a kiss to his chubby cheek.

"Sleep tight, little man," I whisper. I step back and watch as Aria looks into the cot. Her hand brushes over his hair, and she kisses her fingers, pressing them gently to his cheek.

"Night, buddy," she mumbles, and my heart just about

explodes in my chest. She turns around and catches me staring, but I can't drag my gaze from her. "Everything okay?" she asks quietly.

I nod. "Come on, I want to fall asleep with you in my arms," I tell her as I reach for her hand and guide her out of Jacob's room and into mine. She smiles and yawns. As much as I want to make love to her, I know she's tired. I'm more than happy to just have her in my arms.

CHAPTER 17

Aria

The next few weeks fly by, and I spend all of my spare time with Jack and Jacob. I fall asleep in Jack's arms every night, and as much as I don't want to admit it, I know I'm falling in love with him. I'm sure he feels the same. I can feel it in his kisses, and I see it in his eyes when he looks at me. I can't even think about him leaving. Neither of us have mentioned it, and I've no idea how long he plans on staying. It's a conversation we need to have, but for now, I can't bring myself to instigate it.

It's the day before Libby's due date, and her and Jack's parents are arriving this afternoon. If I said I wasn't nervous, I'd be lying. After insisting we just be friends with benefits, we'd never discussed the fact we've become so much more than that.

I want his parents to like me. He and Jacob mean the world to me.

"Morning, beautiful," Jack says on a yawn as he wakes up, his arms tightening around me. I'd been awake for a while but hadn't wanted to move off his chest and wake him up.

"Hey, did you sleep well?" I ask, sitting up on my elbow and staring down at him. His face is soft with sleep, and his dark hair messy. A layer of stubble covers his perfect face and I reach up my hand, brushing my fingers along his jaw.

"I always sleep well when you're wrapped up in my arms," he says, reaching for my hand and brushing a kiss against my palm. There had been a couple of nights earlier in the week where Jacob had been unwell, and he'd wanted to sleep with his daddy. I'd stayed in my own room, and neither of us had slept great. It was surprising how quickly we'd gotten used to being together.

"What time are your parents getting in?" I ask, biting down on my bottom lip.

"They land at two fifteen p.m. I need to leave here just after one." He's borrowing one of the ranch trucks to pick them up.

"What are you telling them about us?" I ask quietly.

Everyone on the ranch knows we're together to some degree, including Claire and Ryan. I have no idea if Claire or Lib mentioned anything when they spoke to Jack's mom on the phone, which I know they do regularly. Before he can answer, his phone chimes from the nightstand. He reaches for it, his whole body tensing underneath me as he looks at the screen.

"Are you okay?" I ask, placing my hand on his arm. He sits up, swinging his legs to the side of the bed, my hand falling from his arm. Frowning, I kneel behind him. "Is it Libby?" I ask, my voice laced with concern.

He shakes his head. "It's Zara."

"Who's Zara?"

"Jacob's mum," he says on a sigh, his hand pushing through his dark hair. "I haven't heard from her in months." I wrap my arms around him and drop my head onto his back. Feeling his hand come over mine, he tangles our fingers together.

"What does she want?"

"She wants to know where we are. She's been to the house I rented, but obviously, we aren't there. She's demanding to see Jacob." His voice sounds strained, and I can't imagine how hard this must be for him.

"I'm sorry," I whisper, pressing a kiss to the bare skin of his back. "What are you going to tell her?"

"That I'm in Texas with Lib, and I don't know when I'll be home. She can demand as much as she wants. She's the one who walked out." His fingers fly over the screen of his phone as he replies, and I move back, not wanting to seem like I'm reading over his shoulder. I can't think of him and Jacob going home, it hurts too much. Climbing out of bed, I pull on a tank and some yoga pants and pad silently to the bathroom, closing the door behind me. Gripping onto the sink, I drop my head, nerves bubbling in my stomach at what this might mean for us. I guess at the back of my mind I had a tiny glimmer of hope he might decide to stay at the ranch, that his parents might see how happy he is here with me. I know he's worried about taking Jacob away from them with Libby already living here. That one text crushed those hopes though, and makes me realize this is so much bigger than just his relationship with his parents. Jacob's mom is in England, and regardless of how rocky their relation-ship is, she will always be his mom. He can never move halfway across the world.

After using the bathroom, I open the bedroom door and see Jack still sitting on the edge of the bed, clutching his phone. "You okay, babe?" I ask, crossing the room and standing in front of him. He raises his head and smiles, dropping his phone onto the comforter. He reaches for me and pulls me to stand between his open legs. His arms wind around my waist and he drops his head on my stomach. My fingers tangle in his hair as I hold him against me. Before either of us can say anything, his phone rings from the side of him, and I glance down, seeing Zara's name flashing across the screen. I feel him sigh heavily, his head still pressed against my stomach. He must have known she was going to call.

"I'll leave you to talk to her," I say quietly, and his head shoots up.

"No, stay. Please. It won't be a long conversation," he says, and I can't say no to him as his eyes bore into mine.

"Okay," I whisper, moving from between his legs and sitting on the bed next to him. He sighs again before picking up his phone.

"Hello," he says, his voice tight. He's silent for a few seconds before he stands and starts pacing the room. "I wasn't aware I needed your permission, Zara," he spits. "Last time I checked, you didn't care!" I can't help but feel awkward as I listen to their heated conversation. I can only hear Jack's side, but I can guess from his responses what Zara is saying. "You know what's not fair? You walking out on your son… I don't know when I'm coming home." He's still pacing the bedroom and I lower my eyes, my fingers fiddling with the edge of the comforter. "That's none of your goddamn business. I don't ask who you're sleeping with. I don't care." My head shoots up and I look across to see him staring at me. He winks at me and I give him a small smile. "Look, Zara," he says with a sigh. "I'll let you know when I'm home, and if you still want to see him, then we can work something out. I won't be home for a while, though." I drop my eyes from his. I don't want him to ever go home, but I know he has to. "What? No! That's not happening, Zara. I have to go. Jacob needs me." I look up as he ends the call and tosses his phone across the room and onto the bed.

I stand up and make my way toward him, wrapping my arms around his neck. "What did she say?" I ask as his arms envelop me.

"That I should have asked her before leaving the country with Jacob, and that she's going to fly out here to see him." I can't believe how calm he sounds after what he's just told me.

"What?" I tilt my head to look at him. "She's coming here? To the ranch?"

He shakes his head. "No, baby. She won't come here. She couldn't be bothered to visit Jacob when he lived in the same city as her, let alone when he's on the other side of the world."

"Do you think she'll call again?"

"I don't know, but I don't want her flitting in and out of his life. That's not fair on him. He deserves so much more."

"He does, but he has you. You're a great dad to him, Jack," I assure him, going up on my tiptoes to kiss him. He smiles before kissing me back.

"You have a better relationship with him than Zara. Even

before she left, she wasn't really present, if that makes sense. He adores you," he says quietly.

"I adore him too, Jack. He's easy to love…" I trail off and voice what I know I've been struggling to say. "I don't know what I'm going to do when you both go home." He wraps his arms around me, and I rest my head on his chest.

"I can't imagine being away from you either." I can feel his heart racing under my cheek, and my stomach flips at his words. Telling him how I feel is on the tip of my tongue, but I hold back. It'll only confuse things. I was the one who pushed for casual, even though we both know it's been far from that for weeks.

"Daddy! Ria!" a little voice calls, and I smile, loving how he's started calling for me along with Jack in the morning. He's been doing it for a few days, and it makes my heart swell with love for him.

"I think someone's awake," Jack says as he brushes his lips against my hair. Reaching for my hand, he guides me out of his room and along the hallway to Jacob's bedroom. Pushing the door open, I smile as I see him standing up in his crib, his little chubby hands holding on to the bars.

"Daddy, up!" he cries when he sees Jack, who walks in and scoops him up, dropping a kiss on his cheek.

"Guess who's coming today?" Jack says to him as he lays him on the changing table and begins to change his diaper. Exposing his tummy, he lowers his mouth and blows a raspberry on his skin. Jacob laughs and I can't help but smile. "Nanny and Pops!" Jack exclaims, and Jacob squeals with excitement. Jack sits him up and he reaches out his arms to me. Crossing the room, I pick him up and put him on my hip.

"Hungry?" I ask, brushing my lips across his blond hair. He nods and I tickle his waist. "Let's get breakfast."

Half an hour later I've left Jack and Jacob in the kitchen finishing off their breakfast. I need to shower and get out to the exercise area. The young horse Savannah and I went to look at a few weeks ago arrived on the ranch yesterday, and today I'm starting to work with her so she's ready for Hope to ride.

Standing under the hot spray of the shower, my mind wanders back to the conversation Jack had with Zara earlier. We hadn't talked about his ex. I hadn't asked and he'd never mentioned her. I knew little bits from Libby, but it wasn't really anything to do with me. It must be so hard for Jack to have her walk out and then just randomly want to see Jacob whenever it suits her. I really hoped she doesn't turn up at the ranch. I know it's likely she was just angry and making empty threats, but she seems unpredictable, so anything is possible.

CHAPTER 18

Jack

Driving to the airport, I glance in the rearview mirror and see Jacob is fast asleep. I'm about twenty minutes from Austin International Airport, and he's been asleep since before we got out of Marble Falls. The car always had that effect on him. I'm looking forward to seeing my parents, and I know Jacob is excited to see them too. I'm a little nervous about introducing them to Aria. I know they'll see how much she means to me when they see us together, and I know my mum especially will worry I'm not going to come home. I want them to enjoy their time here and not worry about me.

I park in arrivals and pull out my phone, groaning when I see two missed calls from Zara. Ignoring them, I check my parents' flight number. The flight's only just landed, so I know they'll be a while yet, getting their luggage and then passing through security. Glancing over my shoulder, I check Jacob is still asleep before stepping out of the truck. Sighing, I pull up Zara's number. I'd tried to forget that I'd spoken to her this morning. I'm finally in a place where I'm happy, and it's like she somehow knows and wants to fuck everything up for me. Why did she have to contact me now? Hitting her name, I put the phone to my ear and wait for her to answer. It rings and rings, and just when I think she isn't going to answer, I hear her voice.

"Hello."

"What do you want, Zara?" I ask, my voice curt.

"Is that any way to speak to the mother of your child?" she asks, her voice like syrup.

"I wouldn't know. I haven't spoken to her since she walked out without even a glance back."

She sighs. "I guess I deserved that."

"Yeah, you did." I pace up and down outside of the truck, dragging my free hand through my hair. "So, I'll ask again, what do you want? Nothing has changed since this morning. I'm still in the US."

"I want to see Jacob."

I sigh, feeling like I'm banging my head against a brick wall. "Like I said, I'm in the US. When I get back, we can arrange something."

"Why are you there?"

"Not that it's any of your business, but Libby is having a baby."

"What about your job? How can you afford to just up and leave?"

"Zara, that's got nothing to do with you."

"I spoke to a lawyer."

I frown, an uneasy feeling settling in the pit of my stomach. "Why?" I ask cautiously.

"You should have asked me before you took Jacob out of the country. You needed my permission."

"You're fucking kidding me! You walked out on us, Zara. You forfeited all rights when you fucked off!" My free hand clenches tightly into a fist at my side.

"That's where you're wrong. I have as much parental responsibility as you."

I laugh, but there's no humor. "Yeah, right! You wouldn't know parental responsibility if it smacked you in the face."

"I want to see my son, Jack." Her voice is calm, and I can't help but wonder what's going on. She's shown no interest in Jacob for the past seven months, and even before she left, she wasn't interested.

"Get on a plane, then, Zara. Wild Oak Ranch and Retreat, just outside Marble Falls in Texas. I gotta go!" I end the call and drop my body back onto the side of the truck. My head contacts with the metal and I close my eyes, breathing deeply. I've told her where we are, but there's no way she'll come. What I said to Aria this morning was right. She hadn't bothered with him when we lived in the same city. She won't fly halfway across the world.

When I've finally calmed down, I gently pluck Jacob from his car seat and hold him against me. He's still asleep, and his head drops onto my shoulder. He's my whole world, and as selfish as it sounds, I don't want Zara back in his life, or mine. Pushing Zara to the back of my mind, I make my way across the car park to the arrivals hall. I stand and watch as people reunite with their loved ones. Jacob is going to be so excited to see my parents. I can't wait to see his face when he spots them. He stirs in my arms and lifts his head, yawning as he looks around.

"Hey, Jacob. Did you have a good sleep?" He nods and drops his head back on my shoulder, his thumb going into his mouth. I chuckle as I hold him against me, dropping a kiss on his head. Another flurry of people drifts through from baggage collection, and I smile as I see my parents. They haven't spotted us yet, and I lift Jacob onto my shoulders, putting him in their line of sight.

"Look over there, Jacob," I say, pointing in their direction. It takes him a minute or so, but I can tell the second he spots them as he starts bouncing up and down on my shoulders.

"Nanny and Pops!" he cries excitedly. My parents see him and, smiling, they make their way over to us. I reach Jacob down off my shoulders and pass him straight to my mum, as she walks up to us, her hands out for Jacob.

"Oh, you've grown so much. Nanny's missed you," she tells him, kissing his chubby cheeks. My dad pulls me into a hug, patting me on the back.

"How was the flight?" I ask as I brush a kiss across my mum's cheek.

"Long, but worth it to see you both. Libby hasn't had that baby yet, has she?" my mum asks, and I shake my head.

"No. You haven't missed it. Don't worry. Let's head to the ranch. Everyone's excited to see you."

An hour later, I turn down the oak tree-lined driveway that leads to the ranch. My mum hasn't stopped talking since she got into the truck, and I can see how excited she is to see Lib. As well as their two suitcases, they'd brought another suitcase full of baby clothes and gifts for Libby. I know how much they missed her. To be here when their grandchild arrives means the world to them.

I park up in front of the ranch house, spotting Libby on the porch swing with a book. When she sees the truck, her face lights up in a smile and she eases herself off the swing and makes her way down the steps. My mum is out of the car before I've even turned the engine off, and she rushes to Libby and pulls her into her arms.

Climbing out of the car, I smile as I watch them both, tears streaming down their faces. I reach into the back seat and unclip Jacob's seat belt.

"Aunt Libby," he cries as I make my way over to them both, my dad following with the bags.

"Hey, little man," Libby says, pulling out of Mum's embrace and wiping her eyes.

"Are you sad?" Jacob asks her, and she comes toward him, brushing her hand against his cheek.

"No, sweetheart. I'm happy," she assures him. He looks confused and I can't help but chuckle.

"Aunt Libby's just happy to see Nanny, Jacob. Like you." He still looks confused but seems to accept my answer.

"Down, Daddy," he shouts as he looks past me toward the stables. He toddles off in the direction of the stables and I chuckle as I follow him. I can see Aria in the exercise area and I'm guessing he's spotted her too.

"Ria," he shouts as he gets nearer. She looks up, her face breaking out into a smile when she sees him.

"Hey, Jacob," she calls out, her eyes flicking past him to me.

She pats the neck of the horse she's working with and climbs over the fence that surrounds the exercise area. Jogging toward him, she scoops him up, tickling him. I smile as he giggles and flings his arms around her neck. My heart stutters as I watch them together. Jacob adores her, and I know Aria feels the same.

"Hi, baby," I whisper as I come up alongside her, snaking my arm around her waist. I brush my lips against her head, and I feel her stiffen. "Is everything okay?"

"I'm nervous to meet your parents," she says, turning to face me. "Did you tell them about us?" Worry is etched on her face, and I squeeze her hip.

"No. I wasn't exactly sure what to say. I'm not sure I know myself what's happening with us, but they will love you, Aria." I want to tell her they'll love her just like I do, but I can't bring myself to say the words. These past few weeks together have been amazing, and the last thing I want to do is spook her by telling her how I feel. "Maybe tonight we can talk?"

"Okay," she whispers, giving me a small smile.

"Jack," my mum calls, and I turn to see her looking over at us.

"Come and meet them." I slide my hand down to Aria's, lacing her fingers with mine. She takes a deep breath and nods. Jacob's on her hip, and we walk hand in hand back toward the ranch house. My mum's eyes go from Jacob in Aria's arms, to our joined hands.

"Mum, Dad, this is Aria. Aria, these are my parents, Emma and Phil."

"Hi," Dad says, raising his hand in a wave.

"Really nice to meet you, Aria," my mom says, a wide smile on her face.

"You too, Mr. and Mrs. Davis."

My mum waves her hand. "Call us Emma and Phil, sweetheart. It seems you've made quite an impression on someone," she says, her eyes falling to Jacob, who's dropped his head on Aria's shoulder. Aria releases my hand and places it on Jacob's back.

"I think it might be the other way around," Aria chuckles, placing a kiss on his head. "He's the most amazing little boy."

"He is." She smiles sadly. "He's changed so much in the few weeks they've been here. We've missed him and Jack."

"I bet," she says quietly.

An awkward silence descends, and Aria drops her eyes to the floor.

"You're here!" Aunt Claire cries from the top of the porch steps, and I breathe a silent sigh of relief that she's unknowingly broken the building atmosphere.

"Claire!" my mum says, turning and rushing up the porch steps to embrace her.

"Let me help you with the bags, Dad," I say, taking one of the suitcases from him.

"Thanks, son. Your mum insisted on bringing far too much stuff."

"Are you okay with Jacob, babe?" I ask, turning to Aria. She nods and I take her hand again, following my dad up the porch steps. I dump the suitcase in the hallway and make my way into the kitchen where everyone is gathered.

"I should get back to work," Aria mumbles from the side of me. "Let you all spend some time together." She places Jacob on the floor, and he walks over to my dad, pulling on his trouser leg.

"Stay for a bit. I'm sure Claire won't mind." I go to wrap my arm around her, but she starts moving backwards.

"I really should get back to Misty. Hope wants to start riding her tomorrow. I'll catch up with you later." Before I can say anything, she's gone. I sigh, knowing the awkward conversation with my parents has likely freaked her out. There's no doubt my parents missed Jacob and me.

"Where did Aria go?" Libby asks as she comes to stand next to me, her hand rubbing her back.

"She had to get back to work." I frown as she moves uncomfortably from foot to foot. "Are you okay, Lib?"

"My back is killing me. I'm so ready for this baby to be born." I push her hand away and rub circles on her lower back.

"Are you sure you're not in labor?"

"I don't think so. It's just a backache."

"Is it the baby?" my mum asks from across the room, concern lacing her voice. Everyone turns to look at us, and Libby laughs.

"No! I just have a backache."

"Are you sure, sweetheart?" my mum asks, coming to stand next to Libby.

"I'm good, Mum," Libby tells her, brushing off her concern. "I might go and lie down though, if you don't mind?"

"Of course I don't mind."

"Come on, I'll walk you home. I need to speak to Aria anyway. Mum, would you watch Jacob for me?"

She nods. "Call me if you need me, Lib."

After a quick round of goodbyes, Libby takes my arm, and

we head down the porch steps. We're slow walking back to the cottage and I glance across at the stables as we pass. Aria's in the exercise area with Misty, and I raise my hand in a wave when she sees us. She waves back and I sigh.

"Is it not going well with you two?" Libby asks, glancing over to where Aria is.

"It's going really well. Too well."

"How can it be going too well?" she asks, her eyebrows drawn together in confusion.

"I love her, Lib." She stops and turns to face me.

"Have you told her?" I shake my head. "Why not?"

"What if she doesn't feel the same? Friends with benefits, remember. She doesn't want anything more."

"You still believe that?" I shrug. "I've seen you together, Jack. She loves you too. You should talk to her."

"We're going to talk tonight."

"Don't wait until tonight. Talk to her now." We come to a stop in the small garden outside the cottage.

"Will you be okay?"

"I'll be fine. Mason will be back soon. I'm just going to lie down." She pulls me into an embrace the best she can with her swollen stomach. "You deserve to be happy, Jack, especially after Mia and then Zara."

"Why does she have to live on the other side of the world?" I whisper.

"You'll work it out. Talk to her." I nod.

"Thanks, Lib."

She goes inside the cottage and I turn and head back to the exercise area. Can I really tell her I love her? If she doesn't feel the same way, I'll be crushed. We've spent every spare minute together since I arrived, but I knew from the beginning she didn't want to get into anything serious, knowing I wasn't staying. I've fallen hard for her though, and the thought of going home and never seeing her again isn't something I can even think about.

CHAPTER 19

Aria

I jog down the porch steps and across to the exercise area. The look on Emma's face when she spoke of missing Jacob and Jack is etched on my mind, and I can't stay at the house any longer. That coupled with Jack wanting to talk tonight is enough to produce a million butterflies in my stomach. I know exactly what he wants to talk about. Us, and what happens next. I'm just not sure I'm ready to hear what he's going to say. I've fallen hard for him, and I can only hope whatever he wants to say to me won't break my heart.

"Hey, girl," I whisper, stroking my hand gently down Misty's nose. She's a beautiful, fifteen hand, midnight black filly, and I know how excited Hope is to finally ride her. I mount her and coax her gently into a trot around the exercise area. She puts up a little resistance, and I lean down, patting her neck until she settles. She's adapted well to having a rider, and although Hope will need to be supervised, I think she's the perfect horse for her. I turn Misty back toward the ranch house and catch a glimpse of Jack and Libby heading toward Libby's place. Jack raises his hand in a wave, and I smile and wave back. I hope Libby's okay. I'll go in and see her later. A few minutes later and I'm dismounting Misty when I see Jack reappear from Libby's. He jogs over, meeting me at the entrance to the exercise area.

"Hey, baby. You about done?" He leans down and brushes his lips with mine.

"Yep. I think she's had enough for today. I'm going to put her back in her stall."

He reaches up and gently strokes her nose. "Can we take a walk?" His eyes slide to mine, and my heart races in my chest.

"Erm... sure. Just give me a few minutes." He follows me into the stables and watches as I get Misty settled. Nerves swirl in my stomach, and I can't help but wonder if his parents arriving has made him re-evaluate things. That, and his phone call earlier with Zara.

"Ready?" he asks as I close the stall door. I nod, and he takes my hand, guiding me outside. "Don't look so worried." He chuckles, squeezing my hand.

"What do you want to talk about?" We walk hand in hand up through the guest accommodations and away from the stables.

"Us."

"Okay," I whisper.

"Aria—" His phone rings loudly from the pocket of his pants and he sighs, closing his eyes. "Hold that thought," he says as he pulls the phone from his pocket, frowning when he sees who's calling.

"Mum, is everything okay?" His eyes widen, and he spins around. "But I just left her…. Okay, we'll be right there." He ends the call and starts tugging me back toward the ranch house.

"Is everything okay?" I ask as he pulls me along with him.

"Libby's waters have broken, and they can't get a hold of Mason. He's up by the river and likely doesn't have a signal. My mum's panicking."

"I'll take Marley and go and get him," I say, releasing his hand and running to the stables.

"Are you sure? I was going to take the truck."

"I'll be quicker on Marley. I can take the shortcut. Go and be with Lib." He's running alongside me and grabs my hand, pulling me to a stop.

"Thank you." He lowers his head and captures my lips with his. "I'm going to be an uncle!" He grins.

"Yes, you are," I tell him with a chuckle. "Now go! Tell Lib Mason won't be long." He nods before kissing me again.

I make my way into the stables and open Marley's stall. I saddle him up in record time and set off in a gallop in the direction of the river. Marley is quick and we make it there in around ten minutes. I can see Mason and Taylor with a group of guests who are fly fishing. I ride Marley as close as I can to the river.

"Mason!" I shout, my hands cupped around my mouth. "Mason," I cry again when he doesn't hear me. Taylor nudges him and points in my direction. "It's Libby. Her water broke." Even from the distance I am, I see his eyes widen and panic cross his face. He wades through the water as fast as he can.

"Is she okay?" he asks as he reaches me, breathless from rushing through the water.

"I think so. I came straight here when they couldn't reach you." He pulls off his waders and tosses them aside. "Take Marley. It'll be quicker than the truck." I quickly dismount and he turns to me.

"How will you get back?"

"Don't worry about that. I'll grab a ride with Taylor. Go!"

"Thanks, Aria." He brushes a kiss on my cheek and climbs onto Marley. In a second, he's racing away from me.

"Good luck!" I shout after him, a huge smile on my face. I watch until he's out of sight before turning back to where Taylor, one of the ranch hands, is still supervising the guests. He sees me and waves before making his way up the river toward me.

"So, baby Walker is on their way?" he asks as he reaches me.

"Seems that way. I hope it all goes well."

"I'm sure it will. Did you want to grab a ride back?"

"If that's okay?"

"Sure. I'll be another hour at least though. We haven't been here long."

"I might walk, then. It's a beautiful day."

"That it is, darlin'. See you later." He waves over his shoulder as he heads back to the guests.

Turning around, I walk back toward the ranch house. It's probably a thirty-minute walk, and the hot Texas sun beats down on me as I make my way through the guest accommodations. The cabins are beautiful and seeing them reminds me I need to speak to Claire and Ryan about moving out of the house and renting Lib and Mason's old cabin. As much as I love living at the house, having my own space would be amazing.

I walk quickly, eager to know how Libby is. As I make my way past Savannah's place, I notice Quinn walking toward me. I haven't seen much of her since she found out she was pregnant a few weeks ago. She and Brody found out at the sonogram they're expecting twins, and the pregnancy is really taking it out of her.

"Hey, Quinn," I say as we get closer. "Did you hear about Lib?"

She nods. "I was coming to find you."

"Is everything okay?"

She reaches me and places her hand on my arm. "Everything's fine. Everyone went with Libby to the hospital and Jack couldn't get hold of you. I offered to come find you."

"*Everyone* went?" I ask in surprise, my eyes going wide.

"I know, right! I'm going to have to speak to Brody when these two are ready to come out." She lovingly places her hand over her still flat stomach. "As much as I love the Parker/Walker clan, there is no way I want them all waiting outside the delivery room!"

I laugh. "It'll serve them right if it's a long labor. Who's got Jacob?"

"Brody. He's showing him the horses." I nod as I take her arm and we walk toward the stables.

"So, how are you feeling? How's the sickness?"

"I'm okay. I'm not going to lie, it's been rough. Today's the first day I haven't thrown up in weeks. Lib and Savannah assure me it gets better. I hope so. I'm really not enjoying being pregnant at the moment."

I squeeze her arm. "How did Brody take the news of two babies?"

She rolls her eyes and laughs. "He thinks he's got super sperm! He's been bragging for weeks."

I burst out laughing. "That sounds like Brody!"

"What sounds like Brody?" he asks as we round the stables, he and Jacob coming into view.

"Nothing," I assure him, a smile on my lips. He looks between us, his eyebrows drawn together in confusion. Quinn laughs from the side of me and steps forward, kissing him lightly on the lips.

"Are you two having fun?" she asks, slipping her arm around Brody's waist.

"Horse ride!" Jacob exclaims before Brody can answer. He chuckles.

"He's been asking to ride one of the horses since Jack went off with Lib."

"I think we can manage that if Uncle Brody will help?" I tell him, sliding my eyes to Brody.

"Sure, what do you need me to do?"

"Come on, I'll show you." I scoop up an excited Jacob and walk into the stables, Brody and Quinn following.

A quick ride on Marley seems to pacify Jacob, and I've taken a few photos, sending them over to Jack's phone, assuring him Jacob is fine. I know he will feel bad leaving me to look after Jacob, but he doesn't need to. I adore spending time with him.

A few hours later and we're back at the ranch house. Quinn

and Brody stayed for a while, but when Quinn started to yawn uncontrollably, they decided to head home. She looked exhausted. After eating dinner, Jacob is sitting cuddled up next to me in the den with his milk. Jack called about ten minutes ago to say not much is happening with Libby, but he's going to stay at the hospital another hour or so, just in case.

When I feel Jacob's head drop against my arm, I gently pull him into my arms and carry him upstairs. He's already dressed in his dinosaur pajamas, and I place him in his crib, dropping a kiss onto his chubby cheek. His eyes stay closed, and his rhythmic breathing tells me he's asleep. I was a little apprehensive knowing I'd be putting him to bed. While I've put him to bed plenty of times over the past few weeks, Jack has always been with me, and I wasn't sure if he was going to settle with just me. Looking at him now though, asleep in his crib, my heart swells with love for him. We've all gotten close over the past few weeks, and I love how Jack trusts me with him.

I close the door to Jacob's bedroom and pad along the corridor to Jack's room. After a quick shower, I climb under the comforter and turn the TV on with the remote control. I try to concentrate on the reality show that's playing, but my mind wanders back to the failed conversation Jack and I had earlier. Nerves bubble up in my stomach as I think about what it was he wanted to say, and I'm torn between wanting to finish the conversation and staying oblivious in my own little bubble.

CHAPTER 20

Jack

I yawn as I park the truck outside the ranch house, the light from the headlights illuminating the driveway. Claire and Ryan had left the hospital a couple of hours ago, but with the house shrouded in darkness, I'm guessing by now they've already turned in for the night.

"I should have stayed at the hospital. What if Libby needs me?" my mum asks from the passenger seat, worry etched on her face.

"She has Mason, sweetheart. He'll ring if she needs us," my dad says from the back seat, his hand coming to rest reassuringly on her shoulder. Despite being at the hospital for hours, Libby's contractions had slowed right down, and baby Walker seemed more than happy to stay where he or she was.

"We can head back to the hospital first thing tomorrow. It didn't look like much was happening tonight," I say, climbing out of the truck and heading up the porch steps.

My parents are staying in the guest bedroom on the ground floor, and after saying goodnight, I go upstairs, stopping to check in on Jacob. Leaning over his cot, he's fast asleep, his thumb nestled firmly in his mouth. Dropping a kiss on his head, I make my way to my room. I smile as I walk in and see Aria asleep in my bed. The TV is on low and she must have fallen asleep watching it. I pad across the room, reach for the remote, and turn it off, plunging the room into darkness. I quickly shower before pulling on some sleep shorts and sliding into bed. Wrapping my arms around her, I pull her against me, and she sighs contentedly as her head drops onto my chest. Suddenly she sits up.

"Did Libby have the baby?" Even in the darkness of the room, I can see the excitement on her face, and I smile.

"No. Not yet. Her contractions slowed right down, so we came home. Mason's still with her."

"Poor Lib. I hope she's not too uncomfortable." She lies back down, pressing her body into my side.

"How was your afternoon? Was Jacob good?"

She nods. "He's always good."

I burst out laughing. "I'll remind you of that next time he's having a tantrum!" She smacks me gently on my chest and I reach for her hand, holding it over my heart. "I missed you," I whisper as I lower my head, capturing her lips with mine. She moans into my mouth as my tongue duels with hers and my cock jumps in my shorts. Rolling her onto her back, my body comes over her as I continue to kiss her. She snakes her hands into my hair, and I brush kisses around her jaw and down her neck. Sitting up, I tug off her tank and drop my mouth to her breast, circling my tongue around her pebbled nipple. She gasps as I suck her bud into my mouth, her back arching off the bed. My hand slides down and under the waistband of her panties, my fingers slipping through her wet folds.

"Oh, God, Jack," she moans as I flick her swollen clit. My fingers find her entrance and I gently push inside her, her body pulling me in. Her hips lift off the bed and I release her nipple from my mouth, capturing her moans with my lips. When her breathing tells me she's close, I remove my fingers from her body, eliciting a whimper from her. I make quick work of removing her panties and position myself between her legs. Lowering my head, I kiss her again as I gently push inside her. Her tight, wet heat envelops me, and I groan into her mouth.

"You feel so good, Aria," I mumble as I gently thrust into her. Her hand reaches up and cups my face. Our gazes lock, and telling her I love her is on the tip of my tongue. Pushing down the words I so desperately want to say, I turn my head, pressing my lips to the palm of her hand. Her breathing becomes labored as I continue to gently thrust inside her. Our eyes remain fixed on each other and there is no doubt we're making love; this isn't just sex, not for me anyway. I can feel Aria's walls fluttering around my cock, telling me she's close, and the familiar stirring in the pit of my stomach builds as I watch her. Her cheeks are flushed with her impending release, and she's never looked more beautiful.

"I'm coming, Jack," she whimpers, her eyes closing and her back arching. My name falls in a whisper from her lips, her whole body shuddering as her orgasm overwhelms her.

Increasing the speed of my thrusts, I groan as my own orgasm hits me and I drop my head into the crook of her neck, my breathing erratic. Her fingers stroke up and down the length of my back as we both catch our breath. When we're no longer panting, I lift my head, my mouth finding hers in a kiss I hope shows her exactly how I feel about her. I slowly pull out of her body, missing her heat instantly.

"I'll just get something to clean you up," I mutter against her lips before climbing off the bed and grabbing a washcloth from the bathroom. Coming back, I gently wipe between her legs. Tossing the cloth in the corner, I slip under the comforter and wrap my arms around her.

"Get some sleep, sweetheart," I tell her, dropping a kiss on her head. Her eyes are already closed, and she sighs contentedly as she presses herself closer to my side. It doesn't take long before her breathing evens out and she's asleep. I brush another kiss on her head. "I love you," I whisper, needing to say the words, but unsure she's ready to hear them. I'm acutely aware that with Libby's waters breaking earlier, we never got to talk. As nervous as I am for her to hear those words from me, I'm getting to the point where I don't know how much longer I can hold back.

Light filters through a gap in the curtains, and I open my eyes as I hear knocking on my bedroom door.

"Jack, are you awake?" It's my mum, and I can hear the panic in her voice. Aria is still in my arms, and she stirs when she hears her.

"Is everything okay?" she asks, her voice thick with sleep.

"I'm not sure." She sits up, pulling the comforter around her as I climb off the bed and slip on some sleep shorts. Crossing the room, I pull the door open, seeing my mum fully dressed, her hands clasped in front of her and worry etched on her face.

"Mum?" Taking her hand, I pull her gently into the room. I'm not sure what time it is, but it's early and I don't want to wake Jacob.

"It's Libby." Her hand flies to her mouth as she holds back a sob, and fear prickles up my spine.

"What's happened? Is she okay? Is the baby okay?"

"Mason's just called. She's being prepped for a C-section. The baby's in distress." Her voice breaks and I pull her into my arms. "Claire and Ryan are already out on the ranch. Can you drive us to the hospital?"

"Of course I can. She's going to be okay. They both are," I assure her, hoping I'm right. I guide her to the bed and have her sit down, my eyes flicking to Aria. "I'll just be a minute." I grab some clothes and head into the bathroom. After using the toilet, I brush my teeth and pull on some jeans and a t-shirt. When I go back into the bedroom, Aria is talking quietly to my mum and holding her hand.

"Babe, are you okay to watch Jacob?" I ask, feeling bad she looked after him yesterday, and I'm asking again today.

"Yes, definitely. Go. Jacob will be fine." She smiles at my mum and I see her squeeze her hand before my mum stands.

Moving toward the bed, I kneel on the comforter in front of Aria. "Thank you," I whisper before I kiss her softly on her lips. "I'll call when I have any news." She nods and I stand up, picking my phone up from the side of the bed. Turning, I see my mum watching us.

"Where's Dad?"

"Getting dressed. He should be ready now."

I nod. "Come on, let's go."

"Thank you, Aria. For watching Jacob," my mum says, and Aria waves her hand.

"I love spending time with him. Give Libby my love." My mum gives her a small smile and I wink at her before taking my mum's arm and guiding her onto the landing and down the stairs. Dad's waiting by the front door and I snatch up the keys to the truck from the small table in the hallway.

Jogging down the porch steps, we all climb quickly into the truck, my mum clutching her phone in her hand. I start the engine and speed away from the house, gravel from the drive spitting up behind us. We drive in comfortable silence for a few minutes until my mum turns to me from the passenger seat.

"Aria seems nice."

"She is. Jacob adores her."

"And you?" She raises her eyebrows in question.

"I really like her."

"I was worried you'd come here and fall in love, like your sister." Her voice sounds sad, but she smiles as I glance across at her. I don't say anything. I'm not sure how to respond. I can't lie. I *have* come to the ranch and fallen in love, but I don't know what that means for my future. Not yet anyway. Not until I've spoken to Aria. I want to ask her to move to the UK, but I know she loves it here. I can't imagine going home and never seeing her again. That just isn't an option.

Fifteen minutes later, I pull up outside the entrance to the hospital. Mum and Dad jump out and rush inside, leaving me to park the truck. When I get inside, I take the lift to the third floor, I tap my foot as I wait for the car to travel upwards. I haven't let myself think that Libby or the baby might not be okay, but as I ride the lift alone, my mind works overtime. When the doors open, I see my mum pacing the waiting area.

"Any news?" I ask as I make my way over to her.

"They're in theatre now," my dad says as he takes my mum's hand and forces her to sit down.

"You're going to wear a hole in the floor, Em," he says, stroking his thumb over the back of her hand.

"Surely we should have heard something by now?" Her eyes find mine and I give her a small smile.

"I'm sure everything is fine, Mum." Before I can say anything else, her eyes go past me, and she gasps. Spinning around, I see Mason standing in the corridor, dressed in blue scrubs. My mum rushes past me and pulls him in for a hug.

"Is Libby okay?" she asks, and he grins.

"She's good. She sent me back here to get you all. We have someone we'd like you to meet." My mum bursts into tears and Mason chuckles, putting his arm around her. "Come on." He guides her down the corridor and through a set of double doors. Dad and I follow, and I can't help smiling as I watch my mum just ahead of me. She's practically bouncing along the corridor and excitement radiates off her.

"This is us," Mason says, coming to a stop outside of a closed door. Swinging the door open, he gestures for my mum to go in first. As I follow, I slap Mason on the shoulder.

"Congratulations, man."

"Thanks, Jack." His smile is wide, and other than the day he married my sister, I've never seen him look happier.

"Oh, Libby!" my mum exclaims, rushing to Libby's side. Her smile matches Mason's, and I can't help but smile myself as I look at her sitting up in bed, holding a baby in her arms.

"Meet your granddaughter, Mum," Libby says, her voice choked with emotion.

"A girl," my mum whispers, and Libby nods.

"Are you okay?" She leans over and presses a kiss on Lib's head.

"I'm okay. Sore, but she's worth it. Would you like to hold her?"

"Yes." Mum takes her from Libby, holding her close to her chest, silent tears running down her cheeks. Standing at the end of the bed, I catch Libby's eye.

"Well done, Lib. She's beautiful."

"Thank you." Her arm goes out to Mason, who crosses the room and takes her hand. Sitting next to her, he drops a kiss on her hair.

"Does she have a name?" my dad asks as he slips his arm around my mum and gazes at his granddaughter.

"She does. We've called her Annie Mia Walker," Libby says, her gaze meeting mine. "We wanted to honor Mia's memory if we had a girl."

"It's perfect," I say quietly, tears stinging my eyes. Blinking quickly, I force the tears away. "Mia would be so proud of you, Lib." She smiles as Mason pulls her against his chest, wrapping his arm around her.

"She's amazing," my mum gushes, and I look across to see her staring at Annie, a wide smile on her face.

"Where's Jacob?" Libby asks, her eyes still on Mum and Annie.

"Aria's watching him." My mom turns to look at me and smiles when I mention Aria.

"I can't wait for everyone to meet her." She turns to Mason. "Did you message Savannah and Brody?" He nods. "Aria too?"

"I haven't told Aria."

"I can tell her. Unless you want to?" I say.

Libby waves her hand. "No, you tell her. That's fine. Will you bring her later so she can meet Annie?"

"Of course. How long do you have to stay in hospital for?"

"A couple of days, I think. I can't wait to get her home."

I smile. "I'll just go outside and call Aria." I make my way toward the bed. "I'm so proud of you," I tell her as I lean down and kiss her cheek. I shake Mason's hand before heading for the door. Placing my hand on the door handle, I turn and look back at everyone. As happy as I am for Libby and Mason, I can't help but feel a little melancholy as I watch them all. I remember how I felt just after Zara had given birth to Jacob, and how excited I was for the future. It hadn't turned out to be the future I'd imagined though. Far from it. My mind wanders to Aria, and watching how happy Lib and Mason are, I know now more than ever I want that happiness with Aria. I just have no idea how I'm going to make that happen.

CHAPTER 21

Aria

After hearing the front door close downstairs, I flop backwards onto the bed. Nerves swirl in my stomach as I think about Lib. Emma looked scared, and I hope everything is okay. It never crossed my mind that something might go wrong.

Reaching for my phone, I illuminate the screen, seeing it's just after 6 a.m. It's still early, and Jacob won't be awake for a couple of hours yet. I lie staring at the ceiling for ten minutes before I sit up and swing my legs to the side of the bed. There's no way I can fall back to sleep, not without knowing Libby and her baby are okay. I pad across the room, go into the bathroom, and turn on the shower.

Twenty minutes later and I'm washed, dressed, and

standing with my ear pressed to Jacob's door. When I'm met with silence, I head downstairs, turning the coffee machine on when I enter the kitchen. I make sure my phone's on loud so I don't miss a call, and place it on the counter before making quick work of throwing together some pancakes. I'm just clearing up after eating when my phone rings. I snatch it up, my heart thundering in my chest when I see Jack's name flashing on the screen.

"Hello," I answer, almost breathless.

"Aria, it's me," Jack says, and I hold my breath as I wait for him to continue. "Libby's had the baby, they're both fine."

"Oh, thank God!" I let out a rush of air, relief flooding my body. "Boy or girl?"

"A girl. Annie Mia Walker."

"That's beautiful. Mia after her friend?" The line goes quiet, and I wonder if the call has dropped. Pulling the phone from my ear, I see we're still connected. "Jack, are you still there?"

"Shit, sorry. Erm, yeah. After her friend." He sounds weird, and I wonder what's changed.

"You okay?"

"I'm good. I should tell you about Mia sometime."

"I'd like that." The line goes quiet again and I don't say anything, knowing he's thinking about Mia. "Lib wants you to come up to the hospital this afternoon and meet Annie."

"I'd love that. Are you staying there until then?"

"No, we'll be coming back soon. Let Lib rest for a bit."

"I'll see you soon, then. Give Lib my love and take a picture of Annie. I'm too excited to wait until this afternoon."

"Okay." He laughs. "Is Jacob awake?"

"Nope, still asleep."

"I might be back before he wakes up. See you soon, baby."

"Bye." He ends the call and I realize I'm grinning. I might only have known Libby and Mason for just over a year, but we've become really close in that time, and I'm beyond happy for them. Glancing down at the phone in my hands, my fingers fly over the screen as I type out a message to Lib. I don't expect a reply, knowing she will have her hands full with baby Annie, but I want her to know how happy I am for them. I've just pressed send when Claire walks into the kitchen.

"Aria, you're up early, and you made coffee," she exclaims, glancing behind me. "Just what I need after an early start." She walks past me and gets down a mug before pouring herself a cup. She takes a sip of the hot liquid and looks around. "Everyone else still asleep?"

"Just Jacob. Everyone else is at the hospital," I tell her with a smile.

She gasps. "Did Libby have the baby?" I nod, and she puts her coffee down and pulls me in for a hug. "Are they okay?"

"It was an emergency C-section in the end, but both are fine now. A girl. Annie Mia Walker."

"I imagine Emma is beside herself with excitement. I remember walking on air when Savannah had Hope. It will be so nice to have another little one on the ranch." Picking up her coffee, she drinks down another mouthful. "I'd better get back to the guest accommodations. I've left Ryan with a leaking faucet."

"As soon as Jack is back, I'll tend to the horses. I know you'll be a ranch hand down now that Mason isn't around."

She shakes her head before putting her mug down on the

counter. "We had someone on standby to help out from the neighboring ranch. Ryan spoke to him yesterday when Libby went into labor. He's coming this morning, so don't worry about the horses. We've got it covered if you need to help out here."

"I'll be in the stables once Jack's back to watch Jacob," I assure her. I don't want to take advantage just because I'm dating her nephew. She smiles and nods.

"Okay. I'll be back later to say hi to everyone." She raises her hand in a wave as she leaves the kitchen, and I hear the front door open and close. Pouring myself another cup of coffee, I carry it into the den and curl up on the sofa while I wait for Jack to get back. Despite not being able to sleep earlier, I now find I can't keep my eyes open as I sink onto the comfortable sofa. Placing my mug on the table in front of me, I drop my head back and close my eyes.

"Aria." I hear my name being called, but it sounds muffled and distant, and I don't want to open my eyes. "Aria, baby." Fingers stroke my cheek, and I sigh as I force my eyes open, smiling when I see Jack kneeling on the floor next to the sofa. "Hey, sleepyhead. Sorry to wake you." I sit up and stretch my arms above my head.

"That's okay. I should get to work now that you're home anyway. What time are you heading back to the hospital?"

"Around three."

"Okay. I'll make sure I'm ready. Did you get any pictures of Annie?" He laughs and pulls out his phone. His fingers move over the screen before he turns it around in his hand. I gasp and take the phone from him, gazing at the picture in front of me.

"Oh, she's beautiful, Jack, and so tiny. What did she

weigh?" I tear my eyes from the phone and look at his blank face. "You didn't ask, did you?" I say with a laugh, and he shakes his head.

"I'm sure Lib will fill you in on all the details later. She is tiny though. Smaller than I remember Jacob being."

"I'm so happy for them."

"Me too," he whispers as he stands and pulls me off the sofa and into his arms. His mouth finds mine and I'm soon lost in his kisses. Someone clearing their throat behind me pulls us both back to reality as Jack pulls out of the kiss and looks over my shoulder.

"Sorry to interrupt. Jacob's awake," Emma says, and I drop my forehead onto Jack's chest, embarrassed to have been caught making out by his mom.

"Thanks, Mum. I'll go and get him."

"Your dad's gone up to him." Stepping out of Jack's embrace, I turn and smile at Emma.

"Congratulations, Emma. Annie is beautiful."

"Thank you, sweetheart. I'm just so glad they are both okay."

"Me too." She smiles at me, and I smile back. "I should get to work." I turn to Jack and press a kiss to his cheek. "See you later."

"Bye, baby."

I leave Jack and Emma in the den and make my way outside and across to the stables. Pushing open the huge wooden doors, I can hear voices coming from the tack room. As I make my way past the stalls, I see they are all empty, the horses seemingly already in the exercise area. I put my head around the tack room door, and Ryan smiles as he sees me.

"Aria, come in. I'd like you to meet Elijah. He's helping out while Mason's off."

"Nice to meet you." I hold my hand out, and Elijah takes it, smiling as he shakes my hand.

"You too, Aria."

"Aria is our horse trainer, and she helps out when we need her. Isn't that right, Aria?"

"It is. Always happy to help. Talking of helping, I need to get started on the mucking out. See you around, Elijah. If you need anything, come find me." I'm just about to leave when Ryan stops me.

"Actually, Aria, I was hoping you'd be able to lead the riding tour this morning? Mason normally does it and I thought you could take Elijah. Show him the route, I know you've done it once or twice before."

"Sure. What time?"

"Ten thirty."

I nod. "I'll get the horses ready." He passes me some paperwork.

"There's only six, so a small group." He turns to Elijah. "I think I've told you everything I need to. I'll leave you in Aria's capable hands." He raises his hand in a wave as he leaves the tack room.

"Let's grab some saddles." I reach up and pull two down, passing them back to Elijah. Grabbing another two, I lead us through the stalls and out into the exercise area. "If you start with Titan." I point across the exercise area to where Titan is grazing by the fence. "I'll get Marley ready." He nods and saddles up Titan. He seems to know what he's doing. I'm not surprised. Ryan wouldn't hire someone who didn't.

"How long have you been a ranch hand?" I ask as I turn and concentrate on Marley.

"Since always, I guess. My grandfather owned a small cattle ranch in Fredericksburg, which my parents inherited when he died. They had to sell it a few years ago, but I loved it. I can't imagine doing anything else. I'd have bought it from them if I'd been able to."

"The new buyers didn't keep you on?" I turn from Marley to look at him.

"A large corporate company bought it and expanded. They weren't interested in keeping on any staff. My parents had other offers, and I begged them to sell to someone else, but they went with the higher offer." I can hear the hurt in his voice.

"I'm sorry."

He shrugs half-heartedly. "It was a few years ago. I had to get away once the sale went through, so I moved to Marble Falls and got a job on the Baker ranch on the other side of town. Been there ever since."

"How come you've ended up here?" I reach for another saddle and walk toward one of the other horses.

"Ryan's a good friend of Tom Baker, my boss. When Ryan asked for some help, I volunteered. It's good to get a change of scenery once in a while."

"Yeah, I guess."

"Erm, Aria, there's a guy waving at you." I look to where he's gesturing and laugh. Raising my hand, I wave back.

"That's Jack, Ryan's nephew." My phone vibrates in my pocket and I pull it out, smiling when I see a message from Jack.

Jack: Hey, baby. Who's the guy?

I can't help smiling as I read the message and wonder if he's jealous. I look sideways at Elijah, only now noticing how good looking he is. Tall, dirty blond hair, well-built. There's not much to dislike, but he's not Jack. My fingers fly over the screen as I type out a reply.

Me: Elijah. Ryan's brought him in to help out while Mason is off. I'm taking him on the riding tour this morning to show him the ropes. Come and say hi?

His reply is almost instant.

Jack: We're just heading into Marble Falls to get a gift for Lib. I'll come and find you when we're back. Have fun, baby.

I look over to the ranch house, and he waves again. Smiling, I wave back.

By 10:30, all the guests booked on the riding tour have arrived. Thankfully, all have ridden a horse before, and after a quick safety briefing, we set off. There are a couple of different routes I know Mason takes, and I choose the one that takes the guests through the pasture where he and Lib got married. I know that's his favorite. I chat to Elijah and the other guests as we ride, and despite not normally having much to do with the guests, I find I'm enjoying myself.

The tour lasts just over an hour, and as we ride back toward the stables, a cab pulls up outside the ranch house.

"Are there guests arriving today?" Elijah asks from the side of me.

"No. Not that I'm aware of. Most guests arrive on a Saturday. Maybe Claire is expecting someone." I don't see who gets out of the cab as I say goodbye to the guests and concentrate on getting the horses settled back in their stalls. Hearing a knock on the stable door, I turn to see a woman in the doorway.

"Hi, can I help you?" I walk toward her, wiping my hands on my jean shorts.

"I'm looking for Jack. Jack Davis. Is he here?" My eyes widen and an uneasy feeling washes over me as I hear her British accent.

"Erm… no. Not right now."

"Great! I've flown halfway across the world and he's not even here!" Her voice is laced with irritation and she reaches up and wipes the back of her hand across her forehead. "Is it always so hot here?"

Her words swirl in my mind and nerves settle in the pit of my stomach. This can't possibly be Zara, can it? She's stunning, even after a fourteen-hour flight. "Is Jack expecting you?"

"Well, no." She places her hands on her hips. "But still, he should be here."

"I can call him?" I offer.

She raises her eyebrows and looks me up and down. "You have his number?"

Folding my arms, I stare at her. She's not making a great first impression. Not that she seems to care. "Yes. I have his number."

She pauses before answering. "Well, I've tried. He's not picking up."

"Oh, okay. Maybe he's driving. I'm Aria. I didn't catch your name."

"Zara." My stomach drops as she confirms what I already know.

"I'm sure he won't be long. He's been gone a while. You can wait on the porch swing until he gets back." I probably sound rude, but I have no idea how long Jack will be and I don't want to make small talk with her. I gesture to the house behind her and she sighs.

"Fine. I hope he's not too long." She turns on her heel and marches away from me.

Sliding my phone from my pocket, I hit Jack's name and pray he answers. I can't believe Zara has just turned up here, and I know Jack is going to be pissed.

CHAPTER 22

Jack

Sitting in the coffee shop in Marble Falls, I groan inwardly as my phone rings in my pocket for the fourth time. I almost don't reach for it, knowing the last three calls were from Zara. I don't want to speak to her today. Something makes me though, and I breathe a sigh of relief when I see Aria's name flashing up on the screen. Smiling, I hit the answer button and put the phone to my ear.

"Hey, Aria. Everything okay?" I ask, standing up and gesturing to my mum that I'm going to take the call outside. She nods, and I make my way through the crowded coffee shop as I wait for Aria to answer me.

"Not really. How much longer are you going to be?"

I pull open the door and walk out into the street. Her voice is weird, and fear prickles up my spine. "Not long. We're just having an early lunch in town. What's wrong?"

"You have a visitor. Zara is here, Jack."

I stop dead and pull my eyebrows together in a frown. I can't possibly have heard her right.

"I could have sworn you said Zara was there," I say, a nervous laugh leaving my mouth.

"I did. She's sitting on the porch swing."

"What?" My voice is barely a whisper and a wave of nausea washes over me. "Are you sure?" I ask, my voice a little louder.

"I'm sure."

"I'm on my way." I end the call and turn around, rushing back inside. I'm at the table in seconds, and I scoop Jacob into my arms, pressing a kiss on his head. "I need to get back to the ranch. Now." My mum stands up, knowing by the tone of my voice that something isn't right.

"What's wrong?"

"Zara's there."

Her eyes widen before her face floods with anger. "What does she want?" she asks, her eyes fixed on Jacob.

I shrug. "To see Jacob, apparently."

"She's flown all the way to America? That makes no sense. How did she know where you were?"

I grimace before turning and walking across the room, my parents right behind me. "I may have given her the address."

"What?" I can hear the confusion in her voice, and I stop and turn around.

"Look, it's a long story. She's been in touch over the past few days, demanding to see Jacob. I told her I was here visiting Lib, and she kept pushing to see Jacob. I yelled the address at her and ended the call. I never imagined she would actually come."

We walk back to the car in silence. My stomach is in knots at the prospect of seeing her again. Jacob has no idea who she is, and the thought that she's going to want to spend time alone with him makes me feel physically sick. It's been just the two of us for so long, I don't want to share him.

Fifteen minutes later and my knee bounces nervously up and down as I pull off the main road and up the driveway that leads to the ranch. My mum has talked nonstop about how much she dislikes Zara, and how I shouldn't allow her to see Jacob after she walked out on us. As much as I love my mum, I wish she'd shut up. I don't want Jacob to see her any more than she does, but she *is* his mother, and there isn't anything I can do about that. Thankfully, Jacob fell asleep as soon as he got into his car seat. I don't like Zara, but I wouldn't let anyone say anything detrimental about her in front of him, even though he'd have no clue what was being said. It's not something I want to start.

I avoid looking at the porch as I park the truck and jump out. Reaching into the back, I pluck a sleeping Jacob from his car seat and into my arms. Taking a deep breath, I finally look toward the house, seeing Zara standing at the top of the porch steps.

"Do you want us to take Jacob while you two talk?" my mum asks from the side of me, a scowl on her face when she looks over at Zara.

I shake my head. "She's here to see Jacob. I've nothing to say to her unless it's about him."

She nods stiffly. "Your dad and I are going for a walk. We'll give you some space." She stands on her tiptoes and kisses my cheek before walking away, her arm linked with my dad, who looks over his shoulder and gives me a small smile. Tearing my eyes off them, I start walking toward the house.

"Oh my God, he's gotten so big!" Zara exclaims as she rushes down the porch steps.

"That's what happens in nine months." My voice is tight, and I see a flash of hurt cross her face, but I'm only speaking the truth. "What are you doing here, Zara?" I walk straight past her and into the house.

"I came to see my son." She follows me inside, pulling her suitcase behind her. "And you." I feel her hand rest on my back, and I stiffen. I take a step forward and her hand falls away.

"Let's make one thing clear, Zara, if you're here to see me, you're wasting your time." Before she can respond, Jacob lifts his head from my shoulder and yawns. "Hey, buddy. Good sleep?" He nods and puts his thumb in his mouth, his head dropping back onto my shoulder.

"Can I hold him?" Zara asks from behind me, and I tense as I hold Jacob a fraction tighter.

"He has no idea who you are, Zara, and he's just woken up. Give him a minute."

She walks toward me, her eyes fixed on Jacob. "Hello, sweetheart." She places her hand on his back and he turns his face away and into my t-shirt. Her face falls, and I wonder if she thought she could just walk back into his life and he'd somehow remember who she was. Neither of us say anything as we stand awkwardly in the hallway for a few seconds.

"Drink, Daddy?" Jacob asks, unknowingly breaking the tense silence. I nod, kissing his hair. I make my way into the kitchen, and Zara follows. I lower Jacob to the floor, his arms immediately going around my leg as he stares uncertainly at Zara.

"Do you want a drink?" I ask as I pour some juice into Jacob's cup.

"Water, please. It's so hot here." I move to the fridge as best as I can with Jacob attached to my leg, and hand her a bottle of water. I pass Jacob his juice cup, and he lets go of the death grip he has on my leg to take it from me.

"Shall we go outside?" I ask, suddenly needing some fresh air.

"Okay. Is there somewhere I can change first? I'm too hot in these jeans." I glance down at the skin-tight black jeans she's wearing and sigh.

"There's a bathroom off the hall. We'll be outside." I scoop Jacob up and walk out, leaving her standing in the kitchen. By the time I reach the bottom of the porch steps, I'm shaking with anger. How dare she just turn up here unannounced and expect to just fit back into Jacob's life? Why would she fly halfway around the world when she hasn't bothered with him for months? She's up to something, and I don't trust her.

"Down, Daddy," Jacob says, pulling me from my thoughts. I lower him to the ground and watch as he runs around the front garden. "Ria!" he cries, and I turn to see Aria walking up from the stables. He runs to her and she picks him up, swinging him around before lowering him back to the ground. He giggles, and I can't help but smile as I watch them. Seeing Aria immediately makes me feel better, and I walk toward her, pulling her against me.

"Are you okay?" she asks into my chest. Keeping my arms around her, I lean back so I can see her face.

"I'm better now I have you in my arms." She smiles, and her cheeks flush pink.

"Did you find Zara?"

I sigh. "Yeah, I did. She's just inside getting changed."

"What does she want?"

"To see Jacob, I think." I leave out the bit about her wanting to see me too. There is no way I'd ever want to go there again.

"Are you really okay?"

I shrug. "I guess. I've just got no idea why she would fly halfway across the world when she's never been bothered before. Makes me think she's up to something, although I've no idea what."

"How long is she here for? Is she staying on the ranch?"

"We haven't got that far yet, but no, she's not staying here. She'll have to find a hotel." She nods, and I lower my head, pressing my lips to hers. As I deepen the kiss, someone huffs behind me. Aria must hear it too as she goes to take a step back, but I stop her. Reaching for her hand, I turn to face a scowling Zara, my hand firmly encased with Aria's. Zara's eyes drop to our joined hands and she folds her arms across her chest.

"Zara, this is Aria, but I think you've already met."

"I guess that explains why you'd have Jack's number," Zara mutters before plastering a fake smile on her face. "But, yes, we've met," she says, her voice louder. "Nice to meet you."

Nice, my arse. She looks like she wants to scratch Aria's eyes out. I've no idea why. We split up months ago. She has no claim over me.

"Nice to meet you too," Aria says. She squeezes my hand. "Maybe I should leave you two to talk?"

"I think that's a good idea. We have a lot to catch up on," Zara says, smiling at me. I glare back at her, my gaze softening as I look down at Aria.

"I'll come find you when we're done. It won't be a long conversation." I lower my head and kiss her, not caring that Zara is standing in front of us.

"Do you really think that's appropriate in front of our son?" Zara asks, and I pull out of the kiss, my whole body tense.

"I should go." Aria slips her hand from mine and walks backwards toward the stables. "I'll see you later. Bye, Jacob." She raises her hand in a wave and Jacob waves back. Turning to Zara, I see she's scowling.

"What the hell was that?" I bite out through clenched teeth when Aria is far enough away not to hear.

"I could ask you the same question! You can't honestly think that's appropriate in front of Jacob?" Her hands go to her hips and she raises her eyebrows in question. My hands clench into fists at my side, and I'm so angry I can barely see straight.

"How dare you!" My voice is raised, but I lower it when Jacob turns to look at me. When he goes back to playing in the garden, my eyes go back to her. "How dare you come here, to *my* family's ranch and tell me how to look after *my* son when you haven't given a fuck about him for the past nine months." I pace up and down in an attempt to calm down. She takes a step toward me and places her hand on my arm, forcing me to stop.

"Jack... I'm sorry. I was out of order." Her voice catches and my eyes fly up to hers. I'm taken aback to see tears in them. I never saw her cry the whole time we were together. Not even when Jacob was born. I'm sceptical though, and I brush her arm off. They're likely crocodile tears.

"Yeah, you were."

"I've been an idiot. I gave up the best thing I ever had." Tears are rolling down her cheeks, and I sigh loudly.

"You'll always be Jacob's mum, and you can still have a relationship with him."

"He doesn't even know who I am," she whispers.

"No, but you can change that. You can't be in and out of his life though, Zara. It's not fair on him. You're either all in, or you're out. I won't stand by and watch him get hurt." I can hardly believe I'm saying this to her, but I'm doing it for Jacob. I want him to have a relationship with her.

"I want to be a good mum."

"I've got to ask, why the change of heart? Why now?"

She shrugs half-heartedly. "My sister had a baby a couple of months ago. Seeing her with Max just makes me realize what I'm missing out on. What Jacob's missing out on. I messed up, Jack." She turns to look at Jacob, who's found one of his toy cars and is driving it along the porch steps. "I went to the house, and when you weren't there I went to your work. Someone told me you'd quit and gone to the US. I panicked. I thought you'd taken Jacob and left, and that I'd never see him again. That's when I called you."

"It's just an extended holiday, Zara."

She nods. "Did Libby have her baby?"

I smile. "Yeah, she did. A little girl, this morning."

"That's great! Congratulations!" She throws her arms around me in a hug, and I awkwardly pat her on the back before stepping out of her embrace. "It wasn't just Jacob that I messed up with, Jack," she says quietly. "I miss you."

I take a step back and run a hand through my hair. "Don't do this, Zara."

"We were good together, Jack. We could be a family again." I can hear the pleading tone in her voice, and my eyebrows pull together in a frown.

"We were a family until you decided we weren't worth the effort."

"It wasn't like that——"

"It felt like that," I say, cutting her off.

She reaches for my hand. "I was scared. I didn't plan on getting pregnant, and I had no idea what I was doing."

"You don't think I was scared? I didn't plan for Jacob either, but he's the best thing that's ever happened to me. We could have learned together." I shake my head. "I really thought we could have had something good, the three of us."

"And now?" she asks, her voice breaking.

"Now it's too late."

"It's never too late. We could try again."

"I've moved on."

"Aria?" I nod.

She holds my gaze, and I can see what she's thinking. She doesn't voice it though. It's what I'm thinking too. Maybe before Zara had shown up, I could have considered staying in Marble Falls and making a life here, but now, that seems impossible. I can't imagine a life without Aria in it, but Jacob can't have a relationship with Zara if we're living in the US, and he comes first. He has to.

CHAPTER 23

Aria

$\mathcal{A}$ ll I can hear is the pounding of my heart as I peek around the partially closed doorway of the stables. I know I shouldn't be spying on Jack and Zara, but I just can't tear myself away from the door. There is no way she is just here for Jacob. She was threatened by me, and for someone who's traveled fourteen hours on a plane to see her son, she's barely spoken to him.

My heart twists in my chest as she throws her arms around Jack. He's facing away from me so I can't see if he's hugging her back, but it's not a long embrace and he's the one to step away. Despite knowing Jack will likely tell me what they're talking about later, I wish I could hear what they're saying. He drags his hand through his hair, and I gasp as she steps closer toward him and takes his hand in hers.

"What are you doing?" Elijah asks from over my shoulder. "Who's that?" I jump and quickly close the stable door, my cheeks flushing as I realize I've been caught spying.

"Erm… I was just…" I trail off and groan as Elijah opens the door and looks out.

"Isn't that the guy who was waving at you earlier? Ryan's nephew?"

"Yeah, that's him."

"And the hot blonde?"

"You think she's hot?" I ask, looking past him to where they're still holding hands. Who am I kidding? She's definitely hot. Beautiful, in fact. "You know what, don't answer that." I turn and walk away from him, picking up the pitchfork to carry on mucking out the stalls.

"Want to talk about it?" he asks as he begins cleaning out the stall next to me.

"There's not much to say. Seems I've fallen in love with someone who not only lives on the other side of the world, but has an ex who looks like a supermodel, is also the mother of his child, and from the looks of things, wants them to try again."

"You got all that from spying on them through a half-closed door?" He leans on the wood dividing the two stalls.

I shrug. "Just saying what I see."

"Looks can be deceiving, and from past experience, an ex is an ex for a reason."

"Maybe." I hardly know Elijah and don't feel totally comfortable talking to him about my relationship, as much as he seems like a nice guy. He must sense I'm done talking, and we spend the next twenty minutes in silence as we finish up our stalls.

I'm in the tack room when I feel my phone vibrate in my pocket. I slide it from my jean shorts and see Jack's name flashing up on the screen. Hitting the answer button, I bring it to my ear.

"Hello."

"Hey, are you almost done? We're leaving for the hospital in about thirty minutes."

I sigh inwardly and bite down on my bottom lip. "Oh, erm, I thought I'd stay here. I can see Lib and Annie when they get home."

He's silent for a few seconds, but I can hear him walking, so I know the call hasn't dropped. "Where are you?"

"In the stables, why?"

"Hang on." The line goes silent again before the call ends. I frown and walk out of the tack room, only to see Jack walking toward me.

"What's going on, Aria?" he asks, coming to stand in front of me, his hand reaching for mine.

"What do you mean?" My eyes drop to the floor, and I feel his fingers under my chin, gently forcing my head up to meet his gaze. "Talk to me. You were so excited to see Annie, and I know Libby wants to see you."

"I do want to see Annie. Libby too. I just wanted to give you some space with Zara…" I trail off and look anywhere but at him. "You looked like you had a lot to talk about. I don't want to get in the way."

"Hey." He squeezes my hand. "You would never be in the way." He steps closer and presses his lips against mine. "I know what you're thinking. She's not coming to the hospital."

"She's not?"

"God, no. Lib hates her."

I can't help but laugh as I drop my head onto his chest. "Is she with Jacob?"

"No. My parents have him. She's trying to find a place to stay."

I lift my head and look at him in surprise. "She flew all the way out here with nowhere to stay?"

"Seems that way. I really think she thought she'd just turn up here and we'd pick up where we left off."

"Let's go and see Lib," I say, wanting to change the subject. Seems like my hunch that she wants another shot with him was right. "I just need a quick shower. I stink."

"You look beautiful."

"I look a mess!"

"Maybe I could wash your back?" he whispers, and I shiver as his hot breath hits the skin beneath my ear.

"I think we'll miss visiting hours all together if you do that." He chuckles and takes my hand, leading me out of the stables and across to the house.

My hand is still encased in his as we walk through the front door and into the entryway. I can hear Zara on the phone in the kitchen, and I drop Jack's hand and head upstairs. After a quick shower, I pull on some clean shorts and a tank and make my way back downstairs. I can hear voices coming from the kitchen, and as I walk in, Zara, who has her phone pressed to her ear, scowls when she sees me.

"What's *she* doing here?" Zara asks, her hand covering the mouthpiece on the phone.

"Aria lives here, not that it's anything to do with you," Jack replies, crossing the room and wrapping his arm around me. I smile as Jacob makes his way to me and holds his arms up. I pick him up and put him on my hip. I don't miss the look of disgust that Zara flashes me when she sees me with Jacob.

"Can you suggest anywhere that might have any rooms?" she asks into the phone, finally dragging her eyes off me. She sighs loudly before pulling the phone from her ear and ending the call.

"Everywhere is booked. There's some town fair on at the end of the week and there are no rooms anywhere."

"I'll have to speak to Aunt Claire when we're back from the hospital," Jack says with a sigh. "They might have a cabin free. I doubt it though. It's their busiest time of the year."

"We need to go," Emma says from across the room, and Jack nods.

"You should explore the ranch while we're gone, Zara. It's really beautiful here," I tell her, determined to be as civil as I can.

She looks at me like I'm crazy. "God, it's too hot for that. I'll just wait here."

"Okay," I mutter, walking past her and out of the kitchen with Jacob still on my hip. I can feel her eyes burning into my back, and I know I should feel sorry for her. I have a better relationship with her son than she does, and that's got to hurt, but I can't get past the fact that she's a bitch.

"You can't possibly be okay with her staying on the ranch?" Emma says to Jack as we drive to the hospital.

"Of course I'm not, but what choice do I have? She said leaving was a mistake, that she messed up and wants to try again." An uneasy feeling settles in the pit of my stomach, and I'm desperate to ask if the second chance he's talking about includes him, but I don't, not with his parents in the truck.

"It's too little too late if you ask me," Emma huffs from beside me in the back seat.

"You don't think I know that, Mum?" He looks in the rearview mirror and catches my eye. "I don't want her in our lives any more than you do, but I owe it to Jacob." I drop my eyes and clasp my hands together in my lap, my heart breaking at his words. Despite initially wanting to keep things casual between us, I can't deny how I feel about him. I can't stand in his way if he wants to give things another shot with Zara. Another shot at being a family. I know too well what it's like to only have one parent. It will just about kill me to let him go though.

I walk with Emma into the hospital, not trusting myself not to burst into tears if I'm too close to Jack, who walks a little behind us with his dad and Jacob. Emma takes my arm and squeezes gently, smiling sympathetically when I look at her.

"She won't stick around, Aria. She's too selfish." I give her a sad smile, wishing I could believe her.

"Even if she doesn't, I'm not sure what future Jack and I have when we live so far apart." Tears burn my eyes and I blink rapidly, praying they don't fall.

"I see how you two look at each other. Talk to him. Promise me you will?" I nod as we come to a stop outside of Libby and Annie's room.

"Let's go and see your granddaughter," I say, taking a deep breath and planting a smile on my face. She smiles back, and I follow her into the room, watching as she rushes to the bed, leaning down to kiss Libby on the cheek.

"How are you feeling, sweetheart?" she asks, and I hang back as Jack, Jacob, and Phil say hello. "Where's Mason?"

"I'm good, Mum. Tired, but good. Mason's just gone to get a coffee. He won't be long." Looking across at me, she waves me over.

"Congratulations, Lib," I say, crossing the room and pulling her into a hug. I look into the plastic crib that sits at the side of the bed and holds the most beautiful baby I've ever seen. She's wrapped in a pink blanket and is fast asleep.

"Pick her up," she encourages. "You won't wake her."

"Are you sure?" She nods and I reach into the crib, scooping her into my arms and holding her against my chest. I gaze at her tiny face, her long dark eyelashes resting on her pink cheeks.

"She's perfect, Lib." My voice breaks, and I swallow down the lump that's formed in my throat.

"Baby?" Jacob asks, and I turn to see him looking at me. Jack picks him up and brings him next to me so he can see Annie. Jack slips his arm around my waist and I watch Jacob stare at Annie before reaching his hand out and poking her cheek.

"Gentle," Jack says, and Jacob pulls his hand away.

"Baby play?" he asks, and I chuckle.

"She's a little small at the moment, but I bet she can't wait to play with you when she's bigger," I tell him, my hand reaching out to brush his cheek. My eye catches Jack's and my heart stutters as he smiles at me. Tearing my eyes off him, I look back at Annie as she stirs in my arms. I'd never thought much about the future. I never really saw beyond the here and now. Despite seeing things clearly for the first time ever, it seems fate has other plans for me, and I won't be getting the future I suddenly realize I so desperately want.

CHAPTER 24

Jack

I can't help but frown a little as I watch Aria holding Annie. She's smiling, but it doesn't quite reach her eyes, and I wonder if Zara turning up is making her question things. I need to talk to her. She needs to know how I feel. While Jacob has to come first, I love her, and not having her in my life isn't an option. Zara might want a second chance with Jacob, but she isn't getting one with me.

"So, Jack has some news," my mum says, and I feel Aria stiffen next to me. My arm is still around her, and I squeeze her waist reassuringly.

"Sounds intriguing," Lib says, a huge smile on her face. Her eyes flick between me and Aria, and from the excited look on her face, I'm guessing she thinks it's something to do with us.

"I don't think you'll be smiling quite like that when he tells you," my mum mutters, and I roll my eyes as Libby pulls her eyebrows together in a frown.

"What's going on?" Libby asks.

I take a deep breath, my arm still around Aria. "I wasn't going to tell you today, but it seems Mum thinks I should." I shoot a look at my mum, who looks anywhere but at me.

"Just tell me!"

"Zara's here."

Her eyes widen. "What? Where?"

"At the ranch. She turned up this morning."

"How does she know you're here? What does she want?"

I sigh again and drop my arm from around Aria as Jacob squirms to be put down. Lowering him to the floor, I slide my eyes to Aria. She has her head down and is gently stroking Annie's cheek with her finger.

"She called me out of the blue a couple of days ago. She wanted to see Jacob. I told her she couldn't as I'm here. Next thing I know, she's at the ranch."

"God, the nerve of that woman! Has she said where she's been for the last nine months?" I can hear the anger in Libby's voice, and I shake my head. "She flew all the way here to see Jacob, when she walked out on you both and didn't bother for months?"

"She said she's made a mistake, that she wants a second chance—"

"You aren't going to give her another chance, are you?" she asks, interrupting me. Her eyes are wide again, and they flick from me to Aria, then back to me.

"Emma, do you think you could take Annie? I need to use

the restroom," Aria says quietly before I can answer. She crosses the room and passes Annie to my mum before slipping silently out of the room.

"Oh God! I meant another chance with Jacob!" Libby cries.

"I know what you meant," I assure her. "There is no way I want any sort of relationship with Zara."

"Does Aria know that? You did speak to her, didn't you? You did tell her you love her?" I shake my head.

"I never got the chance."

"Go and find her! God knows what she's thinking."

The door opens and Mason walks in, two disposable coffee cups in his hands. Smiling, he hands one to Libby before dropping a kiss on her head. "Hey, Jack. Is Aria okay? I just saw her, and she looked upset."

"Shit!" I drag my hand through my hair and make for the door. "Can you keep an eye on Jacob?"

"Yes, just go and find her!" Libby exclaims.

"What did I miss?" Mason asks as I swing the door open and rush into the hallway. There's no sign of her as I look up and down the corridor, and I head for the lift, wondering if she's gone outside for some air.

As the lift doors open on the ground floor, I catch sight of her outside the main entrance. She's sitting on a bench, her head back and her eyes closed. Walking outside, I silently sit next to her.

"Aria," I whisper, my hand resting on the bare skin of her leg. Her head flies up and she jumps.

"Shit, Jack. You scared me."

"I'm sorry, baby." Her eyes are swimming with tears, and my heart twists as I realize I put them there.

"Aria," I whisper again, and she drops her eyes and shakes her head.

"It's okay. I understand."

"Understand what?"

"That you have to try again with Zara. For Jacob."

"Look at me."

She takes a deep breath before her eyes meet mine. "That's not what I want."

"It isn't?" Her voice is barely above a whisper, and I turn to face her, taking her hand in mine.

"No. Zara showing up doesn't change what's happening with us."

She raises her eyebrows. "It doesn't? I can't see how it won't. You have a shot at being a family again, Jack. I don't want to be the reason that doesn't happen."

"You don't get it, do you?"

"Get what?" she asks, confusion lacing her voice.

"I don't want anything with Zara. Not even a friendship. I know I'll have to tolerate her if she ends up being part of Jacob's life, but that's all I'll be doing, tolerating her."

"But—"

"I want a life with you, Aria," I tell her, cutting her off. "The thought of going home and never seeing you again…" I trail off, not even able to think about my life without her in it.

"I just don't know how we can make this work, Jack."

"Do you want to be with me?" I hold my breath as I wait for her answer. She had my heart a while ago, and although I think I know how she feels about me, I know she's guarding her heart.

"Yes," she whispers, and I can't help the smile that fills my face.

"Then we'll make it work." I stand up and pull her into my arms. "I always thought I'd say these words after some romantic gesture where I'd just swept you off your feet." I pause and lean back, waiting for her eyes to meet mine. "But I can't wait any longer. I love you, Aria. I know our relationship isn't going to be easy, but I want to fight for us. I can't imagine my life without you in it." Tears spill down her cheeks and I cup her face, my thumbs wiping away her tears.

"I love you too, Jack." My heart explodes with her words, and relief courses through me knowing she feels the same. "You really think we can make this work?"

"Yeah, baby. I do." I lower my head and capture her lips with mine. It's a soft kiss and one that's full of love. After a few seconds, she pulls back.

"Can I ask you something?" She worries her bottom lip with her teeth, and I frown.

"Anything."

"Does Zara want to give the relationship another shot?"

I groan inwardly. I don't want to worry her, especially knowing what Zara said to me earlier, but I also don't want to lie to her. "Yeah, I think so."

"She's going to make things difficult, isn't she?"

"Only if we let her." I reach my hand up and cup her face. "I'm not saying it's going to be easy, but I know how I feel about you. Nothing and no one is going to change that." She smiles, and this time it reaches her eyes. "Shall we go back inside?"

She nods. "I didn't have nearly enough time cuddling Annie."

"It suited you."

"What did?"

"Having a baby in your arms." Her face flushes with heat, and I drop a kiss on her nose. "Come on." Taking her hand, I keep it tightly encased in mine as we ride the lift back up to Lib's room.

Knocking lightly on the door, we walk in and all conversation stops. Libby's eyes drop to our joined hands and a smile erupts on her face.

"You talked?" she asks, and I nod, dropping Aria's hand and snaking my arm around her waist.

"Everything's good," I assure her. Jacob slides off my dad's knee and walks over to Aria, his chubby little hand pulling on hers.

"Up, Ria?" he asks, and she kneels down, scooping him into her arms. His head rests on her shoulder as his thumb goes into his mouth. Aria crosses the room and sits in the chair at the side of Libby's bed, Jacob nestled against her chest. I can't take my eyes off either of them, knowing now more than ever that I'm looking at my future. I just have to figure out how to make that future a reality when we live thousands of miles apart.

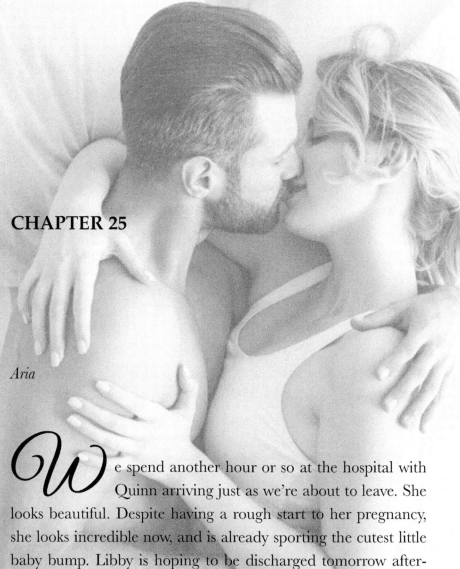

CHAPTER 25

Aria

W e spend another hour or so at the hospital with Quinn arriving just as we're about to leave. She looks beautiful. Despite having a rough start to her pregnancy, she looks incredible now, and is already sporting the cutest little baby bump. Libby is hoping to be discharged tomorrow afternoon, and after saying goodbye she makes me promise to stop by the cottage when they're home. I agree, chuckling to myself. If I know Lib, she likely wants all the details of my and Jack's talk. Quinn looks interested too as she sees us whispering. I'm sure Lib will fill her in as soon as we leave.

I'm nervous as we drive up to the ranch house. Jack and I haven't had a chance to talk anymore about Zara. I'm not stupid though, I know he's going to have to spend time with her while she's here. Jacob doesn't know her. It's not like Jack can just hand him over for them to spend time together. I just know I'm going to hate it.

"You've been gone ages!" Zara exclaims as we climb out of the truck. "There is nothing to do here." Emma shakes her head as she and Phil head inside.

"It's a ranch, Zara. It's about the horses and the land. What did you expect?" Jack walks around the truck with Jacob in his arms. His spare hand reaches for mine and he squeezes it reassuringly.

"I thought there might have been a spa or something. A pool at least!"

Unable to stop myself, I gesture beyond the stables. "The Colorado River is about a thirty-minute walk in that direction." She scowls at me and walks toward Jacob.

"Do you think I could spend some time with my son now?" she asks, her voice tight.

"We should sort you somewhere to sleep for the night first. How long are you planning on staying?" Jack asks, and I watch as her eyes flick to me before landing on Jack.

"I think maybe we should discuss that just the two of us."

"Aria is my girlfriend. Whatever you have to say, you can say in front of her. I'll only tell her later anyway." Her eyes widen before flashing with anger. I barely register her reaction though, butterflies erupting in my stomach when Jack refers to me as his girlfriend.

"Right, well, I've no idea. I didn't book a return flight. I guess I'll just go home when you do." Jack tenses beside me and the butterflies now sit like a heavy stone in the pit of my stomach.

"I'm going to be here for a couple of months at least. Surely you don't want to stay that long? What about your life back home?"

She shrugs. "I'm between jobs at the moment and I could do with a holiday." Apprehension builds in my stomach, and I want to drop Jack's hand and walk away, but I don't. I know he doesn't want her here anymore than I do, but I can't help wondering how her being here is going to change things between me and Jack.

"Where are you going to stay?" He drops my hand and runs it through his hair. I can tell he's pissed, and I don't blame him. No one wants her here. "This is my family's ranch, and if I'm being completely honest, after how you left me and Jacob, I'm not sure how welcome you are."

Her hand flies to her mouth, and she surprises us both by bursting into tears. "I made a mistake," she chokes out through her tears. "The biggest mistake of my life. I just want to make it right."

Jack sighs and walks toward her, Jacob still in his arms. "It's not going to be easy, Zara. It's going to take a lot of hard work to prove to everyone, not only me, that you've changed."

"I'll do it, I promise. I just want that chance." She reaches out and rests her hand on Jack's arm. "Please." Her voice breaks and more tears stream down her cheeks. I only know what Jack's told me about her, but she genuinely looks upset, and I can't help but feel a little sorry for her. Jack nods, and her whole body almost crumples in relief. Pulling herself together, she wipes her eyes and looks past Jack to me.

"Aria." She walks toward me. "I'm so sorry I've been a bitch. I'm not going to lie, I did come here hoping for a second chance with Jack as well as Jacob, but I can see how happy you two are. I'd really like it if we could be friends?" I catch Jack's eye over her shoulder, and he pulls a face and shrugs one shoulder. He seems as surprised by her request as I am.

"I'd like to be friends," I tell her, hoping she can't tell I'm lying through my teeth. I might have felt a little sorry for her, but I can't ever imagine being her friend. It crosses my mind that her whole outburst may be a front, that it's very much a case of keeping your friends close, but your enemies closer. I hope I'm wrong for Jacob's sake. If we're both going to be in his life, it would be good for him if we could be civil.

"Do you think there might be a room on the ranch I could stay in?" she asks, and I look across at Jack.

"Erm… maybe. We should talk to Claire and Ryan." I could offer her my room in the ranch house since I spend every night with Jack, but something stops me. Aside from not wanting her in the room next to us, if things don't go well for me and Jack, for whatever reason, I'd have nowhere to go. Maybe Libby and Mason's old cabin is a better option. I need to speak to Jack first though, see what he thinks.

"I need to bathe Jacob. Zara, do you want to help?"

"I would love to."

"Just give me a few minutes and I'll give you a shout." He turns to me. "Can I have a word, Aria?" I smile and follow him into the house, Zara behind me. Jack goes straight upstairs and into his room and I follow, closing the door behind me. He puts Jacob on the floor with some of his toys and tugs me into the bathroom.

"Are you okay?" he asks as he closes the door, leaving it open a little so we can hear Jacob.

"Yeah, I'm okay. You?" He nods. "Do you think she's full of shit or genuinely wants to make things right?"

He sighs and pulls me against him. "I really don't know. I guess we're just going to have to wait and see."

"What about her staying in Mason and Libby's old cabin?"

"I was thinking the same, but I knew you'd talked about wanting to move in there?"

"I want to stay with you while you're here, if that's okay. I can move in there... later." I can't bring myself to say I'll move in once he's gone home. I can't bring myself to even think about him not being here.

"It's more than okay. I want you with me all the time, Aria." His hand cups my face and his mouth drops to mine. My tongue swipes his bottom lip, and he opens up, our tongues dueling together. His hand slides into my hair and his fingers tugs gently as his kiss consumes me. Heat pools in my stomach and an ache forms between my legs. I want nothing more than to feel him inside me, but with Jacob in the other room, I'll have to wait until later.

"Knock, knock," a voice calls from the bedroom, and the fire raging inside me is instantly extinguished on hearing Zara. Pulling out of the kiss, Jack rests his forehead on mine.

"I'd better get Jacob bathed."

"I'll be in my room."

"I love you," he whispers.

I smile. "I love you too."

Walking out of the bathroom, I see Zara has made herself comfortable on the bed, her fingers flying across the screen of her phone. I'm a little taken aback she isn't trying to interact with Jacob, who is playing with his cars on the floor. Jack is still in the bathroom, running the bath.

"Jack's just filling the tub," I tell her, and she finally looks up from her screen.

"Great. Are you staying to help too?" she asks, and I shake my head.

"No, I'll be in my room."

"Okay." She looks back at her phone, indicating the conversation is over and I can't help but frown. Less than ten minutes ago she was desperate to make a relationship with Jacob and become friends with me. Maybe the tears had been fake after all? It sure seems that way. I make my way to the foot of the bed and kneel on the floor where Jacob is playing.

"Bath time, little man," I tell him, ruffling his hair. "Have fun with Daddy." I'm just about to stand up when he stops pushing his car around and climbs onto my lap.

"Ria come?" he asks.

"Not this time, buddy, but I'll see you downstairs later, okay?" He nods before throwing his arms around my neck, and I hold him tight.

"Who's ready for a bath?" Jack shouts from the bathroom. Zara jumps off the bed and kneels next to me just as Jack pokes his head around the bathroom door. She flashes him a smile and I roll my eyes before kissing Jacob's head. There is no way this woman wants to play fair.

"I'll leave you to it." I stand and head for the door. Closing it slowly behind me, I catch her placing her hand on Jack's arm. She says something to him, but I can't hear what, and he smiles at her. I would never have described myself as a jealous person before I met Jack, but leaving them alone and walking away feels like one of the hardest things I've ever done.

Despite telling Jack and Zara I'm going to my room, I need some air. Jogging down the stairs, I quickly head through the house and out of the front door. I can hear voices coming from the den, but I can't face Emma and Phil. As I make my way to the stables, I pull my phone from my pocket. Scrolling through my contacts, I come to Savannah's name and hit the call button.

"Hey, Aria. How's it going?" Savannah asks as she answers the call.

"Hey, Sav. Are you free for a ride?"

"Erm… yeah, sure. Is everything okay?" I can hear the concern in her voice, and I sigh.

"Yes, no. I really don't know."

"Meet me at my place. Marley is already here. We can go down to the river."

"Thanks, Sav." I end the call and saddle up one of the ranch horses, heading over to Savannah's place at a steady trot.

Savannah waves as I come into view, trotting over to me on Marley. "That was quick."

"I was already in the stables when I called."

"Come on, let's go." I nod and we set off in a gallop. Riding is usually my escape, but not even that seems to be helping today. My mind swirls with thoughts of Jack and Zara, and I groan internally, pushing the irrational thoughts away. They're bathing Jacob, not fucking in the tub.

We ride in silence until we reach the river and dismount. Letting the horses graze, Savannah gives me a few minutes to speak, but when I stay silent, she prompts me.

"What's going on, Aria?"

"Did you hear that Zara showed up?" Her eyes widen in surprise, and the shock on her face tells me she had no idea.

"Zara, Jack's ex?"

"The one and only."

"Fuck!"

"That about sums it up." My voice is deadpan, but Savannah knows me too well and reaches for my hand.

"What does she want?"

"A second chance."

"With Jacob?"

"And Jack, apparently."

"You know he loves you, right?" I smile, my cheeks flushing with heat.

"Yeah, he told me earlier." A wide grin appears on her face and I chuckle.

"You love him too?"

"Yeah, more than I ever thought possible, but I have no idea how we can make things work. I thought the distance was our only obstacle. Now there's Zara…"

"Did Jack know she was coming?"

I shake my head. "No. She called him a couple of days ago, demanding to see Jacob. She was pissed when she found out he was here. Then she turned up this morning." I turn to Savannah. "I don't trust her, Sav. She was a bitch when she first arrived, then put on a big show about how she just wanted a second chance with Jacob. She admitted she wanted to try again with Jack, but could see how happy we are. She's going to make a play for him, I'm sure of it."

"Jack wants you though."

"She's the mother of his son, Savannah. They have a connection, and she's beautiful." I sigh and walk toward the water. Picking up a stone, I toss it into the river.

"She might be beautiful, but she's ugly on the inside. Jack isn't going to forget what she did to them. And he loves *you*."

"God, I hope so. I can't imagine not having him in my life. He's the one, Sav." I choke on my words and she walks toward me, pulling me into an embrace. "He's going to be spending so much time with her. What if—"

"Hey. Stop."

"I'm sorry." I pull out of her embrace and drop my head in my hands. "I feel like I'm going crazy. I've never been this needy. What's wrong with me?"

"You love him, Aria. Simple as that. Love drives you crazy."

"I trust him. I have no reason not to. But…"

"You don't trust her?" Sav finishes for me.

I shake my head sadly. "I'm going to fight if I have to though. I'm not going to let her take them from me."

"If you need any help, Quinn, Lib, and I can go crazy bitch on her. I know Lib hates her!"

I can't help but laugh. I can always count on Savannah to cheer me up and have my back. Libby and Quinn too.

CHAPTER 26

Jack

The next week seems to fly by. Zara is like a different person to the one who walked out on Jacob and me, and no one is more surprised than I am. Not only is she making an effort with Jacob, but also my parents and Lib. It's like she's had a personality transplant.

I'm a little worried about Aria. I've barely seen her this past week. I still fall asleep with her in my arms every night, but I can't get her to open up to me. I've told her Zara being here doesn't change anything between us, but even I'm beginning to wonder if that's true. My feelings for her haven't changed at all, but I'm spending so much time with Zara and Jacob, I can see how it looks. I need to make time for her. I need to put her first. Savannah and Josh are having a pool party this afternoon, and while Zara's been invited, I plan on spending the whole after-noon with Aria.

"You about ready to go, baby?" I call out, pushing myself off the bed and walking toward the bathroom. She's finished work early, and after a quick shower, we have half an hour alone before we're due at Savannah's. Jacob is with Zara, looking at the horses, and it's the first time she's watched him without me. I'm a little apprehensive, but I know it's got to happen at some point. Pushing open the bathroom door, my eyes widen.

"Fuck, Aria! You look incredible." My eyes roam her perfect body, her tiny black bikini leaving little to the imagination. My cock hardens and pushes against the thin material of my swim shorts. A flush of pink spreads up her chest and neck at my perusal, making her look even more beautiful. "Come here." My voice is husky, and her eyes are full of heat as she looks at me. She crosses the small space and I take her into my arms.

"I've missed you," she says softly, her eyes meeting mine.

"I've missed you too, baby." I lower my head capturing her lips with mine. Walking her backwards, I lift her up, placing her on the sink unit. My arms push her legs open and I stand between them, pulling her against me. She moans into my mouth as my erection presses against the thin material of her swimwear. Her hands wind into my hair and her fingers tug gently. I blindly undo her bikini top, not wanting to drag my mouth from hers. Pulling it away from her body, I toss it onto the floor. A moan escapes her lips as my mouth peppers kisses around her jaw and down her neck. When I reach her breasts, I take one in my hand, rolling her nipple between my fingers. I blow gently and then circle my tongue around her nipple before sucking it into my mouth. Her back arches and she pushes her hips against mine.

"What do you need, baby?" I ask against her breast, my teeth biting down.

"Oh, God," she mumbles, her hands pulling on the hair at the base of my neck.

"Tell me what you want, Aria."

"Your mouth," she gasps.

"Here?" I circle her nipple again, and she whimpers.

"No."

"Where?"

"Are you going to make me say it?" Her breathing is labored, and I chuckle against her skin.

"Yes. I want to hear it."

"I want your mouth between my legs," she says quietly. I smile even though she can't see me and kiss down her body. Sliding her hips to the edge of the sink unit, I make quick work of removing her bikini bottoms and put her leg over my shoulder, opening her up to me. She's watching me, biting down on her bottom lip. God, she's so beautiful. I can't believe how much I love her. Dropping my head, I lick through her folds, my tongue seeking out her swollen clit. My cock throbs in my shorts and I reach a hand down, palming myself through the material.

"Fuck, Jack. Don't stop!" I have no intention of stopping as my tongue continues to work her over. Her legs are trembling, and as I raise my eyes, her head is dropped back against the mirror and her eyes are closed. Little moans escape her lips and as I push two fingers inside her, she gasps.

"I'm going to come," she mutters. I can feel her walls gripping my fingers, and as I curl them inside her, she cries out as her orgasm hits. Her whole body shudders and her legs shake. My mouth and fingers continue their assault until she whimpers and pushes my head away. Standing up, I wipe my mouth with the back of my hand and scoop her spent body into my arms.

I carry her into the bedroom and lay her on the bed, then kick off my shorts. She watches me hungrily, her eyes dropping to my cock. She licks her lips and I growl, climbing onto the bed and settling between her legs. "You drive me crazy when you look at me like that," I whisper against her neck.

"Like what?"

"Like you want to devour me."

"Maybe I do." Her voice is low and full of emotion. I lift my head from her neck and capture her lips with mine. Biting on her bottom lip, I pull away.

"Later. I need to be inside you." She moans and my cock jumps. I flip her onto her stomach, and she gasps as I pull her hips up. Stroking my fingers down her spine, my hand gently kneads her perfect arse. Positioning myself, she cries out as I thrust inside her.

"God, Jack! You feel so good this way."

I pound into her, loving how she feels around my cock. My hand reaches up to cup her neck, and I gently pull her up against me, her back to my chest. My fingers brush down to her breast and I pinch her nipple, eliciting a moan from her. Dropping my hand to her clit, my fingers begin to play as I continue to thrust into her over and over again. Her head falls back onto my shoulder and her breathing speeds up.

"I'm close, Jack," she whimpers, her hands coming up to play with her breasts, and I increase the pressure on her clit.

"Come for me, baby. Let go," I whisper against her ear, my

tongue snaking out to lick her skin. I'm close myself, and knowing she is turns me on even more. Her body begins to shudder in my arms, and she cries out as her orgasm crashes into her. Her release triggers my own, and I call out her name as I explode inside her. My legs shake and we both drop forward onto the bed. We're both panting hard, and I roll off her back, pulling her into my arms. Dropping a kiss on her shoulder, I hold her until we've both caught our breath.

"I'll get a cloth, baby," I whisper, before reluctantly unwrapping myself from around her and crossing the room to the bathroom. Reaching for a cloth, I wet it under the tap and pick her bikini up off the floor. Heading back to her, I come to a stop and lean against the unit as I take her in. She's lying on her back with her hand over her eyes. Her legs are open, and I can see my cum running down the inside of her thigh. Despite only just finishing, my cock jumps at the sight of her.

"You're staring," she says with a giggle, her arm lifting off her face and her legs closing.

"Sorry. You're just so beautiful, Aria." A flush of pink travels from her chest, up her neck, settling on her cheeks. I walk toward her and kneel on the bed. I gently push on her knees, her legs drop open, and I wipe between them, my eyes never leaving hers. "I love you so much, baby."

"I love you too." She sits up and sweeps her lips across mine. It's a soft kiss and one that tells me exactly how she feels about me. Reaching my hand up, I brush a strand of hair behind her ear.

"We should get going. Everyone will wonder where we are." I hand over her bikini and watch as she quickly slips it on.

"Are you getting dressed?" she asks, a smile pulling on her lips.

"When I can drag my eyes off you."

"You're great for a girl's ego, you know that?"

"I'm only telling the truth, sweetheart." I finally tear my eyes off her and reach for my swim shorts and t-shirt I tossed on the floor earlier. Pulling them on, I reach for her hand and tug her off the bed.

"I'll just grab some shorts from my dresser," Aria says, dropping my hand and walking out of the room. As she does, my phone chimes with a message. Picking it up, I see Zara's name.

Zara: On my way to Savannah's with Jacob. See you there.

Me: Okay. Won't be long.

Grabbing the bag with towels and a change of clothes for Jacob, I toss it over my shoulder and head out of the room, meeting Aria in the hallway.

"Ready?"

She nods. "Ready."

I reach for her hand and we walk downstairs and out of the house. Part of me wants to take Aria somewhere else for the afternoon so we can be alone. Knowing I can't, we walk hand in hand to Savannah's. Aria's quiet on the short walk, and I can't help but wonder if she feels uncomfortable at spending the afternoon with Zara. I can't blame her. I want to believe Zara has changed, that she really does want a relationship with Jacob, but I can't push down the niggling doubt that she'll up and walk out of his life like before.

CHAPTER 27

Aria

I'm on cloud nine after finally spending time alone with Jack. We've hardly seen each other since Zara arrived. I understand, but I miss him. Despite the mind-blowing sex, it's not enough to take my mind off the pool party, and nerves swirl in my stomach as we walk toward Savannah's house. I've done my best to avoid Zara completely over the past week, and other than a quick "hello" in passing, I've succeeded. The party will be the first time we've spent more than a few minutes together, and I'm not looking forward to it. Jack squeezes my hand, pulling me from my thoughts, and I smile as I look across at him.

"You okay?" he asks, his eyebrows pulled together in a frown. "You're quiet."

"I'm okay, just a little apprehensive about being around Zara. I'm sorry."

"Hey." He tugs on my hand, forcing me to stop walking. He stands in front of me and lifts my chin with his finger. "Don't ever apologize," he says as my eyes meet his. He sighs and drops his forehead to mine. "Part of me wishes she wasn't here. I don't want her in my life, but I have to for Jacob."

I reach my hand up and cup his face. "I want that for Jacob too, Jack. I really do." And I do. I just wish she wasn't living in our pockets.

"It won't always be like this. She won't always be around all the time."

"I know," I whisper, brushing my lips against his. I still have no idea what my future looks like, I just know Jack and Jacob have to be in it.

"Come on, everyone will be waiting for us." I take his hand and we walk in comfortable silence the rest of the way. We haven't even reached the house yet and we can hear screams and laughter coming from the backyard.

"Looks like they started the party without us." He pulls me into his arms. "Think they'll miss us if we sneak off?"

"Yes!" I exclaim, smacking him gently on the chest.

"Yes, they'll miss us, or yes, we should sneak off?" he asks, wriggling his eyebrows.

I burst out laughing. "Yes, they'll miss us! We're already nearly forty minutes late."

He lowers his head and pulls me in for a kiss. "Another half an hour won't hurt, then," he teases, his mouth dropping to my neck.

"No." I giggle. "We can't."

"There you are," a voice shouts from behind us. "Food's almost ready."

"Damn!" Jack whispers in my ear, humor in his voice. "We've been spotted." Turning around. Brody raises his hand in a wave as he heads toward us, a smile on his face.

"What have you two been up to?" he asks, his eyes going from me to Jack. "On second thought, don't answer that. I think I can guess."

My cheeks flush with heat, and he laughs.

"Where are you going?" I ask in an attempt to change the subject. "You're not usually one to pass up on food." I grin at him and he rolls his eyes.

"Quinn has a craving for sparkling water and Sav doesn't have any. She always hated sparkling water before she was pregnant." He shrugs. "I'm just heading into town to grab some."

"I have some in the refrigerator at the ranch house. Just have that."

"If you're sure?"

"Of course." He smiles gratefully before jogging off toward the house, and I grab Jack's hand.

"Come on. I'm starving." I tug him toward Savannah's, and he chuckles.

"Worked up an appetite?"

"Something like that!" When I open the back gate, I can see the party is in full swing. Mason is in the pool with Hope and Jacob, while Josh is on the patio overseeing the barbecue. At the seating area, Libby, Quinn, and Savannah are cooing over baby Annie, who lies in Libby's arms. Zara's sitting with them, but her eyes are on the pool. Glancing over to where she's looking, I wonder if it's Mason who's caught her eye, or Jacob.

"Well, finally!" Savannah shouts as she gets up and makes her way across the yard to us. "We've had to entertain Zara." Her voice has lowered to a whisper, and she pulls a face. "Sorry, Jack. No offense," she says sheepishly.

He shrugs. "None taken."

"Daddy!" Jacob shouts from the pool. Jack squeezes my hand before dropping it and heading to the pool.

"Sorry we're late."

"That's okay. I was only joking, Aria." She links her arm with mine and leads me over to where Lib, Quinn, and Zara are sitting.

"Hi, Aria," Zara says with a smile as she gets up and heads over to Jack. I sigh as I watch her go.

"It must be hard having her here," Quinn says as she gets up and pulls me in for a hug. "How are you doing?"

"I'm okay."

"Really?" Savannah asks.

I shrug half-heartedly. "What choice do I have?"

"She's been so nice this week," Libby says. "She's like a different person. I don't trust her."

"Neither do I," Savannah agrees, and we all turn to look at her sitting on the edge of the pool, talking to Jack.

Needing to change the subject, I tear my eyes away and turn to Quinn. "You look amazing, Quinn." And she really does. She's wearing a pale pink bikini, her small but perfect baby bump on display.

"Thanks. I'm finally past the feeling-like-shit stage, so I'm making the most of it."

"I hear you're craving sparkling water?"

She drops her head in her hands and groans. "I told Brody

he didn't have to go into town. I feel bad he's missing the party."

"We just saw him. I have some at home. He's not going into town."

"Thank you, Aria."

"No problem." I wave off her thanks and move toward Libby and Annie.

"How are you feeling, Lib?" I can't help but smile as I look at Libby. She looks so happy. Her eyes sparkle, even though she looks exhausted.

"I'm really good. Knackered and sore, but good. This one likes to feed every hour, but I'm loving it." My eyes drop to Annie, who is sleeping peacefully in her arms. A wave of longing rushes through me. I want what Lib has. "Do you want to hold her?" I nod and sit down. She passes me Annie and I hold her close. She stirs briefly before going back to sleep.

"Are you okay with her while I use the bathroom?"

"Sure. We're all good here, aren't we, baby girl?" I coo to Annie.

"Thanks." She kisses Annie on the head before heading inside.

"Drink, Aria?" Sav asks, and I nod.

"God, yes! Wine, please, and make it large!"

"Coming right up."

My eyes drift over to the pool. Jack and Zara are sitting on the edge, their legs dangling in the water. Zara's eyes meet mine briefly before she looks away and places her hand on Jack's bare thigh. She whispers something in his ear, and he laughs. Anger bubbles up inside me, and I know for sure now her speech when she first arrived was bullshit.

"Fuck!" Quinn exclaims from the side of me. "I saw that. What does she think she's doing?"

"Whatever it is, she wants me to see. Would you mind holding Annie for me?"

"Are you okay?"

"I'm fine." I pass over Annie and stand up. Slipping off my jean shorts, I kick them to the side and walk over to where Jack and Zara are.

"Jack, could I borrow you for a second?" Jack lifts his head and smiles.

"Sure, baby." Standing up, he comes over to me. Throwing my arms around his neck, I go up on my tiptoes and capture his mouth with mine. He seems a little blindsided, but it only takes him a second or two before he's kissing me back. My hands wind into his hair as my tongue plunges into his mouth. Pressing my hips against his, I feel him harden, and I push harder, eliciting a moan from him. My nipples have hardened, and I gasp as they brush against his chest, only the thin material of my bikini top between us.

"Fuck, Aria," Jack mumbles, as he pulls out of the kiss and rests his forehead on mine. His breathing is erratic, and it matches my own. "You know you've gotten me hard in the middle of a pool party, right?" He chuckles, his hands squeezing my waist.

"I noticed," I whisper, lifting my forehead from his.

"As amazing as that kiss was, is everything okay?"

"Everything is fine. I just wanted to kiss my boyfriend." His face erupts into a smile and I can't help but smile back. "What?" I ask on a chuckle.

"Hearing you call me your boyfriend..." He trails off.

"Well, you are, aren't you?"

"I am, and I love hearing you say it."

He lowers his head and kisses me again. Just as the kiss begins to heat up, a voice shouts, "Jack, man, put her down! This is a family gathering." It's Josh, and his voice is full of humor.

"Leave them alone, Josh!" Savannah shouts back. "They're in love."

A gasp sounds from behind us, and I lift my head to look in the direction of where it came from. Zara is still sitting with her feet dangling in the pool, only now she isn't smiling. A scowl covers her face, and she's glaring daggers at me. If looks could kill, I'd be dead on the spot.

Jack chuckles and takes my hand. "I only want you, Aria," he whispers in my ear. "You don't need to worry about Zara."

"I'm that obvious, huh?" I ask sheepishly.

"A little, but you can kiss me like that anytime you want, and in front of whoever you want. Zara knows the score."

"She does?"

He nods. "And now Savannah's told her we're in love. From her reaction, she clearly didn't think we were that serious."

"I don't trust her."

"I know, but she's proving herself so far with Jacob. I have to give her that chance." Before I can respond, Jacob comes barreling along and slams into my leg.

"Ria, up!" he cries, and I smile as I reach down and pick him up.

"Are you having fun?" He nods and I drop a kiss on his wet hair.

"Food's ready," Josh shouts.

"I'll take him inside and get him dry." Jack takes him from my arms and sweeps a kiss on my lips. "Be right back." My eyes follow him, and I chuckle as I see everyone huddled around the barbecue. Anyone would think they hadn't eaten in a week. I'm just about to head over there when Zara sidles up next to me.

"I know what you're doing, Aria," she says quietly, quiet enough that no one else hears her.

"What?" I ask, raising my eyebrows in question.

"Your little performance with Jack. It's pretty pathetic." Anger courses through me and I really want to slap her in the face.

"Excuse me?" I turn to face her, my hands going to my hips.

"You may as well have just pissed all over him. Like a dog marking its territory." She laughs, but there's no humor in her voice. "Like I said, pathetic." Taking a deep breath, I try to ignore the fact that I'm pretty sure she just called me a bitch without actually saying it.

"I can kiss my boyfriend whenever I want, Zara. It's got nothing to do with you. I give zero fucks what you think." I'm trying to take steady breaths to calm myself down. This party is to celebrate the birth of Annie, and I don't want to cause a scene.

"Of course you don't. That's why you're practically dry humping him on the side of the pool. You're threatened by me, Aria, and you should be. Jack and I have a past, and if I've got anything to do with it, we'll have a future as well. Watch your back." My mouth drops open as she walks away from me, and I'm left wishing I'd slapped her when I had the chance.

CHAPTER 28

Jack

"Hey, do you need a hand?" a voice asks. Looking over my shoulder, I see Zara standing in the doorway to the downstairs bathroom.

"I could have been peeing!" I exclaim as she walks in and closes the door behind her.

Leaning back against the door, she wriggles her eyebrows as her eyes sweep up and down my body. She bites down on her bottom lip and smiles. "Well, I've seen it all before, but I wouldn't mind getting another look. It's been a while."

"You want to see me pee?" I ask as she crosses the small space to stand in front of me.

"That's not exactly what I had in mind…"

"Zara," I warn, turning away from her as I continue to get

Jacob ready. The room is small with just a toilet, wash basin, and shower. With me, Jacob, and Zara in here, it's pretty crowded. There's no denying how beautiful Zara is. Even I can appreciate how good she looks in a bikini, but I feel nothing when I look at her, except maybe uncomfortable when she says inappropriate things like she just has.

"We had some good times, didn't we? It wasn't all bad, right?" Her hand touches my back and I sigh.

"Yeah, Zara, we did, but that was a lifetime ago. I'm with Aria now."

"Really?" Her voice is dripping with sarcasm. "I never would have guessed."

"What does that mean?" I turn around to face her, and her eyes drop to my chest again.

"Her little performance by the pool. Talk about marking her territory."

I roll my eyes. "We're together, Zara. She's allowed to kiss me."

"Oh, please. That show was for me. I'm not stupid."

"Don't flatter yourself. Most couples in a relationship are affectionate in public. Just because you never wanted me to kiss you…" I trail off, wondering why I'm even having this conversation with her. "We should get back."

Her eyes finally leave mine and focus on Jacob. She's been in the bathroom for at least five minutes, and it's the first time she's acknowledged him. "Hey, gorgeous. Did you have fun in the pool?" Jacob nods shyly. "Let's get some food." He cheers, his shyness disappearing at the mention of food. She picks him up and places him on her hip as she carries him out of the small space. I grab Jacob's wet shorts off the floor and follow them out. By the time we get outside, everyone is either standing around the barbecue, eating and talking, or sitting on the decked area. Everyone except Aria. As my eyes sweep around the garden, I see her sitting on the edge of the pool, her legs dangling in the water. Grabbing two burgers from Josh, I head over, sitting down next to her.

"You okay?" She turns and smiles, taking the burger from my outstretched hand.

"Yeah, I'm okay." Her smile doesn't quite reach her eyes though, and her voice sounds weird.

"Are you sure? Why are you sitting over here on your own?"

She shrugs. "No reason."

"Let's go and sit with everyone." She nods, and I take her hand, pulling her up to stand.

Aria is quiet as we sit with Libby and Mason, and I can't help but wonder what's changed in the ten minutes I was inside. Zara comes over with Jacob, who sits on the floor next to Hope.

"Are you free for a ride tomorrow, Aria?" Sav asks as she comes to sit with us.

"I can in the afternoon. I have an excursion with Elijah in the morning."

"The afternoon's good."

"Any chance I can tag along?" Zara asks. "I've never been on a horse before."

Aria tenses beside me.

"Erm… Aria?" Savannah says, her eyes widening.

"Yeah. If you want," Aria says with a shrug.

"Great. Jack and I have plans in the morning, so the afternoon works perfectly for me too." Aria's eyes flick to mine, and I swear they flash with hurt before she looks away. Zara asked me earlier to take her into town to pick up some groceries, although now she's making it out to be much more than that.

"It's just grocery shopping, Zara."

"Yeah, but I was thinking we could do something afterwards with Jacob. Maybe the park?"

"I'm not sure I'll have the time. We can talk about it later." I'm pissed she's putting me on the spot in front of everyone. I don't want to spend time with her like that. I'm happy for her to see Jacob, but we're not a family. I'm only taking her grocery shopping because she has no transport while she's here. I might suggest she rents a car if she's going to be staying a while. I'm not going to be her taxi service.

An uneasy silence descends, and Aria shifts uncomfortably in her seat. Zara doesn't seem to notice and continues to drink from her large glass of wine.

"Hope, why don't you take Jacob on the swing set?" Savannah suggests, breaking the silence.

"Okay, Mommy."

"Do you mind if I help myself?" Zara asks Savannah, holding her almost empty wine glass in the air.

"Not at all," Savannah replies, a fake smile on her face. Drinking down the last of the red liquid, she stands and goes inside.

"Anyone else want to punch her in the face?" Savannah asks when Zara is out of earshot.

"Me!" Libby exclaims. "I just don't want to pop a stitch!"

"I can't believe we have to take her riding tomorrow. Why would she even want to come with us? Surely she knows we don't like her."

"She's so self-involved, I don't think she even realizes," Libby scoffs.

"Come on, guys. Stop with the bitching. I don't like her any more than you do, but she is Jacob's mum."

"And what a great job she's done of that!" Libby says sarcastically. "In case you'd forgotten, Jack, she walked out on him, and you."

"I haven't forgotten, but how can I deny him a relationship with her?"

I can't help but feel a little annoyed. I know Lib hates Zara, and I know why. But everyone seems to have an opinion. Really, what choice do I have? I have to let her try.

"He doesn't need her. He has you, and me, and Aria."

"And you all live on the other side of the world. When we go home, it's just me and Jacob again."

"I'm just going to use the restroom," Aria says quietly. It's not lost on me that she hasn't uttered a word since agreeing to take Zara riding. She's walked away before I can stop her, and I groan, dropping my head into my hands.

"Can you really go home and never see Aria again?" Mason asks, and my head flies up to look at him.

"What?"

"You remember Lib and I had a week apart just after we got together? She flew home without telling me and wouldn't answer my calls when my crazy ex faked a pregnancy?" Libby's cheeks flush pink and she presses herself against Mason, his arm curling around her as he pulls her close.

"I remember. You flew to England to bring her back. This is nothing like that, Mason."

"Maybe not, but I think your feelings for Aria are as strong as mine were for Libby."

"Were?" Libby exclaims, pushing away from him.

"Yes, baby. Were," he says, pulling her back into his arms. "Of course I loved you then, but it's nothing compared to how I feel about you now. You and Annie are my whole world." Libby lifts her head and stares at him before bursting into tears, sobbing against his chest. "Hormones," he mouths to me, and I chuckle. "The point I'm trying to make is that I could barely breathe knowing she was so far away from me. It was the longest week of my life, Jack."

"I can't stay, Mason. No matter how much I want to." I turn and catch sight of Aria coming out of the house. "I do love her, more than I ever thought possible, but Jacob's whole world is back in England. I can't take him away from that."

"You're Jacob's whole world, Jack," Savannah says softly.

"And Zara?"

"All I'm going to say is, she didn't think of you when she up and left. Why should any decisions you make about the rest of your life be based on her?" Savannah says with a shrug.

"They aren't based on her. They're based on Jacob and what he needs."

"And what about what you need?" she asks.

"I want to be with Aria. I can't imagine my life without her in it, but it's not as easy as that. Zara has parental responsibility. Legally I can't just take Jacob away. Sometimes we don't get what we want."

"So you're just going to give up?" Libby asks, as she wipes away her tears.

"I'm not giving up. I'm being realistic."

"I just want you to be happy."

I stand and pull her up into a hug. "I am happy."

"Yeah, but for how long?"

Sighing, I hold her close. Seeing Aria heading back, I say, "Where's that niece of mine? I haven't had a hold yet."

"Nice change of subject," she says with a sad smile. Mason reaches into the pram that sits at the side of them and scoops up a sleeping Annie. He hands her to me, and I lift my eyes to see Aria smiling at me.

"I'm just borrowing Annie," I say over my shoulder to Lib. "We'll be right back." Walking the short distance to Aria, I place my hand in hers. "Walk with me?"

"Okay." I lead her across the garden and out of the gate.

"Are you okay?" I ask when we're a little way from the house.

She nods. "I just hate to hear you talking about going home. I can't think of you not being here." Her voice breaks and her eyes drop to the ground. "I'm sorry. I know you can't stay. I don't mean to be so needy."

"Hey, look at me." I wait until her gaze meets mine. "You are not being needy." I pull her as close as I can while holding Annie. "If it were just me, I'd stay in a heartbeat. You know that, right?" It's the first time we've spoken about me not being able to stay. We both knew it, but saying it aloud makes it more real somehow.

"I know," she whispers. "I wish things were different."

"So do I, baby." I rest my forehead on hers and close my eyes. "Come home with us?"

"What?" She gasps as she takes a step back.

"When we go back to England, come with us." Her eyes are

wide, and I know they mirror my own. "I can't imagine my life without you in it, Aria. I can't stay here, but you could come with us." I can almost see her mind working overtime as she stares at me. "Say something," I beg when she stays silent, her eyes still fixed on me.

"I can't imagine my life without you either, Jack, but what would I do in the UK? Everything I know is here..." She trails off, her teeth worrying her bottom lip

"We have stables and riding schools in the UK." I pause and drag my hand through my hair. "I know what I'm asking of you is huge, but how I feel about you, Aria, it's a once-in-a-life-time love, and I know we can make this work." She's quiet again, and I've no idea what her decision's going to be.

"Okay," she mouths, her voice barely audible.

"Is that a yes?"

She laughs and throws her hand over her mouth. "That's a yes," she says between her fingers. "Are we really doing this?"

"You bet we are! I love you so much, Aria." I kiss her, a feeling of relief washing over me. Mason was right, I wouldn't have been able to breathe without her.

"I love you more."

"Not possible," I whisper against her lips. Annie stirs in my arms, and Aria takes a step back.

"Do you know how sexy you look, shirtless and with a baby in your arms?"

"Well, I do now," I tell her with a smile. "Let's not say anything about you coming to England. Not until we have a place to stay and everything is sorted."

"Okay. Are you going to tell Zara?"

"Yeah, I'll talk to her."

"She's going to be pissed."

"Let her be pissed. I don't care. This was meant to be, Aria. I was meant to come here and find you." Annie stirs again and opens her eyes. Looking down at her, I smile. "I think someone is going to be wanting a feed soon. We'd better get you back to your mummy."

With my hand encased tightly in Aria's I walk slowly back to Savannah's place feeling happier than I have in a long time. Judging by the smile on Aria's face, I know she feels exactly the same way.

CHAPTER 29

Aria

"I can't wait for this to be over," Savannah hisses from across the stall. "I was hoping she'd be too hungover to want to bother after the amount of wine she drank last night. Have you spoken to her today?"

"Hmm," I mutter, as I saddle up Marble.

"Are you even listening to me… Aria?"

I shoot my head up when she shouts my name. "Shit. Sorry, Sav. I think I zoned out."

She narrows her eyes and crosses the small space to stand in front of me. "Okay, spill!"

"Spill what?" I ask, not meeting her eye.

"Whatever it is you're thinking about."

"I can't. Not yet." I realize I've said too much the second

the words leave my mouth. There is no way Savannah will let me get away without telling her now.

"Oh my God, you're pregnant!" she cries.

"What? No, I'm not pregnant, and keep your voice down! Zara will be here any minute." My eyes quickly flick around the stables, a wave of relief washing over me as I see we're alone. Her eyes narrow again before dropping to my stomach. I roll my eyes and laugh. "Savannah, even if I *was* pregnant, which I'm not, you wouldn't be able to tell just by looking at me!"

"Well, if you're not pregnant, what is it?"

I pull my eyebrows together in a frown as I stare at her. It could be one of a million things, but I think I know why her mind went straight to a baby. I see the longing in her eyes when she holds Annie. She might think she hides it well, but not from me. Anyone can see how much she adores Hope, and while Josh is Hope's father in every way that's important, he's not her biological father. An illness as a child robbed him of fathering a child of his own, but seeing her with Annie, I wonder if she longs for more.

"Have you spoken to Josh?" I ask, hoping I'm not speaking out of turn.

"Does Josh know what's going on and he hasn't told me?" she exclaims, her hands going to her hips.

"No. Not about me. About a baby?"

"A… a baby?" she stutters, her eyes dropping to the floor. "What do you mean?"

"Have you talked to him about having another baby?" I ask gently. She's quiet for a few seconds before she finally looks at me, tears filling her eyes.

"How did you know I want another baby?"

I shrug. "I've seen the way you look at Annie."

Her eyes widen. "Do you think Josh has noticed?"

"I don't know, Sav. I'm guessing that means you haven't talked to him?"

She shakes her head. "How can I? He knew how much I wanted a family, and when he found out he couldn't give me one, he pushed me away for so long. Getting pregnant with Hope after a one-night stand wasn't my finest moment, but it's what brought us together." She pauses to wipe the tears that have begun to fall down her cheeks. "I told him he was enough. How can I tell him I want another baby? He'll think…" she sobs, her hand flying up to her mouth. Rushing toward her, I pull her into my arms.

"Josh loves you, Savannah. Anyone can see that—"

"And I love him. God, I love him so much," she cries, interrupting me.

"I know you do, and that's why you have to talk to him. He would hate to know you're feeling like this."

"He'll think—"

"You don't know what he'll think until you speak to him," I tell her gently, cutting her off. "There are options, Sav. Adoption, sperm donation, maybe even IVF. Has he ever seen a fertility doctor?" She shakes her head. "Promise me you'll speak to him?"

"Okay. I promise." She steps out of our embrace and wipes her eyes. "Thank you, Aria," she says quietly.

"There's no need to thank me. That's what friends are for."

"Don't think I haven't noticed that you changed the subject." Her hands are back on her hips and she raises her eyebrows in question. "Come on, tell me."

I roll my eyes and groan inwardly. "Fine! But you can't say a word, Savannah. Not one word to anyone. Do you promise?"

She bounces on the spot. "I promise, just tell me already!"

"Okay. Jack asked me——"

"Oh, good. You're still here," a voice shouts from the other end of the stables. "I thought you might have gone without me."

"Urgh, Zara!" Savannah mumbles. "Impeccable timing as ever! Did I say I hated her?"

"You might have mentioned it once or twice." I chuckle. "Now shhh, she'll hear you!"

"I hope she does! And where's the apology for being half an hour late?"

"I'm not sure we're getting one," I mouth at Savannah, before turning and flashing Zara my fakest smile.

"Zara, hi. We're almost ready to go." I turn away from her and finish off saddling up Marble.

"I had a great time yesterday, Savannah. Looking forward to the next party."

"I'm glad you had fun." Savannah's voice is dripping with sarcasm, and I sneak a glance at Zara, seeing Sav's sarcasm is lost on her.

"So, which one is mine?" Zara asks, looking between Marley and Marble. "Don't we need three horses?"

"Savannah's lending you Marley. He's better with beginners." I gesture with my head to the horse by Savannah. "I'm riding Titan. He's already outside."

"I'll grab you a helmet," Savannah says as she heads for the tack room.

"I'm not wearing a helmet," Zara exclaims, flicking her blonde curls over her shoulder. "I don't want hat hair."

Savannah stops in her tracks and flashes me a "what the fuck" look.

"You really should, Zara. You've never ridden a horse before. What if——" Savannah starts.

"Are you wearing one?" Zara asks, cutting her off.

"Well, no, but——"

"Then I'm not wearing one either."

"Fine. Suit yourself." Savannah shrugs. "I can't be bothered to argue," she mutters under her breath as she walks past me.

"Mind if I join you?" a voice calls from the stable door, and I smile as I recognize the voice as Jack's.

"Of course not. You can ride Titan. I'll saddle up Cookie," I tell him as I walk toward him. Going up on my tiptoes, I brush my lips against his.

"Who's looking after Jacob?" Zara asks, her voice tinged with annoyance. Looking past me, he glares at her.

"He's with my parents. I'm not going to leave him on his own, Zara."

"I was just asking." She pouts.

"Right! Let's get going," Savannah announces, breaking the awkward silence that's descended. "Zara, I'll help you mount Marley." Taking Marley's reins, Savannah leads him outside and Zara follows, glancing over her shoulder at Jack and me.

"Thank you," I whisper to Jack once we're alone.

"What for?" He wraps his arms around me, dropping a kiss on my hair.

"For being here."

"Always, baby."

Ten minutes later and we're all heading away from the stables. "Can we go and see the lake where Mason proposed to Libby? She was telling me about it a few days ago. It sounds so romantic," Zara says.

"Erm… sure, we can head that way." I'm a little taken aback at her request. She doesn't seem the romantic type, but if that's where she wants to go, it's fine with me. I just want this afternoon to be over. Jack is taking me on a date tonight, and I can't wait to be alone with him.

Conversation while we ride is a little slow, and we're reduced to discussing the weather and other menial topics. I really have nothing in common with Zara, so I'm struggling to make conversation. Thankfully, Savannah is more than happy to chat, even if she is asking things I'd never dare to.

"So, Zara," Savannah starts. "How are things going with Jacob? I bet he's changed a lot since you last saw him?"

My eyes widen and I steal a glance at Zara, whose face is like thunder.

"They're going good. Great actually," she bites out. "Can we go any faster?" she asks after a few minutes. "It's a little boring." We're riding at a steady pace, knowing this is her first time on a horse. I glance at Sav, who rolls her eyes.

"Yeah, I guess," I tell her. "If you just tap your heels, he'll go into a trot." I watch her do as I say, and Marley takes off in a trot. She bounces a little in the saddle, a small yelp coming from her. "If he's going too fast, pull back on the reins," I shout as I nudge Cookie into a gallop. Before I can reach her, Savannah screams behind me.

"Jack!" she cries, and I turn just in time to see Titan rearing up. As if in slow motion, I watch in horror as Jack is thrown from the horse. Fear engulfs me as I force Cookie to stop. Jumping from her, I race to where he's landed, my heart in my mouth. He's on the ground and unconscious. Dropping to my knees, I panic as I see blood on the ground.

"There's blood, Savannah. He hit his head. Call nine-one-one," I cry.

"Oh my God! Is he okay?" Zara asks as she falls to the ground next to me.

"I don't know. He's not awake. We need an ambulance, now!" I take his hand in mine, my thumb stroking his skin. "You're going to be fine, baby," I whisper, my voice catching.

"The ambulance is on its way. I'm going to take Marble and meet them. They'll never find us out here otherwise," Savannah says. Her hand squeezes my shoulder, and my scared eyes find hers. "Are you okay?" I nod as silent tears roll down my cheeks. "He's going to be okay, Aria."

"Please hurry, Sav." I watch her ride away on Marble before looking back at Jack. Blood is beginning to pool on the ground beneath his head, and I know I need to try and stop the bleeding. Dropping his hand, I pull my tank over my head.

"Help me, Zara. We have to try and stop the bleeding." Her hands shake as she gently lifts his head. Placing my tank on the back of his head, I hold it against the wound, praying it stems the bleeding. His face is pale, and as I brush my fingers across his cheek, his skin is cool but clammy. I hope the ambulance gets here soon.

I don't know how long we've been waiting for help, but it feels like hours and Jack is still unconscious. Zara hasn't said anything since asking if he was okay, but tears streak down her cheeks. Despite not liking her, she looks as scared as I feel.

"They should be here soon. They have to be." Her eyes meet mine and she nods. Picking up her hand, I squeeze it and she smiles gratefully at me.

A few minutes later, I hear the welcomed sound of an emergency vehicle in the distance. "Oh, thank God," Zara mutters, dropping her hand from mine and standing. She waves her arms, and within minutes, the ambulance pulls up. Two EMTs jump out, and after briefly explaining what's happened, I reluctantly step away from Jack. My whole body begins to shake as I watch the EMTs work on him. Savannah appears by my side and pulls me in for a hug.

"Where's your shirt?" she asks as I shiver in her arms. "Are you cold?"

"She's in shock, I think," Zara answers from beside me. "She used her top to try and stop the bleeding." Pulling out of the embrace, Savannah removes her shirt, leaving her in just a tank.

"Here, put this on. Are you going with him in the ambulance?" I nod, unable to find my voice. "Hey, Aria. Look at me." She waits until I lift my head. "He's going to be okay."

"God, I hope so, Sav. I can't lose him," I whisper. "I've only just found him."

"You aren't going to lose him."

I hope she's right.

CHAPTER 30

Aria

"Aria," Emma shouts, and I lift my head from my hands and stand from the uncomfortable plastic chair I've been sitting on. She rushes across the waiting room, Phil and Zara following. "Oh, sweetheart," she says, her voice breaking as she reaches me. She pulls me into her arms and I promptly burst into tears. "Is there any news?"

I shake my head. "A nurse came out about five minutes ago to say they were taking him for a CT scan. He's still unconscious," I tell her through my tears.

"What happened? Savannah said he was thrown from the horse?"

"Something must have spooked Titan. It happened so fast. Where's Jacob?"

"Savannah's taken him to her house. He's okay."

The four of us sit in silence in the waiting room. What seems like a million people come and go while we sit waiting for news. Nerves creep up my spine the longer we wait. Surely if everything was okay, someone would have come out to us by now? Phil suddenly stands and begins to pace the small waiting area.

"What's taking them so long? Why is no one telling us anything?" He closes his eyes and drags his hand through his hair. Emma stands and takes his hands, forcing him to stop pacing.

"I'm sure they'll be out to speak to us as soon as they can." Her voice sounds calm, but her face is etched with worry.

"Are you the family of Jack Davis?" an older man in scrubs asks as he comes to stand in front of us.

"Yes, we're his parents," Phil says. "Is he okay?"

Taking a deep breath, I stand up, my hands clasped nervously in front of me.

"I'm Dr. West. He's still unconscious and I'm afraid to say he's fractured his skull." Emma gasps and reaches for my hand. My heart pounds in my chest and I swear the whole room can hear it. "It's not as bad as it sounds," he assures us. "It's a mild fracture, and he'll definitely have a headache for a few days, but there's nothing to suggest that he won't make a full recovery."

"When will he wake up?" I ask, my voice shaky.

"That I don't know. There was some swelling on the CT scan, so it could be hours, it could be days. He will wake up though." Relief courses through my body and my legs give way. Emma must notice as her arm snakes around my waist, keeping me on my feet.

"Can we see him?" she asks.

"Yes, of course. Come with me." I reach behind me and take Zara's hand.

"He's going to be okay," I tell her, and she nods slowly, following me as I pull her across the waiting room.

"We've admitted him," Dr. West says. "He'll need to stay in for at least twenty-four hours once he's regained consciousness, maybe longer." He leads us through a set of double doors and along a corridor. "His room is just here." We come to a stop outside of room 120. "If he wakes up, press the buzzer and someone will be with you."

"Thank you, Doctor," Phil says, shaking Dr. West's hand. He nods his head before walking away.

Emma pushes on the door and I follow her in. She rushes across the room to where Jack lies, unconscious in the bed. A large bandage is wrapped around his head, and the clothes he was wearing have been replaced with a hospital-issued gown. I slowly walk to the other side of his bed and take his hand in mine. Leaning down, I press my lips against his.

"Wake up, baby," I whisper. "Please." I watch his face for any sign that he can hear me, but there's none.

"He will, Aria," Emma says quietly. "We just have to be patient."

I sit in the chair next to his bed, his hand still encased with mine. Zara comes and sits next to me and I offer her a small smile. She's hardly said anything since we arrived at the hospital, but I can't worry about her. I have enough to worry about with Jack.

Several hours pass and there's no change. Nurses come in and out of the room every hour to check his vitals, offering encouraging smiles, but they still have no idea how long it will be until he wakes. We take it in turns to talk to him, hoping our voices will pull him from his darkness, but nothing seems to work.

I've no idea what time it is, but it's dark outside and my back aches from sitting on the uncomfortable chairs. Standing, I pace the room, trying to get some feeling back into my legs.

"Let's take a walk, Aria," Emma suggests, and she takes my arm and guides me to the door.

I look over my shoulder at a still sleeping Jack. "I don't know. What if he wakes up?"

"Zara and Phil will be here. You haven't left the room since we got here. You need a break."

I bite down on my bottom lip and slowly nod my head. "Okay." I let her lead me out of the room and back through the seating area. It seems like days have passed since we were in here waiting for news. Stopping at a vending machine, I get a bottle of water. "What time is it?" I ask Emma as we get outside.

"It's late. Two twenty-five a.m."

"Savannah messaged me earlier. I never replied. It's too late to reply now." My hand flies to my mouth. "Oh, God! Jacob!"

She places her hand on my arm. "He's fine, Aria. Savannah still has him. She knows Jack's going to be okay, but is still unconscious." She pauses. "You really love him, don't you?"

"Jack? Yeah, I do."

"No. I mean Jacob."

"Oh. Well, yes, I love Jacob. I love them both."

She smiles. "They love you too."

"Can we go back inside? I want to be there when he wakes

up." She nods and we walk back toward Jack's room in comfortable silence. As we near his room, I notice an orange light flashing above the door. "What's that?" I ask as we get nearer. Before Emma can answer, a doctor and nurse run from the other end of the corridor and into Jack's room. The unopened bottle of water drops from my hand and I sprint the short distance to his room. I fling the door open. It bangs off the wall, and everyone turns to look at me.

"Is he okay?" I ask desperately, almost afraid to hear the answer.

"He's waking up," Zara exclaims. "He squeezed my hand."

"It could have just been a reflex," the nurse explains. "Dr. Lewis is just checking him over."

I nod as I hold my breath, waiting for them to do their checks.

"Jack, can you hear me?" the doctor asks.

"Where am I?" he croaks.

"He's awake," I whisper, looking at Emma, who's smiling widely.

"You're in the hospital, Jack. You had an accident. How are you feeling?" Dr. Lewis asks as he flashes a light in Jack's eyes.

"My head hurts."

"That's to be expected. I'm afraid you've fractured your skull. We did a CT scan, and it showed a small swelling. It's a mild fracture though, and you should make a full recovery. Nurse Carter will get you some painkillers, and I'll be back to check on you later." He looks overwhelmed and I've no idea if he took everything in that the doctor told him.

"Thank you," Emma says as Dr. Lewis and Nurse Carter leave the room. My eyes go to Jack, who's staring at Zara.

"Zara," he whispers, holding his hand out to her. Her eyes widen in surprise before a smile erupts on her face and she moves closer toward him. His outstretched hand reaches for hers, his eyes fixed on her stomach. "The baby?" he asks, panic lacing his voice. "How long have I been asleep? Did I miss it?" Emma gasps from the side of me and suddenly I can't breathe. My fingers begin to tingle and black spots dance in front of my eyes.

"What?" Zara whispers.

"Did you have the baby?" he asks, confused. "Why aren't you pregnant?"

"He thinks it's three years ago," I mumble. Emma reaches for my hand and pulls me into her side.

"I'll get the doctor," Phil says, his voice sounding distant and muffled. Seconds later the same doctor and nurse return, their eyes full of concern.

"What year is it, Jack?" the doctor asks as he comes to the side of his bed. Jack's eyes are still focused on Zara and a frown appears on his face.

"What?" he asks, dragging his eyes off her.

"What year is it?"

"It's 2017. Why are you asking me that?"

"And where are you? Which country?"

"Which country? England, of course. What's going on." He turns back to Zara. "Why aren't you pregnant? Did I miss the birth?" he asks again.

"Would you give me a minute, Jack?" the doctor asks. Jack nods, his frightened eyes looking around the room. My heart breaks when his gaze passes me by without even a flicker of recognition. "Would everyone mind stepping outside while

Nurse Carter takes Jack's vitals?" Emma squeezes my hand and I let her lead me into the corridor with them, Zara following.

"Why does he think it's 2017?" Emma asks once we've been led along the corridor and into a relatives' waiting room.

"It seems the head injury has caused some short-term memory loss. What baby is he referring to?" Dr. Lewis asks.

"Jacob, his son. He's almost three," Zara replies. "I'm Jacob's mother." Dr. Lewis nods in understanding.

"Will his memory come back?" I ask quietly, terrified to hear the answer.

"As the head injury heals, there is every chance he will regain his memories. The most important thing is to allow him to remember things himself. Obviously, he will need to know about his son, and that he is indeed in America and not England. But overloading him with information on the missing three years of his life will cause him confusion. He won't know what are memories and what are things he's merely being told. As hard as it will be, he needs to remember what he can by himself."

I feel like I'm going to throw up. Jack has no idea who I am, and I'm not going to be able to tell him. "How long will it take for him to remember?" I ask desperately.

"There is no way of knowing. It could be days, or weeks, or even longer. I'm sorry." He smiles sympathetically at me. "The best thing you can all do for Jack is be there for him. He's going to be confused and scared until he figures this out."

"So we should lie to him?" Emma asks, her gaze flicking between me and Zara.

"Just let him take things at his own pace. Everything he

knows has changed. If he's overloaded with information, his memories might never return."

"Thank you, Dr. Lewis," Phil says, shaking his hand.

"I should get back to him. He'll wonder where I've gone," Zara announces as she makes for the door. Stopping, she turns around. "I think I should be the one to tell him about Jacob. He thinks we're together, after all." She's gone before anyone can respond. Exhausted, I slump onto the worn leather sofa that's pushed against the wall. Dropping my head in my hands, silent tears fall down my cheeks. In the space of ten minutes, I've gone from the highs of seeing Jack wake up, to the depths of despair at knowing he has no idea who I am or what we've shared over the past few weeks.

"I should go," I say as I stand and wipe away my tears.

"Go?" Emma asks, surprised. "Go where?"

"Home. Jack has no idea who I am."

"But he loves you."

"He loves Zara. I'm nobody to him." My voice breaks, and I swallow down the golf ball-sized lump in my throat. "Zara wants to be with him, Emma. That's what she came here for, to get him back. Now she's going to get her wish."

"And you're just going to stand by and let her? I thought you loved him?" She sounds annoyed. I know how much she dislikes Zara.

"I do love him… but I can't tell him. He thinks he's happy with Zara and she's going to take full advantage of that." I sit down heavily on the sofa.

"Then you have to make him fall in love with you again, Aria." She sits down next to me and takes my hand. "I've *never* seen him as happy as he is when he's with you. I knew as soon as I saw you two together… I knew he'd fallen in love with you." Fresh tears streak down my face and she pulls me into a hug. "Please don't give up on him," she whispers. I want so badly to say I won't, but I know Zara isn't going to play fair. How can I stand by and watch them be together? It's going to break my heart. Can I really make him fall in love with me all over again? I have no idea, but thinking about a life without him in it is too painful to comprehend.

CHAPTER 31

Jack

Dazed and confused, I drop my head onto the pillow as the nurse leaves the room. My head is pounding, and I wish it would stop so I can pull my thoughts together. Something is wrong. Why isn't Zara pregnant? Did she have the baby and I missed the birth? Did something happen to the baby? Panic begins to set in, and I sit up, reaching for the call button the nurse told me about. Before I can press it, the door swings open and Zara walks in.

"Zara," I say, relief rushing through me. "What's going on? Where is everyone?"

She sits on the bed next to me and takes my hand in hers. "You had an accident, Jack. You hit your head."

"Were you… were you hurt too? The baby?" My eyes drop to her flat stomach and I furrow my brows in confusion.

"No. I'm fine. But when you fell and hit your head, you lost your memory."

I laugh. "If I lost my memory, Zara, how come I remember you?"

"You're remembering things from three years ago, Jack. I had the baby. Jacob's almost three."

I laugh again and shake my head. "What? That can't be true. I think I'd remember my own son!" The laughter dies on my lips when I see she isn't joking, and an uneasy feeling settles in the pit of my stomach.

"You're telling the truth, aren't you?" I say quietly. She nods. "I have a son?" She nods again. "I missed almost three years of his life?"

"No! You were there for every second. You're a great dad. Jacob adores you."

"God, this is fucked up!"

A knock sounds on the door and I turn as it opens, relieved to see my parents walk in. "Honey, how are you feeling?" my mum asks as she crosses the room and sits on the other side of the bed.

"Confused. I have a son, Mum. A son I can't remember."

"I know, sweetheart, but the doctor said there's no reason why you shouldn't regain the memories you've lost."

My dad comes to stand beside her. "It'll all come back to you, son. Just give it some time."

I sigh loudly and Zara lowers her head, brushing her lips against mine. Hearing a small gasp from across the room, I look around Zara to see a woman standing awkwardly by the door.

Her eyes are fixed on the floor and I find myself willing her to look up so I can see her face. After a few seconds, she lifts her head, and my breath catches in my throat as her beautiful blue eyes meet mine. She's stunning, but there's a sadness on her face, and I can't help but wonder who or what caused it.

"This is Aria," my mum says.

"Aria," I whisper, my eyes still fixed on her.

"She works on the ranch." My head swings around to look at my mum.

"The ranch? As in Texas?"

"I hadn't gotten around to telling him that part yet," Zara bites out, her voice tinged with annoyance.

"We're in Marble Falls, Jack," my dad says, ignoring Zara's tone. "You came out here with Jacob. Me and your mum followed a few weeks later."

"I guess that explains why the doctor and nurse have American accents. Wait. Why are we here? In Marble Falls, I mean. Is Libby okay?"

"She's fine. In fact, you're an uncle. She and Mason had a baby a few days ago. That's why she's not here. She wanted to be."

"A baby? But they only just got married…" I trail off, dropping my head back on the pillow, wincing as pain shoots through my head. "They didn't just get married, did they?" I ask, looking at the ceiling.

"No, Jack," my mum says gently. Sighing, I sit up again, slower this time. Looking across at Aria, I smile as I find her looking at me. "I'm guessing we're friends?" I ask her. "I'm sorry I can't remember."

"That's okay, and yes, we're… friends." She smiles and my

heart pounds in my chest as our eyes lock. After a few seconds, Zara clears her throat from the side of me and I snap out of my daze.

"Maybe you should all leave and let Jack get some sleep," Zara says.

"No, wait," I shout. "I want to see Jacob. Where is he?"

"He's fine, Jack. Savannah is looking after him," my mum assures me. "We'll bring him to see you in the morning."

I turn to Zara and take her hand. "Do you have a picture on your phone? Maybe seeing a picture of him will help me remember."

"Erm… I don't have my phone with me. It's back at the ranch."

"I have a picture," Aria says quietly, and she reaches into the pocket of her shorts and pulls out her phone. She spends a few seconds finding the picture before walking toward the bed and handing me the phone. Aria's sitting on top of a horse, her arms wrapped around a little boy who's laughing as the picture's being taken. He looks a lot like me, but I don't recognize him, and that breaks my heart.

"Anything?" my mum asks. I shake my head and hand the phone back to Aria.

"Did he like going on the horse?" I ask her.

"He loved it. He thought he was a cowboy."

I smile, wishing I could remember. "Who took the photo?" Her eyes go from me to Zara, then back to me.

"You did, then you sent it to me." I frown, thinking we must be good friends if I have her number and trusted her to take Jacob on a horse. I suddenly feel exhausted and can't stop the yawn that escapes my lips.

"I think that might be our cue to leave," my dad says with a chuckle. He pulls me into a hug while my mum presses a kiss on my cheek. "We'll come back in the morning with Jacob. Try and get some rest."

"See you tomorrow, Jack," Aria says quietly from the end of my bed.

"Bye, Aria."

"Zara, are you ready to leave?" my mum asks as she links her arm with Aria.

"Oh, no. I'm staying with Jack." She reaches for my hand, pressing her lips across my knuckles.

"There's no need, Zara. I'm fine. You should go back to the ranch and be with Jacob."

"Jacob will be fine with Savannah. I almost lost you today. I'm not letting you out of my sight." She climbs onto the bed, pressing her body against mine. Hearing the door open, I look up to see Aria leaving.

"Is she okay?" I ask my mum, who's glaring at Zara.

"She suddenly feels a little sick. She's just gone for some air. I'll make sure she's okay. We'll see you tomorrow."

Once the door closes behind them, I wrap my arms around Zara and kiss her on the head. "Is everything okay between you and my mum? You haven't had an argument or anything, have you?"

"What? No! Why would you think that?"

I shake my head. "She seemed a little off, that's all. It's probably nothing."

"She's just worried about you. You gave us all a scare."

"Yeah, I guess." I yawn again. "I have loads of questions,

Zar, but right now I need to sleep. Maybe I'll wake up and remember everything."

"Maybe," she whispers before tilting her head and capturing my lips with hers. She moans as her tongue pushes into my mouth. I kiss her back, but something feels off, and I pull out of the kiss, a niggling doubt creeping into my mind. Dropping my head back onto the pillow, I feel guilty as I tighten my hold on her and close my eyes, giving in to sleep.

I GROAN as daylight filters through the blinds. It's a welcome change to be woken by sunlight as opposed to nurses taking my vitals every hour. By the time I'd manage to fall back to sleep, it was time to be woken again. Zara had slept through every check and is still nestled against my chest. There is still a pounding in my head, but it seems a little less than yesterday, which is surprising considering my lack of sleep. I've no idea what time it is, but I need to pee. Gently moving Zara off my chest, I wince as I slide off the bed, my whole body aching.

After using the toilet, I glance in the mirror above the sink and frown looking at the large bandage wrapped around my head, dried blood matting my dark hair. Desperate for a shower, I make my way through my room and out into the corridor. I head for the nurses' station and I hear someone call my name.

"Mr. Davis, what are you doing out of bed?"

Turning, I see one of the nurses rushing toward me. "I needed to pee."

"You do know you have a bathroom in your room?" She takes my arm and ushers me back along the corridor.

"Yes, I know. I wanted to ask if I could have a shower. I have blood in my hair."

She looks up at me as if I've asked her to give me a lap dance. "Mr. Davis—"

"Jack, please," I tell her, cutting her off.

"Fine. Jack. You have twelve stitches in the back of your head, not to mention a fractured skull. You need to be in bed."

"Well, when can I have a shower?"

"You can't get the wound wet for a couple of days. You can have a shower later this morning if you don't get your hair wet." She pushes open the door to my room and leads me inside. "You'll need help in the shower. I'll ask one of the nurses to come after the doctor's been. Now, please, get into bed." She gestures to the bed, only to see Zara fast asleep. "Mrs. Davis," she says loudly, waking Zara up.

"We're not—" I'm about to tell her we aren't married, but the truth is I've no idea if we are or not. A feeling of foreboding washes over me at the thought I might be married and not even know.

"Your husband needs to be in his bed. This is not a hotel."

"What?" she asks, sleep lacing her voice.

I chuckle, and the nurse flashes me an annoyed look.

"You need to get out of my patient's bed."

"Oh, right, of course. Sorry." She looks sheepish as she rubs her eyes and swings her legs over the edge.

"Get in, please, Jack. I'm not leaving until you do." Sighing, I sit on the edge of the bed and raise my eyebrows in question. She shakes her head. "Legs as well." I do as she asks. "Stay there." After watching me for a few seconds, she seems satisfied and finally leaves.

Once the door closes behind her, I look across to Zara, who's sitting in the reclining chair next to the bed. "Are we married? The nurse called you Mrs. Davis."

She shakes her head. "No. She must have just assumed." She leans forward and takes my hand. "I like how it sounded though."

She smiles, and I give her a small smile back, uncomfortable at how relieved I feel knowing we aren't married. I can't help but wonder what our relationship is like. Why aren't we married? If Jacob is almost three and we're happy, then surely marriage is the next step? Questions swirl in my mind. Questions I don't have the answers to, and for some reason, can't bring myself to ask Zara about.

CHAPTER 32

Aria

Opening my eyes, I sit up quickly, taking a few seconds to realize I'm in my old bedroom rather than in Jack's. I haven't slept in my own room for weeks, but it felt too strange to sleep in his bed when he barely knows my name, despite desperately wanting to feel close to him.

I hardly slept at all last night. My heart physically aches when I think of Jack not remembering me, or anything we've shared in the past few weeks. It had taken everything in me to walk away from him in the hospital, knowing Zara would waste no time in filling his head with lies of their "relationship."

Swinging my legs over the side of the bed, I pad across the room to the bathroom. After turning the shower on, I use the bathroom and brush my teeth as I wait for the water to warm up. When the room fills with steam, I pull off my sleep shorts and tank and step under the hot spray. Tipping my head back, I close my eyes. Tears pour down my cheeks, hidden by the water from the shower. I rarely cry, but I seem to have cried more in the last twenty-four hours than I ever have before. I guess that's what happens when your heart shatters. Emma had tried to assure me on the way back from the hospital that Jack will remember, that he won't be able to forget a love like we shared. But the fact is, he *has* forgotten, and not even the doctor could guarantee he will ever remember again.

I spend far too long in the shower, not wanting to get out and face the day. Knowing I have to, I eventually turn off the water and dry off. After getting dressed, I pick up my phone and make my way downstairs. It's later than I thought when I check the time, and I can hear voices coming from the porch. Making my way to the door, I pause.

"Someone has to tell him! He has to know they aren't together! What about Aria?" Libby asks.

"The doctor said we have to let him remember himself. If we influence him, he might never remember Jacob's birth or the first two years of his life," Emma replies.

"I get that, Mum, but Zara is influencing him! She'll be telling him all sorts of crap!" Taking a deep breath, I push the door open and walk out onto the porch. "Aria!" Libby rushes toward me and pulls me into a hug. "Are you okay?"

"Not really," I say.

She steps back and out of the embrace. "You have to tell him, Aria. He loves you. He loves you so much."

"I love him too, but your mom's right. He has to have the chance to remember Jacob..." I trail off and burst into tears, embarrassed to be breaking down in front of Jack's parents, but powerless to stop it. She pulls me back into her arms as I cry on her shoulder.

"Oh, sweetheart. Please don't cry. Everything will work itself out," Emma says. I feel her hand on my back. I wish I could believe her, I really do.

"We need to speak to Zara. Surely she knows she won't get away with lying to him. When his memory comes back—"

"*If* his memory comes back," I say through my tears, cutting her off.

"It will come back, Aria. It has to."

Pulling back, I wipe my tears. "What time are you heading to the hospital?" I ask.

"As soon as we have Jacob," Emma says with a frown. "You are coming, aren't you?"

I shrug one shoulder. "I don't know."

"Please come," Emma begs. "Jack will want to see you."

I only wish that were true. I imagine he hasn't even thought about me once since I left the hospital.

"Come with us to get Jacob and then decide?"

"Okay," I sigh, giving her a small smile.

We walk in silence to Savannah's house. I don't have the energy to make small talk, and I know nothing they can say will make me feel better.

"Does Savannah know about Jack's memory loss?" I ask as we climb the porch steps to the front door.

"No. I only managed to speak to Libby this morning. It was too late when we got home last night." The door swings open before I can respond.

"Is Jack awake?" Savannah asks, worry etched on her face.

"Can Jacob hear us?" Emma asks from the side of me.

She frowns. "No, he's in the backyard with Josh and Hope. What's happened? Come in, come in." She gestures to the entryway, stepping to the side so we can pass her. Closing the door behind us, she looks at me expectantly.

"Jack's awake," I tell her, her whole body seeming to sag with relief.

"Oh, thank God!" she exclaims. "And he's going to be okay?"

"Yes. The doctor said he should make a fully recovery, but…" I pause and take a deep breath. "He woke up thinking it's 2017 and that Zara was pregnant with Jacob." I rush out the last part. I don't know why, it's not like saying it quickly makes it any less true. Her eyes widen before flicking between me, Emma, and Phil.

"Shit! Is it short term?"

"We hope so," Emma says.

"You told him it's 2020 though? And that he's with you now?" she asks me.

I shake my head. "He knows what year it is, and that Jacob is almost three. He doesn't know anything else. He thinks he's still with Zara."

"What? Why? Why wouldn't you tell him?"

"The doctors have advised that we tell him as little as possible to give him the best chance of regaining his memory," Emma explains. Coming to stand next to me, she takes my hand.

"That makes no sense."

"He won't know what are memories and what are things he's just being told. I want him to remember all the milestones with Jacob. Telling him could confuse him even more and the memories never come back," I say sadly.

"But what about you and him?"

I shake my head. "He has to remember," I whisper.

"Ria!" I hear Jacob shout before I can respond. Looking past Savannah, I see Jacob running toward me.

"Hey!" I say, blinking away the tears that sting my eyes. "Have you had fun with Hope?" He nods as he slams into my legs, and I reach down to pick him up, placing him on my hip. I bite the inside of my cheek. If Jack doesn't remember, I not only lose him, but Jacob too. My stomach churns at the realization.

"Are you heading to the hospital?" Savannah asks, her worried eyes fixed on me.

I nod and glance at Emma. "Jack wants to see Jacob."

"Come back here when you've seen him and we can finish our conversation, okay?"

"Okay."

AN HOUR later and I park the ranch truck in the parking lot of the hospital. To say I'm nervous is an understatement. When I woke up this morning, I wasn't sure I was even going to come. The need to see Jack and to know he's okay won over though, but now that I'm here, I'm wondering if I've made the right decision.

Climbing out of the truck, I stand and look at the imposing building, my hands wringing nervously in front of me.

"It'll be okay," Emma whispers in my ear. I don't see how,

but I don't voice that, instead offering her a small smile. She links her arm with mine and gently tugs me toward the entrance. Phil follows with an excited Jacob.

We're silent on the walk to Jack's room, nervous butterflies taking flight in my stomach the closer we get. Just as Emma is about to open the door, I pull my arm from hers. "You go in, I just need a minute," I say quietly.

"Aria," she starts.

"Please," I beg. "Just a minute."

She holds my gaze for a few seconds before nodding. Taking a step away from the door, I turn and watch the three of them disappear inside. Leaning against the wall, I drop my head back and close my eyes. Part of me so desperately wants to see Jack, but another part can't bear to see him and Zara playing happy family, not when I know their relationship is so far away from that. Taking a deep breath, I stand in front of the door, my hand on the door handle. Should I knock? I guess I should, it's not like Jack or Zara will be expecting me. Knocking lightly on the wood, I wait.

"Come in," Jack shouts. Opening the door, I walk in, plastering a fake smile on my face. My eyes go straight to Jack, my heart pounding as he smiles when he sees me. "Hey, you came back," he says. My eyes flick to Zara, who's scowling.

"How are you feeling?" I ask, my eyes back on him.

"Good. My head is still pounding, but I can't wait to get out of here."

"Have they said when you can be discharged?"

"Not yet, but I'm hoping I won't have to spend another night here. The bed's not big enough for two." He laughs.

The smile slips from my lips and a wave of nausea washes over me. "That's great," I mutter, my eyes dropping to the floor.

"Has the doctor seen you yet this morning?" Phil asks, and I couldn't be more grateful that he's taken over the conversation.

"No, not yet. I'm waiting for one of the nurses to come and help me shower. Apparently, I'm not allowed to shower alone." He shrugs and Zara smiles as her eyes meet mine.

"You don't need a nurse for that. You have me," Zara says as she stands from the chair she's sitting in and sits next to him on the bed. Jacob is sitting with Jack, and seeing the three of them together makes my heart ache. Clearly, seeing Jacob hasn't brought any memories back for him like I was so desperately hoping it would.

"I think you should leave the showering to the nurses, Zara," Emma says. "You wouldn't know what to do if he were to pass out."

Zara glares at Emma, changing her expression when Jack looks at her.

"Ria, play?" Jacob asks, holding one of the cars in the air that Emma and Phil brought to the hospital with them.

A look of surprise flashes across Jack's face as he looks from Jacob to me. "Sure, buddy. You know how much I love to play cars." Crossing the room, I take the car from his hand and drive it up and down Jacob's leg, loving hearing him giggle.

"Daddy too!" he cries, his face lighting up in a smile.

I laugh, "Okay. Should we see if Daddy is ticklish?"

"Yes!"

Taking the car, I slowly drive it up Jack's blanket-covered leg, moving it from side to side, trying to get him to laugh. "I don't think it's working," I whisper to Jacob. "Why don't you drive your car on his other leg? I bet between us we can get him laughing." I look up at Jack, and he smiles. Jacob takes his car and copies what I'm doing. After a few seconds, Jack bursts out laughing, reaching for Jacob and tickling him.

"Are you ticklish too?" he asks Jacob, who is squealing with laughter.

"Stop," he says through his laughter, pushing Jack's hands away.

"Do you and Jacob play a lot?" Jack asks when he finally stops tickling Jacob.

"Erm… yeah. We like to play with the cars, don't we, Jacob?" He nods and climbs off the bed. Standing in front of me, he puts his arms up and I bend down to pick him up, settling him on my hip. His thumb goes in his mouth and he drops his head onto my shoulder.

"He's got a great relationship with Aria," Emma says. "They've really bonded while you've been here." I can't help but steal a look at Zara who's scowling at me. When I look away, I notice Jack staring at me. Butterflies erupt in my stomach again, but this time not because I'm nervous. The way he's looking at me is like how he did before the accident, even if he doesn't realize it.

"We must have spent a lot of time together." He turns to Zara. "How long have we been at the ranch?"

"Erm, I don't know. A few weeks?" Zara stumbles over her words, making her reply sound more like a question than an answer. Jack gives her a funny look, but before he can respond, she jumps up and makes her way to me. "I'll take him," she says. "I am his mum, after all." She mutters the last part so only

I can hear as she leans in to take Jacob from me. He squirms in her arms, but she holds him tightly.

"Stop it, Jacob," she says through gritted teeth. Jacob stills and then bursts into tears.

"Daddy," he whimpers and leans his arms over to Jack. Zara huffs and hands him to Jack before heading to the door.

"I'm going to get some air." She walks out, slamming the door behind her.

"Am I missing something?" Jack asks as he holds a sobbing Jacob against his chest. "What was all that?"

I bite down on my lip, desperate to tell him Zara isn't his girlfriend and that I'm head over heels in love with him. I sneak a glance at Emma and Phil, who look as torn as I do. All three of us are saved from answering when a knock sounds on the door, and the doctor from yesterday walks in.

"Jack, how are you feeling? You're looking a lot better this morning," the doctor says, picking up his chart from the end of the bed.

"We'll wait outside while you speak to the doctor," Emma says.

"Want me to take him?" I ask Jack, holding my arms out to a still sobbing Jacob.

"Will he be all right?" Jack asks, and I nod.

"He'll be fine." Jacob lets me take him from Jack, his arms going around my neck and hugging me tightly. Jack reaches for my free hand, his fingers brushing mine. A zip of electricity shoots up my arm, and I know he feels it too when he pulls back his hand, his eyes flying up to mine.

"Thank you," he whispers, and I smile as I follow Emma and Phil out of the room.

Walking down the corridor, we find Zara at the vending machines. "What was that back there?" she spits, her hands going to her hips.

"I could ask you the same question." I turn and hand Jacob to Emma, not wanting him to hear my conversation. When they've walked away, I turn back to Zara. "What are you doing? You know you and Jack aren't together. What are you going to do when he starts to remember?"

"There's no guarantee that he will."

"So, you're happy to be in a relationship knowing that if Jack could remember, he wouldn't want to be with you? That's enough for you, is it?"

"I love him, Aria, and I'm going to fight for him."

"Well, I love him too, and he loves me. You're going to have a fight on your hands. He *will* remember, Zara, and he's going to hate you even more than he did before the accident." I turn and walk away before she can respond. My whole body is shaking, and when I turn a corner, out of her line of sight, I drop down to a crouched position, my hands covering my mouth.

I saw something in his eyes today, and I know the feelings he had for me are there, even if they're hidden from view at the moment. I will fight for him. I love him too much to walk away. Anything else just isn't an option.

CHAPTER 33

Jack

It's been the longest of days, and I'm finally being discharged. Mason is coming to pick us up, and I can't wait to get out of this hospital room. Mum, Dad, Aria, and Jacob left a few hours ago, leaving me alone with Zara. Conversation has been difficult, and despite asking about the last three years, she's struggled to answer a lot of my questions. I have no idea what our relationship is like, but being stuck in a room with her for hours has highlighted that we have very little in common. She doesn't seem to know a lot about Jacob either, and I can't stop thinking about how he reacted when she took him from Aria. Sighing, I shake away my thoughts and climb out of bed.

"Did I have my phone on me when I fell off the horse?" I

ask, as I pull off the hospital gown and reach for the clothes I was wearing when I was brought in. She stands from the chair she's been sitting in and walks around the bed, her eyes fixed on me. Her small hands reach out to touch me, her eyes dropping to my chest. She drags her hands up and over my shoulders, her fingers linking behind my head. I drop the clothes in my hands, my arms involuntarily going around her waist as I tug her against me.

"What are you doing?" I whisper, my eyes dropping to her lips.

"I can't see you half naked without wanting to touch you," she mutters before her lips crash against mine. Bringing one of my hands from her waist, I tangle it in her hair. She bites down on my bottom lip and I open up to her, her tongue stroking against mine. She moans into my mouth, but I struggle to concentrate on her; the same niggling feeling from when she kissed me yesterday bubbles to the surface.

"God, I've missed you," she mumbles as I pull out of the kiss. My forehead crinkles in confusion.

"What do you mean? You've been with me the whole time I've been here?" She steps away from me and turns around, picking up the clothes I dropped when she kissed me.

"I just meant we hardly get any alone time anymore." She holds my clothes out to me and I slowly take them from her.

"Are we happy, Zar?"

"What?" she asks, her eyes wide.

"Are we happy?"

"Of course we are." She looks anywhere but at me, and an uneasy feeling settles in the pit of my stomach. Pulling on my shorts and shirt, I can't help but think that I don't believe her. I need to talk to my mum. I'm pulled from my thoughts by a knock at the door.

"Come in," Zara calls out, and I lift my head as the door opens, seeing Mason in the doorway.

"Hey, how you feeling?" he asks as he walks in.

"Better. Ready to get out of here." I cross the room and pull him into a one-armed hug. "I hear congratulations are in order."

"Thanks, man. Libby's desperate to see you. She's waiting at the ranch house with Annie."

I shake my head. "I can't believe you've been married for four years and have a baby. For me, the wedding was only a few months ago."

"It'll *all* come back to you, Jack." He stresses the word all as his eyes flick to Zara.

"Shall we get out of here? I can't wait to have a shower," she says, taking my arm and ushering me out of the door. I shrug half-heartedly as she pulls me past Mason and into the corridor. Thanking the nurses as we pass the nursing station, I suddenly can't wait to get out of here.

It's ALMOST dark as Mason parks the truck outside the ranch house. I look up to see Libby on the porch swing. Her Kindle is in her hand, and I can't help but smile. I might have lost my short-term memory, but it's good to know some things never change. After climbing out of the truck, I head up the steps, meeting Libby at the top.

"I'm so glad you're okay," she chokes out, tears swimming

in her eyes. "I'm so sorry I couldn't come to the hospital." She steps toward me and pulls me into a hug. I hug her back fiercely, suddenly needing that familiarity of someone I've known all my life and who has always been there for me.

"That's okay. I understand, you've had your hands full." My eyes go past her to the pram behind her. "Congratulations, Lib. I'm so happy for you and Mason."

"Come and meet her again." She looks sheepishly at me. "Sorry, I didn't mean to say again."

I chuckle. "It's okay, Lib." She turns and reaches inside the pram, scooping up a tiny bundle dressed in pink.

"This is Annie. Annie, this is Uncle Jack."

Smiling, I stare at Annie. "She's beautiful."

"Come inside and you can hold her. Mum and Dad are in the den with Jacob." I nod and follow her inside. I turn around, expecting to see Zara behind me, but it's just Mason.

"Where did Zara go?" I ask, looking past him.

He shrugs. "Said she needed to go do something and disappeared." I frown and look out over the ranch. Not seeing her, I turn back around and head on inside.

After a round of hugs from my parents and Jacob, I finally sit down and meet my niece. She's tiny and perfect and sleeps the whole time I'm holding her. Jacob seems to adore her too and climbs onto my lap so I'm holding both of them. I can't believe I can't remember either of them. It makes my heart hurt to think I can't remember Jacob's birth, or his first step, or first word. I hope to God I get those memories back.

Annie begins to cry, and I hand her back to Libby, who starts to feed her, her cries instantly stopping. "I guess I should get Jacob to bed. It's getting late."

"Let me help you. You should be resting. Where's Zara?" my mum asks as she stands and picks Jacob up from off my lap.

"I don't know." She rolls her eyes and I frown.

"Did something happen between you and Zara, Mum?" I ask.

"What? No!" Her cheeks flush pink and she walks out of the den with Jacob. I notice Libby looking at me sadly, but I don't have the energy to question her. Instead, I say a quick goodbye to everyone before following Mum and Jacob upstairs. They're not on the landing when I get there, and I stand on the top step, realizing I have no idea which room Jacob is in. Remembering I stayed in Savannah's room the last time I was at the ranch, I make my way to that room, knowing the first room on the left is Brody's, although I have no idea if he still lives here four years later. Pushing the door open, I walk in, stopping in my tracks when I see Aria coming out of the bathroom with a tiny towel wrapped around her. She screams when she sees me, her hand flying to her chest.

"Shit! You scared me."

"Aria! I'm so sorry." My eyes track up and down her body, her hair wet from the shower. When my eyes finally find hers, she's staring at me. "My mum brought Jack up to bed, but I don't know which room is his. Or even where I'm sleeping, for that matter."

"It's okay. Your room is next door, and Jacob's is just across the hallway."

"Do you live here? At the ranch house?"

She nods. "I rent a room from Claire and Ryan. It was supposed to be short term while I helped Savannah with a new horse. Twelve months later, I'm still here." She laughs and I find myself smiling at her.

"You have a great laugh." A flush of pink travels up her neck and onto her cheeks, and I close my eyes, wondering why the hell I said that.

"I'm sorry." I shake my head. "I don't know where that came from."

"It's okay," she whispers, her eyes fixed on mine.

"I should…" I gesture over my shoulder and take a couple of steps backwards.

"How are you feeling? How's your head?" she asks softly.

"Still a little sore. The doctor says I need to be woken every hour, so I think I'm in for a long night. Zara too." Her eyes drop from mine when I mention Zara, but not before I see the hurt that flashes through them. I frown at her reaction and take a step toward her. "Aria—"

"There you are," Zara exclaims from behind me. "Where's Jacob?" I close my eyes and sigh inwardly as Zara interrupts us. "What are you doing in here?" I turn to see her scowling at Aria.

"Jack just got a little lost, that's all," Aria says, her voice tight. "I was just telling him where Jacob's room is. I should get dressed." I turn back around, but she's already disappeared into the bathroom, and I find myself wishing I could talk to her for longer. I haven't been able to stop thinking about her since I saw her with Jacob at the hospital. I feel drawn to her, but I've no idea why. It's clear to see there is tension between Zara and Aria, as well as between Zara and my mum. I just wish I could remember, as it seems everyone has taken a vow of secrecy when it comes to the past three years.

CHAPTER 34

Aria

The next week is pure hell. I can't seem to get a minute alone with Jack. Zara is always with him and makes a big deal of hanging all over him whenever I'm around. Jack's tried to strike up a conversation on more than one occasion, but Zara always interrupts us. She must have also discreetly moved her things from the cabin and into Jack's room, as the cabin now sits empty. I lie in bed at night trying not to think about what they are doing with only a thin wall to separate us. I'm beginning to think I was mistaken about what I saw in his eyes at the hospital that day, and again in my room after he was discharged. Maybe it was wishful thinking and nothing more. I don't want to go against what the doctor told us, but seeing them together is killing me.

It's late afternoon and I'm in the stables, lost in thought as I brush one of the ranch horses. I've almost forgotten what it feels like to be wrapped in Jack's arms, and I wonder if that's something of a blessing. My brain's way of blocking out something that's becoming too painful to remember.

"Aria," a voice shouts, pulling me from my thoughts. Looking up, I smile as I see Savannah and Quinn walking toward me. "Girls' night tonight. You haven't forgotten, have you?" Sav says. The smile slips from my lips and I groan inwardly. I haven't forgotten, but I'm not in the mood for a night out.

"Rain check? I'm really not good company at the moment."

"No way!" Quinn says, taking the brush from my hand. "What are you going to do if you don't come?"

I try to get the brush, but she holds it out of my reach. "I don't know, watch a movie maybe."

"Haven't you done that every night for a week? Mom says she hardly ever sees you around the house anymore, that you're always in your room," Savannah says, her eyebrows raised in question.

I shrug one shoulder, my eyes dropping to the floor of the stables. "It's just easier to stay in my room. I don't have to see them then," I whisper.

"This is bullshit!" Savannah exclaims, and my head flies up to look at her. "Jack needs to know about you!"

"I agree," Quinn says. "If I'd lost my memory, I'd want to know everything, especially who I was in love with."

"That bitch Zara *knows* you and Jack belong together. She's taking advantage of him not remembering," Savannah says exasperatedly.

"I know!" I shout. "You think I don't know that?" Tears streak down my cheeks, which I angrily wipe away. "What am I supposed to do? I'm no one to him, barely a friend. Even if I tell him, he doesn't love me back. He doesn't remember. Telling him won't change how he *feels*."

"God, this is messed up," Quinn says as she pulls me in for a hug. "I'm so sorry, Aria." She holds me as I sob against her shoulder. I want nothing more than to tell Jack everything, but it won't change anything. He's in love with Zara, not me.

"Please come out tonight. You can get drunk and dance and forget about everything for a while?" I can hear the pleading tone in Savannah's voice, and as much as I want to crawl into my bed, pull the comforter over me and hide away, I know she isn't going to give up.

Pulling out of Quinn's arms, I wipe my tears and take a few minutes to calm down. "Okay," I say eventually. "I'll come."

"Let's go back to the house and you can grab some clothes. We can get ready at my place. A real girls' night, like before we had to be responsible. We can be drunk on cheap wine before we even leave." Savannah glances at Quinn. "No wine for you though, Quinn. You'll still have to be the sensible one tonight."

"I guess one of us has to." She chuckles.

"Thank you," I whisper. "I love you guys."

"We love you too, Aria," Quinn says. "Come on, let's grab your stuff."

An hour later and we're at Savannah's. Josh has taken Hope up to the ranch house to play with Jacob, and we're currently making cocktails in the kitchen. Quinn insisted on styling my hair, and it falls in loose waves over my shoulders. My black bodycon dress hugs my curves in all the right places, and I feel much better after making an effort.

"I think this definitely calls for a margarita!" Savannah exclaims as she dances around the kitchen, Lady A blasting from her iPod. I can't help but smile as I watch her prepare two cocktails. I should have known she would never let me wallow in my own self-pity, Quinn too.

"I thought we were having cheap wine?" I say with a chuckle, referring to her earlier comment in the stables.

She waves her hand. "I think we can stretch to something a bit more sophisticated now that we're legally allowed to drink!"

"Fair enough! Make mine a large one."

"What other one is there?" She winks at me, and I burst out laughing. Despite wanting to hide away from the world and everyone in it, I'm beginning to think a night out with the girls is exactly what I need.

"Hey, you ready to go?" a voice shouts from the entryway, and I turn to see Brody in the doorway. His eyes are fixed on Quinn, and he looks at her like he's seeing her for the first time.

"You look beautiful, baby," he says softly as he crosses the room and kisses her. "Too beautiful. Where are you going tonight?" His eyebrows pull together in a frown as he waits for an answer.

"We're going to the Brass Hall," Savannah replies. "Don't go getting all protective, she'll be fine."

"Does Josh know you're going there?"

She narrows her eyes at him. "Why?"

He lets out a sarcastic laugh. "Because I'm sure if he knew you were going there, wearing that." His eyes drop to the electric blue pencil dress she's wearing. "He'd be pissed."

She scoffs. "I'm a grown woman, Brody. Josh isn't going to tell me where I can and can't go, or what I can wear."

"You *do* know Josh, right?"

"Urgh, what is it with you cowboys?" She slides my cocktail across the breakfast bar to me before taking a mouthful of her own drink. "So, are you going to tell him?"

He laughs. "What happened to, 'I'm a grown woman, Josh isn't going to tell me where I can and can't go'?" She rolls her eyes and glares at him.

"Are you going to tell him or not?"

"I'm wondering what it's worth."

"Brody!" Quinn chastises.

"Okay, okay. I think I have a solution where everyone is happy, including me. I don't want anyone hitting on my girl either."

"No one is going to be hitting on me, Brody. I'm four months pregnant!" she admonishes.

"You have no idea how hot you look, do you?" He lowers his head again and kisses her.

"Put her down and tell us this solution where everyone is happy?" Savannah says, rolling her eyes again.

"I come with you."

"What? How is that a solution where everyone is happy? This is a girls' night, Brody."

He shrugs. "I'd be happy."

"No!"

"Look, Jack is in the truck." His eyes flick to me and my heart pounds in my chest when he mentions Jack. "Between Aunt Emma and Mom asking him if he's okay every thirty seconds, and crazy Zara, he could do with a couple of hours out of the house. We were going to go for a drink once we'd dropped you off anyway. Why don't we just come to the Brass Hall? We won't get in your way. You can still have your girls' night." He smiles and wriggles his eyebrows. "See, everyone's happy!"

I feel three pairs of eyes looking at me, and heat travels up my neck and over my cheeks. Picking up my drink, I swallow down the whole glassful.

"I'll just use the bathroom. Let you three talk." Brody slips out of the kitchen and Quinn comes to stand next to me.

"It's your call, Aria. It might be the perfect chance to spend some time with Jack, away from Zara. If you don't want to, I'll tell Brody to go and I'll drive us into town?"

I sigh and drop my head onto the breakfast bar. I'm torn. A huge part of me wants to say yes. I want nothing more than to spend some time with Jack without Zara hanging all over him. I miss him so much it hurts. But another part wonders what the point would be. I won't be able to touch him, hold his hand, kiss him like I so desperately want to. I groan. Who am I kidding? There's no chance I'm going to pass up the opportunity to spend some time with him. I'll deal with my broken heart tomorrow.

"Okay," I mutter, my head still on the breakfast bar. Savannah squeals excitedly and I lift my head. "Who is she calling?" I ask Quinn when I see Sav walk out of the kitchen, her phone pressed to her ear.

She shrugs. "I have no idea. Look, are you sure you're okay with this? I know we promised you a girls' night."

"I want to see him, Quinn. I'll take any time I can get with him right now. I haven't spoken to him in days, even though we live in the same house. I hate it."

"I can't even imagine how hard this is for you, Aria. It sucks."

"Okay, baby. See you soon," Savannah says as she walks back into the kitchen, ending her call. "Josh is going to come with us. Mom said she'd watch Hope and Jacob."

"Where's Zara? Why can't she watch Jacob?" I ask, frowning.

"She went to bed with a headache, so she'll have no idea we're all going out." She grins wickedly and I can't help but laugh.

"Ready?" Brody asks from the doorway, obviously having overheard our conversation.

I stand up, nerves bubbling in my stomach. A wave of panic washes over me and I shake my head. "Oh, God. What am I going to say to him?" I look frantically between Savannah and Quinn, who both just smile.

"Be yourself, Aria. It worked last time," Quinn assures me.

I nod. "Okay, let's go before I change my mind." Savannah links my arm, and we head through the house to the front door. It's dark when we get outside, and the porch light comes on, illuminating the driveway. I can make out a figure sitting in the passenger seat of Brody's truck, but it's too dark to see his face. I know he'll be able to see me though, so I try not to stare too long in his direction.

I'm nervous, but excited to spend time with him. I'm determined to make the most of it though, knowing this might be the only time I can get him away from Zara. In a strange way, I feel like Cinderella without the fairy godmother or the glass slippers. Only for me, it's not my horse-drawn carriage that turns into mush at midnight, it's my heart when he goes back to her.

CHAPTER 35

Jack

"*A*re you coming inside or waiting here? I'm hoping they're ready to go," Brody asks as we park outside Savannah and Josh's house.

"I'm good here." He nods and heads into the house, the porch light coming on as he climbs the steps. When the light goes out, I'm plunged into darkness and I drop my head back onto the seat, grateful for a few minutes alone. I think this might be the first time I've been alone since being discharged from the hospital. I know my mum means well, but she's driving me a little crazy asking me if I'm okay every ten minutes. When Brody said he was driving the girls into town, I jumped at the chance to get out of the house for half an hour, plus, I knew Aria would be going and I've barely seen her all week. Jacob is asking for her all the time, and something tells me that, before the accident, she was an important person in both our lives.

My mum isn't the only reason for wanting to get out of the house. Zara is driving me crazy as well. I have no idea how we've managed to stay together for the last three years. She pays no attention to Jacob, except when she thinks someone is watching her, and she constantly moans about how bored she is on the ranch. I can't imagine we're happy, although she assures me we are. She's not happy with me at the moment though. We haven't slept together since I got back from the hospital, and I don't know why. It's not for lack of trying on her part, but something feels off, and I can't bring myself to be intimate with her. She's beautiful, there's no doubt about that. I'm just not attracted to her. I can't help wondering if I felt the same before the accident.

Sighing, I go to reach for my phone, forgetting I've lost it. I really need to get a replacement; it feels strange to be without one. I'm guessing I lost it when I fell off the horse, but despite going back to where I had the accident, I haven't been able to find it.

Suddenly, light illuminates the truck, and I look toward the house. My breath catches in my throat when I see Aria on the porch. She looks stunning, and I can't take my eyes off her. I haven't been able to push down the bizarre connection I feel toward her since talking to her at the hospital, and if I'm honest, I was hoping I'd see more of her this past week than I have.

As my eyes travel over her body, I take in the tight black dress that falls mid-thigh and hugs her curves perfectly. I groan inwardly as my eyes drop to the black heels on her feet that seem to make her legs look impossibly long, even though she isn't tall. Her blonde hair is curled and falls loosely around her beautiful face, and I'm thankful the truck is in darkness so she can't see me staring. My eyes follow her down the steps as she makes her way to the truck, her arm linked with Savannah's. Other than stumbling into her room the night I was discharged from the hospital, I've hardly seen her, despite us staying in the same house. I can't help but wonder why. We must have been good friends before the accident for her to have developed such a good relationship with Jacob. It was clear from the hospital that Zara has a problem with her, so the friendship can't be theirs.

The rear door opens, illuminating the cab, and Aria slides across the back seat. "Hi, Jack," she says quietly, and I smile as I look over my shoulder at her.

"Hey, Aria. You look beautiful."

"Thank you," she says, her cheeks flushing pink. I can't seem to take my eyes off her, and it's only when someone clears their throat that I'm snapped out of my daze. Turning back to the front, I hadn't even noticed Brody, Quinn, or Savannah getting in the truck.

"Change of plan, Jack," Brody says, a smile pulling on his lips.

"Please don't tell me we have to go back to the house?" I groan, and he laughs.

"No. Well, yes, actually, but only to pick up Josh. We're tagging along with the girls on their night out."

"Oh…" I turn to look in the back again, my eyes finding Aria's. "That sounds fun." She smiles at me and my stomach flips. What the hell is going on?

Ten minutes later and Brody is parking outside the Brass Hall in Marble Falls. Josh rides in the flatbed of the truck and jumps out as we park, holding the door open for the girls. The two couples walk hand in hand across the car park, leaving Aria and me to walk together.

"How are you feeling?" she asks as we join the queue to get in.

"Much better. I only get the occasional headache now, and usually when I'm tired."

"That's great. I hope it's not going to be too loud in here for you. There's normally a live band playing."

"I'm sure it'll be fine. I'm looking forward to getting out of the house for a bit." We've reached the front of the queue, and I gesture for her to go ahead of me to the security guy. The others have already gone in, and I watch as the guy on the door goes through her bag, chatting with her and making her laugh. A strange feeling of jealousy washes over me as I watch him hit on her. It's irrational to feel jealous when we're only friends, but nevertheless, I can't push down the feeling. I'm glad when he waves her through, and I follow her into the crowded bar.

"Wow, it's busy. Do you see the others?" she shouts, going up on her tiptoes, her mouth close to my ear. I look around, but I'm distracted by having her so close.

"No. Maybe they're at the bar?"

She nods and gestures with her head to the back of the room. "Bar's this way." She goes to walk away but I grab her hand, the same bolt of electricity shooting up my arm as when I touched her in the hospital. She stills and turns to face me, her eyes dropping to our joined hands.

"We were friends, right? Before the accident, I mean," I shout in her ear as I reluctantly drop her hand. She nods.

"Yeah, we were… friends."

"How come I haven't seen you around the house this week?"

"I guess I've been busy with work. Some weeks are like that."

I hold her gaze, wondering if she's telling the truth. "Surely you have to eat though? You haven't eaten one meal with us, and Jacob's been asking for you."

Her face lights up in a smile. "He has?"

I nod. "He keeps asking for Ria to play. He misses you."

"I miss him too." It might be loud in the bar, but I can hear the sadness in her voice.

"Maybe we could do something with him tomorrow, the three of us, if you're not busy?" I can see the indecision on her face, and I frown. "If you don't want to—"

"No!" she says, cutting me off, her hand coming to rest on my arm. "I want to, but what about Zara?"

"She won't mind." I say the words, but I don't believe them.

"I think she might. We're not exactly the best of friends."

"Why is that?"

She closes her eyes and shakes her head.

"Aria!" a voice shouts, interrupting our conversation. Dragging my eyes off her, I see Savannah waving to us from across the bar.

"Can we talk later?" she asks, her hand dropping from my arm. I nod, seeing Savannah making her way toward us.

"Promise me we will?"

"I promise."

"It's so busy in here! We thought we'd lost you. Come on, Josh is at the bar," Savannah says, grinning at us before taking Aria's arm and tugging her toward the bar. I follow, wishing we could have finished talking.

When we've all got a drink in our hands, we head across the room, managing to find an empty table on the edge of the dance floor. The girls waste no time drinking down their drinks and announcing they're going dancing. I smile as I watch Josh and Brody telling Savannah and Quinn to stay where we can see them, only for Savannah to roll her eyes and ignore them. Aria looks at me and smiles as Savannah pulls her into the crowds and out of view. I chuckle as I watch them go.

"I don't know why I even bother," Josh says, rolling his eyes as he stands to try and see where the girls are.

"They'll be fine. I can see them," Brody assures him.

Josh sits down and picks up his Bud. "You seem to be getting along well with Aria, Jack," he shouts over the noise of the crowd. Brody punches him on the arm and Josh turns to him. "What the fuck!" he cries, rubbing his arm. Brody shakes his head at Josh and looks over at me.

"Ignore him. How are you feeling?"

I frown as I look between the two of them. "I'm fine. Aria and I are friends, aren't we? I mean we were, before the accident?"

"You could say that," Josh mutters before taking a pull of his Bud.

"Josh! Enough!" Brody warns. "Yes, Jack. You were friends before the accident. Good friends."

I look between them again and take a mouthful of Coke.

"What aren't you telling me? Come on, guys. Don't you think I deserve to know?"

"Maybe Zara isn't who you think she is," Josh says.

"I fucking give up!" Brody exclaims, rolling his eyes. "No filter, just like your wife!"

"What does that even mean, Josh?" I ask, ignoring Brody.

"It means things aren't what they seem."

I frown, more confused than ever. "That's not an answer."

"Ask Zara, Jack."

"But I'm asking you," I say, a little annoyed. "Why won't someone just tell me?"

"It's not for us to say," Brody says before Josh can answer. "It's fucked up and I'm sorry, man."

"Tell me this, then, am I happy with Zara? We've been on the ranch at least a few weeks. You must have seen us together? Are we happy?" They're both silent for a few seconds before Josh answers.

"Ask yourself the question. You've been home from the hospital a week. Are you happy?"

"No," I reply immediately, not even having to think about it. There's been a niggling doubt in my mind since before I left the hospital. If my relationship with Zara before the accident is like it is now, then I can only think I stayed for Jacob. I'm not happy. Not at all. "Something's missing. I just don't know what the hell it is!" I slam my bottle of Coke down on the table in frustration.

"Look, lost memories or not, you can change your life whenever you want, Jack. You don't have to stay in a relationship where you aren't happy. Life's too short, man," Brody says sympathetically.

"Urgh, I hate this! Why can't I just remember!"

"Come and dance!" Quinn exclaims as she suddenly reappears at the table and unwittingly interrupts the conversation. She sits down in Brody's lap.

"Hey, baby. Having fun?" he asks, and my eyes drop to the hand he places protectively over Quinn's small baby bump. I can't help but feel a little envious of their relationship. They clearly adore each other, Sav and Josh too. Even with what I can remember of my relationship with Zara, it was never like that. We only decided to make a go of things because she fell pregnant. It was never that all-consuming love. I could only hope it had grown into that in the years we'd been together, the years I couldn't remember. It didn't feel that way though. Not even close. I have to speak to her when I get back to the ranch.

"Come and dance," she says again. "You guys too." She points to me and Josh, pulling me from my melancholy.

"You up for that, Jack?" Josh asks as he drinks down the last of his Bud.

I shrug. "Sure. Why not?" I finish my drink and follow Quinn as she leads us to where Aria and Savannah are dancing. Some guy is trying to dance with Aria, and I can see how uncomfortable she is. The guy, however, seems to have no idea. I hesitate for a second before walking up behind her and winding my arms around her waist.

"It's me, Jack. Play along," I whisper in her ear. She stiffens for a few seconds before relaxing and dropping her head back on my chest. She smells of strawberries, and I inhale, her scent invading my senses.

"She's taken, man. Move on," I shout to the guy, who's now glaring at me. I can't say I blame him for being pissed. She's the most beautiful woman in the room, and I try not to think about how good it feels to have her in my arms. I thought it might feel awkward, but if anything, it feels the opposite. Familiar and like home. The guy's disappeared, but I make no move to let her go, and I wonder if she can feel the pounding of my heart on her back.

"Thank you," she shouts, her head tilting back to look at me. "I've never needed rescuing more." It's dark on the dance floor, but I swear I can see tears swimming in her eyes, and my heart twists as I realize she's upset. I turn her in my arms, but she keeps her head down, and I use my fingers to lift her chin so she's looking at me. Her hands go to my chest and I inhale sharply as she touches me.

"Are you okay? You look upset."

"I'm okay." I hold her gaze, knowing she isn't telling me the truth, but I don't want to push her. "Will you dance with me?" she asks, just loud enough for me to hear. I hadn't noticed the music change to a slow song, and I nod as I pull her closer. Her arms go around my neck and she drops her head on my shoulder. We dance in silence, and I know for sure this time she can feel the racing of my heart, just like I can feel hers. The song ends, and I don't want to let her go. Knowing I have to, I reluctantly remove my arms from around her and take a step back. The music changes and Savannah takes her hand, spinning her around. She laughs and I can't pull my gaze off her. She's mesmerizing.

As the night goes on, I catch Aria's eyes on me more and more, and while I haven't danced with her again, I'm itching to. I don't know how to react to my developing attraction to her. I'm with Zara and would never cross a line with someone else while I'm in a committed relationship, but even my morals are being tested as I watch her dance.

When Quinn starts yawning, we decide to call it a night. Both Savannah and Aria are drunk, and getting them out of the bar proves difficult. Josh is practically carrying Savannah, and I end up with my arm around Aria's waist as I guide her through the crowds. We're almost to the door when she grabs my hand and pulls me into a corner.

"What are you doing?" I chuckle as she stumbles and reach out to grab on to her so she doesn't fall.

"Shh," she mumbles, her finger going to her lips.

"I'm not making any noise." I can't help but smile at her and she grins back at me.

"Just a few more minutes before we have to go back to reality," she slurs, winding her arms around my neck. I don't hesitate to pull her close, frowning at her words.

"What do you mean, back to reality?" Her shoulders shake, and I realize she's crying. "Aria, talk to me. What do you mean?" I try to pull out of the embrace to look at her, but she holds on to me tightly. After a few minutes, she composes herself and steps back, wiping her eyes.

"I'm sorry," she whispers. "Ignore me. I always cry when I'm drunk. We should go. Everyone will be waiting." She goes to walk past me, and I reach for her hand, stopping her.

"Aria."

She shakes her head. "Please don't ask me, Jack. I can't... I'm sorry." Her voice catches and I squeeze her hand.

"Okay," I say quietly, seeing how whatever it is she can't tell me is killing her.

I'm quiet on the way back to the ranch, my mind swirling with all that Aria didn't say. Looking in the rearview mirror, I see she's fast asleep when Brody pulls up outside the house. Climbing out of the truck, I open the back door and scoop her into my arms, her head dropping on my shoulder. She doesn't stir, and after a round of goodbyes, I silently carry her up the porch steps, managing to open the front door without dropping her. The house is dark, and I navigate the hallway and up the stairs to her bedroom. Her door is slightly ajar, and I push it gently with my foot. I cross the room, lower her onto the bed, and gently remove her shoes. Kneeling, I push a strand of hair off her cheek and tuck it behind her ear, my fingers softly stroking her cheek. Leaning down, I brush a kiss on her forehead. I know I'm hurting her. I can see it in her eyes. I just have no idea how, and I pray I don't carry on doing so.

I pad down the hallway and silently check on a sleeping Jacob before heading for my room. Zara's asleep, and I get changed into some sleep shorts, my mind swirling with Josh's comments from earlier. I want to speak to her, but I know she won't appreciate being woken up. I'll speak to her in the morning. Maybe, for once, I'll get some answers.

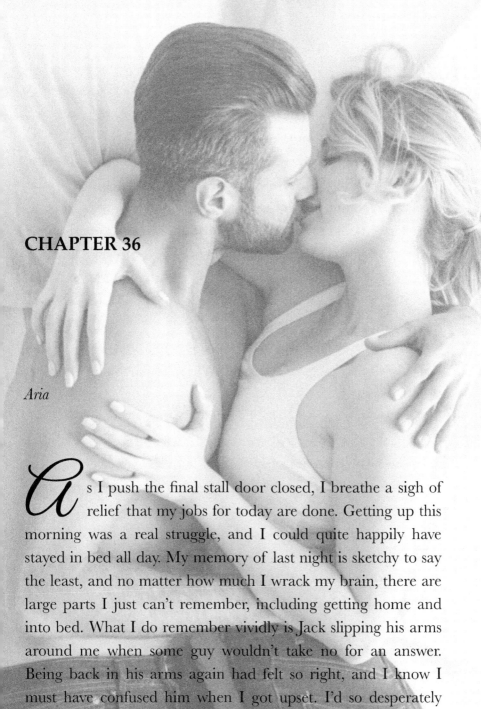

CHAPTER 36

Aria

*A*s I push the final stall door closed, I breathe a sigh of
relief that my jobs for today are done. Getting up this
morning was a real struggle, and I could quite happily have
stayed in bed all day. My memory of last night is sketchy to say
the least, and no matter how much I wrack my brain, there are
large parts I just can't remember, including getting home and
into bed. What I do remember vividly is Jack slipping his arms
around me when some guy wouldn't take no for an answer.
Being back in his arms again had felt so right, and I know I
must have confused him when I got upset. I'd so desperately
wanted to kiss him, to make him remember how good we were
together, but I knew I couldn't. I just pray he remembers soon.

The pounding in my head has just about subsided, and I'm

left with that sickly feeling in the pit of my stomach that screams hangover. I want a long soak in the tub, followed by a nap, and maybe some food somewhere in between. I walk slowly back to the house, enjoying the sun beating down on me. My mind swirls with thoughts of Jack, and I'm a million miles away when a little voice brings me back to earth.

"Ria!" Looking up, I see Jacob running toward me. Smiling, I stoop down, and when he reaches me, he throws his arms around my neck. Losing my balance, I fall backwards onto my ass. With Jacob's arms still around me, he falls too, and we both burst out laughing.

"Are you okay?" Jack asks, his voice full of concern. I look up to see him standing above us. When he sees us laughing, he smiles.

"We're fine, aren't we, Jacob?" I say tickling his side. He squeals with laughter as I continue to tickle him, his tiny hands trying to push mine away. He finally manages to scramble away, and Jack holds his hand out to me. Taking it, he pulls me to stand up.

"How are you feeling after last night? Sore head?" he asks, a smile pulling on his lips. I look sideways at him, my cheeks flushing pink.

"Oh, God! I didn't do anything stupid, did I? My memory of last night is a little sketchy."

"I know that feeling," he says wryly.

I gasp. "I'm sorry. I didn't mean to compare my drunken night out to…"

"Hey, it's fine. And no, I don't think you did anything stupid."

"How did I get to bed?"

"You fell asleep in the truck and I carried you upstairs. I put you to bed."

I drop my head in my hands and groan. "Urgh, I'm sorry! I'm never drinking again."

He laughs. "Well, if it makes you feel any better, you look a lot less hungover than Savannah. We've just come from there and she looks rough."

"I'll tell her you said that!" I joke, bumping my shoulder with his. We're both silent for a few minutes as we watch Jacob running around.

"So, what do you remember of last night?" he asks quietly, his foot kicking at the ground.

"Erm, I remember you rescuing me from some handsy guy. Thanks for that, by the way."

"Anytime."

"And I remember us dancing. It's patchy from there."

He nods. "What about when I mentioned the three of us doing something today? I know Jacob misses you." He chuckles. "I think him tackling you to the ground is proof of that."

"I remember," I whisper. "I miss him too."

"Jacob, come here," he shouts, and he comes running over. Jack scoops him up and whispers in his ear, but it's loud enough for me to hear. "Do you remember what we were going to ask Aria?" Jacob looks at me before shaking his head. "You do, the picnic?" He nods and turns to me.

"Ria, picnic!" Jacob shouts before squirming to get out of Jack's hold. Jack lowers him to the ground, and he takes off running again.

"So, that was Jacob asking if you'd like to go on a picnic." He laughs. "What do you say? Are you free?"

What feels like a hundred butterflies take flight in my stomach at the thought of spending time with them. I'm desperate to say yes, despite feeling hungover and tired.

"Zara isn't around if that's what you're worried about. I know last night you said you aren't the best of friends."

"Where is she?"

"Austin, apparently. She was gone when I woke this morning. Mum said she invited herself when Aunt Claire said she was going."

"Okay then," I say quietly. "I just need a quick shower though. I stink."

"You look beautiful."

"I look a mess!" He frowns. "What's wrong?"

"Nothing. I just had the strangest feeling of déjà vu. Like I've said those words to you before." He shakes his head, as if brushing off the feeling, and my eyes widen as I remember he *has* said those words to me before, the day Zara arrived. He'd come to the stables to find me. We were going to visit Libby at the hospital after she'd had Annie. I want to tell him, but I don't. Hope sparks in my chest that it might mean he's beginning to remember.

"You definitely have time for a shower. I need to get the picnic ready anyway. Jacob and I can do that while you're getting ready."

I nod, and we walk in comfortable silence to the house. Once inside, I stop at the foot of the stairs. "I can help you with the food once I'm ready."

He waves off my offer. "I'll be fine. Take your time. You might want to put your swimsuit on. We're going to the river."

He grins at me and I smile back before turning and heading upstairs.

I'm quick in the shower, eager to get back downstairs. Plus, I don't want to be alone too long, overthinking whether I should be spending time with Jack and Jacob regardless of how much I want to. I put my black bikini on under my shorts and pull on a tank. I don't do much with my hair, it's wet, so I braid it and leave it to dry naturally. Jogging down the stairs, I hear voices coming from the kitchen and I find Jack and Emma packing a wicker picnic basket.

"Hi, Emma. How are you?" I ask as I walk in.

She turns and pulls me into a hug. "I'm good, sweetheart. It feels like forever since I've seen you." She looks from me to Jack and smiles. "I hear you're going on a picnic?"

"We are. Is there anything I can do?" I ask, looking across to where Jack is still packing the basket.

"No, we're all done," she assures me.

"Where's Jacob?"

"He's outside with Phil. That child has so much energy, I can't keep up," she says with a smile.

"The picnic's ready, I'm just going to run and get changed." He winks at me as he jogs out of the kitchen, leaving me alone with his mom.

"I'm so glad you're spending some time together," she says. "I'm worried about him, Aria. He seems so lost."

"I hope it helps him to remember. I miss him so much."

"I think he knows he isn't happy with Zara. I still have no idea why she flew all the way out here. She barely notices Jacob."

I shake my head. "He's the most amazing little boy. I don't understand her."

"Do you think we should tell him? There's no sign of him remembering?"

"I don't know, Emma. What if telling him messes up him ever remembering Jacob? I want him to get those memories back more than anything."

"More than remembering you?" I nod. "You love him that much?" I nod again, tears filling my eyes. She pulls me into a hug, holding me tightly.

"Everything okay?" Jack asks, reappearing in the kitchen. I pull out of Emma's embrace and my mouth goes dry as I look across at him in his black swim shorts, his t-shirt pulled tight across his chest. It's a good job Jacob's coming with us. I don't know how I'd manage to keep my hands off him otherwise.

"Everything's fine," Emma says when I don't answer.

"Aria?" he asks when I still don't speak. Realizing I'm staring at him, I drop my eyes to the floor and play with the hem of my tank as my cheeks rush with heat.

"Yep. I'm good. Let's go." I keep my eyes off him as I head into the entryway, hearing Emma chuckling in the kitchen. Picking up the picnic blanket, I stand on the porch steps, watching Phil and Jacob in the yard. They are both on their hands and knees, driving cars and trucks around the grass.

"Ready for our picnic, Jacob?" I shout.

"Yes!" he cries, and I laugh, loving seeing him so excited.

"Pops is ready for a lie-down, I think," Phil groans as he stands up and stretches out his back. "I think I'm getting too old for this."

"What? Never!" I tell him with a smile.

After saying goodbye, we head to the ranch truck. With the picnic basket, towels for swimming, and Jacob's little legs, Jack decides driving to the river will be easier. We could have gone on horseback, but I don't want to suggest that after Jack's accident, and it would be tricky with the basket anyway.

"Do you want to drive, Jacob?" Jack asks, and Jacob's face lights up.

"Yes!"

Jack laughs. "Come on, then." He climbs into the driver's seat and lifts Jacob in, settling him on his lap. I slide into the passenger seat, my heart exploding with love for them as I watch an excited Jacob grip the steering wheel tightly.

"You might have to give me directions. It's been a while since I was at the river. I think the last time was when I visited for Lib and Mason's wedding."

His words cause a wave of sadness to crash over me. We made love for the first time by the river, and hearing him say he doesn't remember being there hurts. Even though I know he doesn't remember, it's like a knife to my heart, another reminder that he remembers nothing about our relationship.

I'm quiet on the short journey, and I know Jack's noticed. I'm looking out of the passenger side window, but I can feel his gaze on me. I hadn't even thought of the feelings being back at the river would evoke. I don't want to ruin the afternoon by overthinking everything, so I take a deep breath, pushing my emotions down as I feel the truck come to a stop. Jack opens his door and lifts Jacob down.

"Stay away from the water," he shouts as Jacob runs off. We can see him through the windshield, and we watch him for a few seconds in silence. "I've been here since the wedding, haven't I?" His gaze is fixed on Jacob and I'm grateful he can't see the tears that are beginning to sting my eyes.

"Yes," I whisper. He sighs and nods before climbing out of the car, and I sit there feeling torn. I can't decide if I'm relieved or disappointed he hasn't asked about it. It's not like I could tell him if he asked anyway. I guess he assumes we came here in a group. Maybe being here again will jog his memory. I really hope it does.

CHAPTER 37

Jack

I glance across the cab at Aria, whose head is turned away from me as she stares out of the window. I've done it again. I've unwittingly hurt her. It was one innocent comment, but I saw the flash of hurt in her eyes, and I knew straight away I've been here after Libby and Mason's wedding. The more time I spend with her, the more I question whether something happened between us before the accident. Would she look so devastated at me not remembering if we're only friends? But if that's true, where does Zara fit into everything? I refuse to believe I'd cheat on Zara, no matter how unhappy I was.

Jacob squirms on my knee, and I open the door, lowering him gently to the ground. "Stay away from the water," I shout as he runs off. I watch him running around for a few seconds, and with my eyes still on him, I ask, "I've been here since the wedding, haven't I?"

She pauses for a second before answering. "Yes," she whispers, confirming what I already knew. I sigh and nod before climbing out of the car. I hate that I'm hurting her, but I seem to be doing it more and more.

Going to the flatbed of the truck, I pluck out the picnic basket and head over to a large tree, the canopy of which provides some shade from the hot Texas sun. Aria follows me a few seconds later with the blanket. Laying it out, she sits down on it and smiles at me.

"I'm starving. What have we got?" I know she's trying to put our conversation in the truck out of her mind, but her smile doesn't quite reach her eyes, and I have to stop myself from asking her to tell me everything. I remember the torment on her face in the Brass Hall last night when I tried to talk to her. I don't want to see that look on her face again.

Calling Jacob over, we sit on the blanket, and I lay out everything I prepared at the house. There's far too much food for the three of us, especially as Jacob barely eats anything. He's too excited to go swimming, and I have to ask him three or four times to sit down, bribing him with swimming only if he eats something.

"Did you bring sunscreen?" Aria asks when we've all finished. "I'll put some on Jacob before we go in the water."

I reach into the bag I've brought containing a change of clothes for Jacob, pulling out the sun cream, along with a swim nappy.

"Are you sure you don't mind?" I ask, unable to stop myself from thinking that Zara hasn't bothered once to put sun cream on him in the past week.

"Of course not." I watch as she calls him over and removes his clothes, making quick work of pulling his swim nappy on. He's practically bouncing with excitement and I can't help but smile. He lets Aria cover him in sun cream without any moaning, something he doesn't do for me, and she even talks him into sitting on the blanket playing with his cars for ten minutes while the cream soaks in and his lunch goes down.

"Would you mind putting some on my shoulders? My British skin isn't quite used to this heat yet." I chuckle. Looking at her, I swear I see her eyes flash with heat before she swallows.

"Erm… okay."

I peel off my t-shirt and turn so my back is to her. I look over my shoulder as she kneels up and squirts the cold cream onto my shoulders. Tearing my eyes off her, I close them as she touches me, her soft hands gently rubbing the cream into my skin. Despite the temperature, goose bumps erupt where she's touching me, and I have to stop myself from turning around and kissing the hell out of her. My hands itch to touch her, and I have to adjust myself as I start to get hard in my shorts. What is wrong with me? I've never felt this drawn to someone. The desire to kiss her is overwhelming.

"You're done," she says quietly, handing me back the sun cream. Taking it from her, I stay with my back to her while I put everything away, knowing if I turn around now, she'll see the effect she's having on me.

"Thank you," I whisper eventually, when I can trust myself

to speak. The air seems to crackle with tension, and I hope I haven't made things awkward.

"Who wants to go swimming?" she asks.

"Me!" Jacob cries, breaking the tension. She laughs and stands up, removing her jean shorts and tank. I try not to stare, but I'm not very successful as she kicks her shorts away, leaving her in a tiny black bikini. I knew she was beautiful, but seeing her like this takes my breath away.

"Did you bring his floaties?" she asks, pulling me from my haze of lust.

"Erm, yeah. I think I left them in the truck." Tearing my eyes off her, I jog to the truck, finding them in the flatbed. When I get back to them, they are paddling hand in hand in in the shallow water. I stand and watch them for a few minutes, laughing when I see Jacob kick his little legs in the water, splashing Aria. The section of the river they're in is like a small lagoon, edged with large rocks making it almost like a pool. The water is calm and crystal clear.

"Let's get these on," I say as I walk up behind them, slipping the floaties on his arms. With Aria on one side of him and me on the other, we each take a hand and walk with him into the water. Despite the blistering hot sun, the water of the river is cool, and he squeals as the cold water hits him. I pick him up, allowing him to get used to the temperature before letting him go.

"I'd forgotten how cold this river is!" Aria exclaims, her voice breathless. "Best to get your head under and get it over and done with," she says before disappearing completely under the clear water. She reappears seconds later, dragging her hand down her face to wipe away the water.

"Better?" I ask with a chuckle.

"Not really! I'm sure I'll get used to it in a few minutes."

She's right, and within a few minutes, we're all acclimatized. After tossing Jacob into the water what feels like a hundred times, he's happy on his own, splashing anyone who tries to get near him. Keeping an eye on him, I swim over to Aria, who is floating on her back, her eyes closed.

"How's the hangover feeling?" I ask.

She stands up and treads water in front of me. "I think this is the perfect hangover cure. I was planning on a bath and bed before you invited me here, but I think this is much better." My eyes drop to her bronzed smooth shoulders, glistening from the water, and I can't help thinking I'm glad she decided not to opt for the bath-and-bed option. She clears her throat when I don't respond, and I realize I'm staring. My eyes flick to Jacob, and she follows my gaze.

"He really loves the water, doesn't he?"

"He does. He's going to be disappointed when we go home and there isn't a pool or a river in the back garden to swim in." I laugh, but the laughter dies on my lips when I see her face. Tears fill her eyes, and she turns away from me, disappearing under the water. Following her, I wait for her to surface.

"Aria, what's wrong? Talk to me, please," I beg, my hands going to her waist. She gasps as my fingers touch her bare skin.

"Nothing's wrong." She pushes my hands away and swims to the shore. Making her way out of the water, she sits down on the blanket. I frown and swim over to Jacob, coaxing him out of the water with the promise of a cookie that we brought as part of the picnic. Picking him up, I carry him the short distance to the blanket, pull off his floaties, and wrap him in a towel. I give him the cookie, and he eats it quickly before putting his head in Aria's lap and promptly falling asleep. The sun and the swimming have clearly worn him out.

There isn't much room on the blanket, and Aria and I sit pretty much shoulder to shoulder. "I know something is off, Aria. I feel it. I wanted to talk to Zara this morning, but she'd left for Austin before I could. Everyone just acts like everything is fine when I know it isn't." Her hand strokes Jacob's hair as he sleeps. When I don't say anything else, she looks up. Her steel blue eyes fix on me, and I can see she's torn. She wants to tell me something, but she's holding back. "Please, Aria," I beg. "I feel like I'm living someone else's life."

"Jack... I." Her eyes drop to my lips before meeting my gaze again. "I so want you to remember..."

"Strawberries," I whisper.

"What?"

"You smell of strawberries." I'm so close to her, her scent invades my senses, and I'm overcome with a feeling of familiarity.

"It's my shampoo."

"I remember." Her face lights up with a smile.

"You remember?"

"I remember the smell."

"Do you remember anything else?" she asks, and I can hear the excitement in her voice.

"No," I say sadly. "But I want to, Aria. So much."

"Maybe it means your memories are starting to come back?" She sounds hopeful and I don't want to bring her down.

"God, I hope so."

The sun has moved while we've been in the water and the

canopy of the tree no longer provides the full shade it did when we arrived. My eyes go to Aria as she tilts her head back, lifting her face to the sun. The movement exposes her neck, and it takes everything in me not to lean over and press my lips against her skin. I've tried to push down these crazy feelings I have for her, but what if I'm not meant to push them down? What if we're meant to be together? But how can we be? My mind swirls with unanswered questions and I wish to God someone would just tell me what I'm meant to feel.

We spend the next hour talking. She tells me all about her childhood and her move from Vermont to Texas when her dad left. I get the impression she's told me all this before, but it's new to me, and I soak up every word, desperate to know everything about her.

"I'm guessing you already know a lot about me?" She nods. "Do you know what hurts the most about not being able to remember?"

"I think I can guess," she says sadly, her eyes dropping to a still sleeping Jacob.

"I missed everything with him. First smile, first laugh, first step, first word. The list goes on. What if I never get that back?"

She reaches her hand across and laces her fingers with mine. "You didn't miss it, Jack. You were there for every one of those things, you just don't remember at the moment. It *will* come back to you. It has too." She whispers the last part, her voice barely audible.

"Zara has no photos of him on her phone. Don't you think that's weird? The only photo I've seen of him was the one you showed me in the hospital."

"Libby has photos. She was always showing me ones you'd

sent her. You used to send her new ones every week. I know how much she missed you two. You should ask her."

"I will. Thanks, Aria. Maybe seeing some old photos will help." I smile at her. "How's the rest of your week looking? Got any plans?"

"I'm going to Llano with Sav tomorrow. She's looking at buying another horse. Then on the weekend we're off to Austin, bridesmaid dress shopping."

"Brody did tell me he and Quinn are getting married. Isn't the wedding in a few weeks? How come you don't have your dresses?"

"We were waiting for Lib to have the baby. She didn't want to pick a dress and have to guess her size."

"That makes sense."

"Do you think you might still be here for the wedding?" She looks nervous as she asks and bites down on her bottom lip.

"Yeah, I think so. My parents told me I took voluntary redundancy at work and gave up the lease on the house we were renting to spend a few months out here." I shake my head. "I've got to admit, I was a little surprised when they told me. I don't remember loving my job, but to just give it all up…" I shrug. "Seems a little extreme to just walk away from every-thing, even for a few months."

"I think you missed Lib and wanted to be here when she had the baby. I'm sure it will all make sense when you get your memory back."

I nod but don't say anything. Everyone seems so sure I'll remember, but I'm sceptical. Other than a random smell, I have nothing that makes any of the last three years any clearer, and the more days that pass, the farther away I seem to get from them.

CHAPTER 38

Jack

After spending a few hours by the river, I bundle everything in the back of the truck, and we head home. Jacob sits on my lap again as I drive, his little chubby hands gripping the steering wheel. Aria's quiet on the ride back, and I want to ask her if she's okay, but I know she'll tell me she is, even if she isn't.

"Oh, great," I mutter as the ranch house comes into view and I see Zara standing on the porch steps. Even from here I can see she looks annoyed.

"What's wrong?" Aria asks as she looks across the cab at me.

I gesture with my head to the house. "Looks like Zara's back from Austin."

She swings her head around to look at where I'm gesturing. "Did you tell her we were going on a picnic?"

I shake my head. "She never would have gone to Austin, and I really wanted to spend some time with you."

"I thought you said it was Jacob who'd been asking for me?" she asks, her eyebrows raised in question.

"It was. He has…" I trail off as I park the truck.

"Why do I feel like we did something wrong?"

"We did nothing wrong. I'm allowed to have friends."

"Looks like it. I should go." She leans over and strokes Jacob's face. "Bye, little man. I'll see you soon, okay?"

"Aria, wait." I don't want her to leave like this. I'm a grown man. No one is going to tell me who I can and can't be friends with.

"I'm just going to cause an argument if I stay. I don't want Jacob to see that. I'll see you later. Thanks for the picnic. I had fun." She climbs out of the truck before I can stop her, my eyes following her as she walks up the porch steps. When she gets to where Zara is, I frown as Zara grabs her arm, forcing her to stop. Jumping out of the truck, I walk toward them, Jacob in my arms.

"What's going on?" I ask as I reach the bottom of the steps.

"Just reminding Aria what's mine, that's all," Zara spits, her eyes fixed on Aria, whose back is to me.

"Excuse me," Aria says quietly, shaking off Zara's hold on her.

"Aria." She ignores me and walks into the house, the front door closing behind her. I drag my eyes off the door and turn to Zara. "What the hell was that?" My voice is low so as not to alarm Jacob, but my tone is laced with annoyance and I know she hears it.

"I could ask you the same thing! Where have you been?"

Before I can answer, my mum appears at the door, her face a picture of worry. Her eyes are fixed on me and I know she can't see Zara from where she's standing.

"Why is Aria crying? What happened?" My heart twists knowing she's upset, and I drag my free hand through my hair in frustration.

"Hmph," Zara says. "I've no idea why *she's* upset. I should be the one crying, knowing my boyfriend spent the day with another woman."

On hearing Zara, my mum steps out of the house, her eyes narrowing as she glares at her.

"Really!" my mum exclaims. "You've no idea? Are you sure about that?"

My eyes flick between my mum and Zara, and I wonder what the hell their cryptic conversation means. Zara doesn't back down though and glares back at my mum, which leaves me feeling uncomfortable.

"Like I said, I've no idea." She holds my mum's gaze determinedly, and there is a silent standoff between the two of them until my mum shakes her head. She sighs loudly and walks down the steps toward me. I'm more confused than ever after watching their exchange.

"Let me take Jacob so you two can talk." I nod and she reaches her hand up, cupping my face. "Follow your heart, Jack," she whispers, her eyes boring into mine. Dropping her hand, she reaches for Jacob, placing him on her hip. "Do you want some ice cream?" she asks, and he nods, bouncing excitedly in her arms. "Come on, then, let's get some and find Pops." She disappears inside with Jacob and I'm left alone with Zara, who looks like she wants to kill me.

"Where have you been with *her*, Jack?"

"We went to the river for a picnic. We're friends."

She lets out a sarcastic snort and walks down the porch steps to stand in front of me. "Can't you see it?" she asks, her tone softening as she puts her hands on my bare chest.

"See what?" I ask, confused.

"She wants you, Jack. She's trying to come between us."

I laugh and shake my head. "And how exactly is she doing that? I asked her to go on the picnic, and I've hardly seen her all week."

"I've seen her looking at you like a lost puppy." I roll my eyes and step away from her, her hands falling from my chest.

"You're being ridiculous, Zara."

"Am I? She was always hanging around you before the accident. Why do you think Jacob is so attached to her? She never left you or him alone. I hated it, and even you were beginning to get sick of her."

"That can't be right," I voice, my head pounding with everything she's telling me. I'm so confused. This is the most anyone's told me about what happened before the accident, other than finding out about Jacob, but what she's telling me feels wrong.

She shrugs half-heartedly, closing the small distance I'd put between us. She winds her arms around my neck and brushes her lips against mine. "It's the truth, you just don't remember. I wouldn't lie to you, Jack."

I look down at her, realizing I hardly know the woman in

front of me. In my head, it's three years ago and she's six months pregnant. I've known her for just over six months, and we argued a lot in those six months. I've no idea if she'd lie to me. The Jack before the accident does, but I'm not him, not anymore.

"You're right, I don't remember, but she seems nothing like how you're describing."

"I don't want to talk about her anymore. I'm sorry I got mad, I just don't want to lose you." I sigh and wonder if she's struggling with my memory loss as much as I am. If we were happy before the accident, then she must see a change in me. Maybe it's that that's making her act a little crazy.

"Are we happy, Zara? Really happy?"

"What?" she asks, her voice wobbling.

"Are we happy?"

"You asked me that at the hospital."

"I know, but I'm asking again."

"We've had our ups and downs like any couple... but I'm happy. Aren't you?" Her voice is low, and when her eyes meet mine, tears are pooling in them. Sighing, I drag my hand through my hair before wrapping my arms around her. Maybe this is my fault. I guess I'd be insecure if my girlfriend lost her memory and then spent the day with a guy I felt threatened by.

"Let's go inside. I need to shower." My voice has softened, and I kiss her gently on the head. Taking her hand, we head inside. Once upstairs, I go into the bathroom and turn on the shower. When I turn around, Zara's standing in the doorway.

"You haven't answered," she whispers.

"Answered what?"

"Whether you're happy or not?" Her eyes search mine and I feel like an arsehole, but I can't lie to her.

"I'm confused, Zar. I don't know how I should feel. I just want the last three years of my life back." She goes to say something but changes her mind and offers me a sad smile instead before turning and leaving the room. I seem to be hurting everyone at the moment, and my head pounds under the stress of it all.

Once I've showered, I come out of the bathroom to find the bedroom empty. Zara must have gone downstairs, and I can't help feeling a little relieved she didn't try to join me in the shower. I think I've hurt her enough today without rejecting her any more. I dress quickly and knock on Aria's door before I go downstairs. I want to check she's okay after her run-in with Zara, especially knowing she was upset. There's no response to my knocking though, so I push gently on her door, only to be met by an empty room. Sighing, I make my way downstairs, knowing I won't be able to speak to her alone if she's with everyone.

Aria isn't downstairs when I get there though, and I don't see her again for the rest of the night. She's clearly avoiding me, or Zara, or both of us, and I can't say I blame her. I manage to speak to my mum alone, and she tells me Aria has gone to Libby and Mason's to see Annie. She tries to ask me about my talk earlier with Zara, but I brush off her questions, not wanting to talk about it.

307

"Jack, wake up!" Zara whisper shouts in my ear. I groan and roll over, not wanting to open my eyes yet. "Jack!" Her voice is more urgent, and my eyes fly open, the chink of sunlight sneaking through the curtains burning my eyes.

"What's wrong?" I ask, sitting up. "Is it Jacob?" My head spins after sitting up too fast and I close my eyes until the spinning stops. Turning to face her, I see her phone in her hand.

"No. It's my dad." Her voice breaks and she bursts into tears. Reaching for her, I pull her into my arms and let her sob against my chest, waiting for her to calm down. When she does, I pull back slightly.

"What's happened? Is he okay?"

"He's had a… a… stroke. He's in hospital. My sister just messaged me."

"I'm so sorry, Zar."

"We need to go home." She jumps up and pulls her suitcase from under the bed, frantically emptying drawers and tossing the contents into her bag.

"Go home?" What I can only describe as a wave of fear crashes over me at the thought of leaving the ranch. She stops her wild packing and turns to look at me.

"Yes, Jack! My dad just had a stroke." She shakes her head and turns away from me. "You do what you want. I need to go home."

I instantly feel like a jackass and jump out of bed and go to her. "Of course I'll come with you," I find myself saying, my hands on her waist. "Jacob too. You shouldn't be on your own. I'm sorry, you just took me by surprise." She drops her head back on my chest and I feel her sigh.

"That's okay. It's not what I was expecting either."

"I'll go and look for flights. I'm sure Aunt Claire won't mind if I use the laptop." I kiss her gently on the back of the head and make my way downstairs. I can hear voices coming from the kitchen, and I find my parents eating breakfast. They always were early risers. Not even Jacob is awake yet.

"Morning, Jack. Everything okay?" my dad asks, the look on my face clearly giving me away.

"Zara's dad had a stroke. We need to go home."

"Go home?" my mum asks, standing from the breakfast bar. "You can't." Her eyes flick to my dad and I look between them.

"Didn't you hear what I said? Her dad had a stroke, he's in hospital."

"Can't she go on her own?"

I frown, despite thinking the same thing briefly upstairs. "I can't let her go on her own, she's a mess. I know you don't like her—"

"How do you know that?" she asks defensively.

"Just how you've been around her since I got back from the hospital. I don't know what's gone on between you two, because no one will tell me anything," I say exasperatedly. "But I'm not blind."

"What about Aria?" she asks.

"Emma," my dad warns, subtly shaking his head.

"I *have* to go with Zara. What sort of man would I be if I let her go on her own?" I pace the small space, dragging my hand through my hair. "What I want doesn't come into it." She goes to say something, but I hold my hand up. "Don't, Mum. Don't say anything. I have to do this and that's all there is to it. I need to look for flights." I leave them in the kitchen and head to the den in search of the laptop. Finding it, I sit down heavily on the sofa, spending the next half an hour searching for flights. I find one leaving Austin International at 11:50 a.m. If we hurry, we can just make it. That's the only flight out today, so it's that or wait until tomorrow, which I know Zara won't want to do.

After booking the tickets, I make my way back upstairs. Thankfully, Jacob is still asleep, giving us time to finish packing our stuff before he wakes. Zara has done a lot while I've been downstairs and it's only the last few bits left. By the time we're finished, Jacob is awake, and my parents have given him breakfast and gotten him dressed. I need to do what I've been putting off all morning and say goodbye.

"I'm going to see Lib and everyone before we go. We have about thirty minutes before we need to leave. Do you want to come?" I ask Zara.

She shakes her head. "I'll wait here." I nod and leave her in our bedroom. I check Aria's room just in case, but find it empty, knowing she'll be in the stables by now. When I get downstairs, I scoop Jacob from his high chair. Everyone will want to say goodbye to him too, and I'm just about to head outside when my mum comes out of the den, phone in her hand.

"Jack," she calls, stopping me in my tracks. "I've just spoken to Claire. Aria and Savannah aren't here. They left early this morning for Llano. Josh and Hope went with them," she whispers. "I'm so sorry."

I remember Aria telling me she was going to Llano with Sav while we were at the river yesterday. With everything that's happened this morning, I'd forgotten. An unwelcomed pain settles in my chest knowing I won't get to see her again. I'm devastated for her too. I know how much Jacob means to her. She'll be gutted not to be able to say goodbye to him. I can't find the words to reply to my mum, so I stay silent, giving a small nod of my head before turning and jogging down the porch steps with Jacob in my arms.

I can't stop thinking of Aria as I walk to Libby and Mason's cottage. It would have been hard to say goodbye, but knowing I'm never going to see her again makes me feel like I'm going to throw up. I frown as I reach the cottage, not seeing Mason's truck out front. An uneasy feeling settles in the pit of my stomach and I know before I even knock on the door they aren't going to be home. I knock anyway, praying I'm wrong. When no one answers, I sigh and look at Jacob.

"I guess Aunt Libby and Uncle Mason are out too."

We slowly make our way back to the ranch house, finding Zara on the porch with all our bags. Her eyes are puffy from crying and I give her a sympathetic smile as I go to her, pulling her against my chest. "Seems everyone is out." I haven't been to Brody's place, but he's likely to be on the ranch and could be anywhere. I'll have to FaceTime everyone when we get back home.

"I'm sorry you can't say goodbye," she says softly.

"It's not your fault. Come on, let's get everything in the truck." I grab as many bags as I can carry, my dad getting the rest, and we load up the truck. My dad is driving us to the airport and my mum is coming too. She's still inside though, and my dad gestures for me to go and get her.

"Mum," I call out as I walk into the house.

"Jack, are you really sure about this?" she asks as I find her in the hallway. "Going home with Zara is what you want?"

"Does it matter? It's the right thing to do. She's the mother of my child and she needs me." I sigh loudly. "I don't know who

I am anymore, Mum. Maybe going home will help. I'm so confused about everything." Her face is etched with worry and she pulls me to her, wrapping her arms around me.

"I've spoken to your dad. Here's the key to our house. You won't have anywhere to stay when you get home, and I don't want you in a hotel." She pulls out of the embrace and pushes a silver key into my hand.

"I'm sure we'll be able to stay with Zara's family," I tell her, looking down at the key.

"Take it anyway… just in case."

"Okay."

"Libby's going to be so upset she missed you."

"I wish I could have said goodbye to everyone."

"Have you tried calling Aria?" I shake my head. "I have her number."

"I wouldn't know what to say to her. It's better this way," I say sadly.

"Jack—"

"Please, Mum. Drop it." She nods and we walk to the truck in silence.

My dad drives us away from the ranch and I look over my shoulder, watching the ranch house get smaller and smaller. The whole time, the feeling of dread in the pit of my stomach gets larger and larger. I'm doing the wrong thing, but I'm powerless to change it.

CHAPTER 39

Aria

*I*t's mid-afternoon, and I stare out the window of the truck as we drive back from Llano. Savannah and I had left early to look at a horse she wanted to buy, and at the last minute, Josh and Hope had decided to come with us. I smile as I remember how excited Hope had been to help choose the newest ranch horse. She'd talked the whole way there about how this horse was going to be a friend for Misty, and that she couldn't wait for them to meet. There was no doubt she'd inherited Savannah's love for horses.

We stopped for lunch on the way home, and now we're almost back at the ranch. I can't push down my nerves at the thought of seeing Zara and Jack again, especially after my run-in with Zara after the picnic. God, I hate her. I'd gone to visit

Lib and Mason last night, needing to be out of the house and away from the possibility of bumping into her. The ranch house is big, but when we're all there together, it's suffocating, and it feels like the walls are closing in on me. Now more than ever I need to ask Claire and Ryan about moving into the old cabin.

I realize I'm lost in thought when I feel the truck come to a stop outside the house.

"We'll come in and say hi. I'm sure Hope would like to see Jacob," Savannah says as she glances over her shoulder at me. "Plus, if she sleeps any longer, she'll be awake all night." I glance across at Hope to see she's fast asleep. The excitement has clearly worn her out.

Climbing out of the truck, I follow Josh, who's carrying a sleeping Hope in his arms, into the house. There are voices coming from the kitchen, and I take a deep breath, steeling myself to come face-to-face with Jack and Zara. They aren't there though, and I breathe a sigh of relief when I see Emma, Phil, and Claire. They fall silent when we walk in, and I find three sets of eyes trained on me.

"Is everything okay?" I ask, frowning when they all continue to stare at me.

"Aria, sweetheart, come in and sit down," Emma says, taking my hand and guiding me to a stool at the breakfast bar. My eyes flick to Savannah, who shrugs. It seems she has no idea what's going on either.

"You're kind of scaring me," I admit. "Did something happen?"

"Zara had a phone call this morning. Her dad's had a stroke," she says gently, her hand still holding mine.

"Oh, that's awful! Is he okay?" I ask, looking at Emma and then across to Claire.

"They aren't sure yet. He's in the hospital." She sighs. "Honey, there's no easy way to tell you this, but they went back to the UK. Their flight left at eleven fifty a.m."

"What?" I whisper, my eyes wide. A wave of nausea crashes over me, and I swear I'm going to throw up.

"I'm so sorry, Aria," Emma says.

"This is bullshit!" Savannah exclaims from behind me. "If he'd been told the truth when he woke up, none of this would have happened."

"Savannah," Claire warns. "This is no one's fault. Everyone was just doing what they thought was best for Jack."

"And what about what's best for Aria…"

Her voice becomes muffled along with all the other sounds in the kitchen, and all I can hear is the pounding of my own heart, and it's deafening. He can't have gone back home, he just can't. I can't never see him again. My breathing becomes shallow and my hands begin to tingle. Black dots dance in front of my eyes as I struggle to get air into my lungs, and I begin to panic that I can't breathe. Suddenly, I feel someone stand in front of me, their hands on my shoulders as they force me to breathe into a paper bag. After a few minutes, the tingling in my hands stops, and my breathing evens out. The voices become less muffled and I look up into worried faces. Needing to get away, I push back the chair I'm sitting on and stand, hearing it crash to the floor behind me.

"I'm sorry. I need to go." I run out of the kitchen and out of the house. I can hear Savannah behind me, shouting my name, but I keep running and I don't stop until my legs give way. Breathing hard, I drop to my knees in the middle of one of the fields.

"Fuck, Aria!" Savannah gasps. "I haven't run that far since high school." I can't answer her as I sob, ugly tears streaming down my face. "Shit," she mutters, dropping to the ground next to me. Her arms go around my shoulders and I stiffen at first, eventually giving in to her embrace. My head drops onto her lap and I can't seem to stop the flow of tears. She doesn't say anything, her hand softly stroking my hair.

I have no idea how long I cry for, but when I finally manage to stop, my eyes are sore and my head is pounding. Sitting up, I wipe my eyes and draw my knees up to my chest, my arms wrapping around them. "I'm sorry," I whisper to Sav. "I just couldn't stay in the house and let everyone watch me fall apart." My head is down, and I pull at the grass with my fingers.

"I understand, Aria. So what are you going to do?" My head flies up and I look across at her.

"What do you mean?" I ask, frowning. "He's gone. There's nothing to *do*."

"Go after him, Aria. Enough of this 'waiting for him to remember' crap. He needs to know the truth."

"Knowing the truth and feeling it are two different things, Sav," I tell her sadly.

"You think he doesn't have feelings for you? I've seen him with you, Aria. I've seen the way he looks at you. He might not remember you were together, but I know he was falling in love with you all over again."

"You don't know that! We've hardly spent any time together since he was discharged from the hospital."

"And whose fault is that? Zara knew exactly what she was

doing! She knew if you two spent any time together, sparks would fly, which is exactly what happened at the Brass Hall the other night."

I shake my head. "Even if that is true. He still left." My voice breaks and I take a deep breath, not wanting to fall apart again.

"He's a good guy, Aria. In his head he's in a relationship with Zara, no matter how conflicted he feels. He'd be an asshole if he let her travel home on her own after she'd received news like that. Just because he left doesn't mean he wanted to."

I pull myself together and look across at her. "You really think that?"

"You belong together. Zara might think she's won, but you're the one in his heart. It's only a matter of time." I desperately want to believe what she's saying, but am I just delaying the heartbreak by clinging on to something that might never happen? I don't have the answers, and neither does anyone else right now.

"He asked me to go back to England with him," I say quietly.

"What?"

I nod. "Before the accident. He asked me to go home with him when the time came, and I said yes. That's what I was going to tell you in the stables the day of the accident, but Zara interrupted us."

"Oh, Aria." She pulls me into a hug, and I bite down on the inside of my cheek in an attempt to hold it together. It doesn't work and silent tears fall down my cheeks.

"Don't you think it's a little convenient her dad had a stroke, just as you and Jack start to get close?" she says, and I pull out of her embrace and wipe my eyes.

I stare at her, my eyes wide. "You think she's making it up?"

She laughs sarcastically. "I think that woman would do anything to get Jack away from you."

"How would she explain that when they get home and her dad's fine?"

She shrugs her shoulders. "A miraculous recovery maybe?"

"Surely not!"

"I wouldn't put anything past her."

"Why don't you call him?" Savannah suggests. "I know he's lost his phone, but he'll get a replacement when he gets back home?"

"Yeah, maybe." I have no idea what I'd say to him, or even if I could talk without bursting into tears.

She gives me a sad smile, and we sit in comfortable silence for a few minutes. I tear absentmindedly at the grass again while everything Savannah said sinks in. Is she right? Was he falling in love with me? I want to believe it so badly, and I know this pain in my chest that's been ever present since Jack woke up not knowing me won't go anywhere unless we're back together. I also know we don't always get what we want.

Eventually, we head back to the ranch house with Savannah promising to call me later. I can hear voices coming from the den, but I bypass everyone. Unable to face them, I go straight to my room. It's not long before the tears begin to fall again, and I lie curled up on my bed, sobbing into my comforter. Feeling exhausted, I close my eyes, praying my dreams take me to Jack and that I'll wake up and realize this whole thing was a mistake.

CHAPTER 40

Jack

Jacob sleeps for most of the flight and Zara barely utters a word, which leaves me with far too much time to think, and I can't stop thinking of Aria. I can't help but wonder if she was upset when she found out we'd had to leave. I know for sure she'll miss Jacob. She adores him. I wonder if she'll miss me too. My heart hurts every time I think about her, and knowing I won't see her again just isn't something I can comprehend.

It's early morning when we land, and Zara's brother-in-law, Dean, is at the airport to pick us up. I can only remember meeting him once, although I'm sure I've met him multiple times over the past three years. He eyes me warily when we meet though, and I have no idea why. Maybe we don't get on. I make a mental note to ask Zara later.

Once we're in the car, I'm surprised to hear Zara's dad is out of hospital and back home.

"Didn't he have a stroke?" I ask from the back seat, my voice tinged with confusion.

Dean looks across to Zara, his shoulder rising in the subtlest of shrugs.

"Of course he did," Zara snaps. "It must have been a mild one, so they let him go home."

"I'm confused. Didn't we just fly halfway across the world because you thought your dad was going to die?" I hate myself for thinking it, but I'm beginning to wonder if Zara's being completely honest with me.

"I had a message from my sister to tell me my dad had a stroke, Jack," she spits. "What did you expect me to do? It's been a long flight. He's obviously recovered a little while we've been in the air. Would you rather he'd died so your flight back from Texas was worth it?" I sigh, knowing for sure I'm an arse-hole saying that to her. I lean forward and squeeze her shoulder.

"No, of course not. I'm sorry. I'm just tired from the flight."

She doesn't reply, and we're silent for the rest of the journey, eventually pulling up outside what I'm assuming is her parents' house. After unclipping Jacob from his car seat, I open the door.

"Why don't you wait here? I'll just check they're awake," Zara says, looking over her shoulder at me.

"Okay," I say with a frown. I guess it's still early. My body has no idea what time it is with all the traveling. I still climb out of the car and let Jacob run around on their front garden. He's been cooped up for hours and needs to let off some energy. I look up and down the unfamiliar street as I wait for Zara to call us inside. When we first got together, she didn't have much to do with her parents, and I'd only met them twice, both times at our house. We must have been here since Jacob was born though, more than once, I'm guessing. God, I wish I could remember.

I'm pulled from my thoughts when I hear Jacob cry out. He's fallen on the driveway and I rush over, picking him up. I quickly scan my eyes over him, seeing blood on his jeans by his knee. He must have grazed it when he fell. I manage to calm his cries down before walking with him in my arms to the front door which Zara has left slightly ajar. Needing to clean up his knee, I knock lightly on the wood before walking in. Seeing the kitchen right ahead of me, I make my way down the hallway, stopping in my tracks when I hear voices coming from what I assume is the sitting room to my right.

"No!" a woman's voice cries. "I don't want that man in my house!" My eyes widen in surprise when I realize she must be talking about me. "How can you stand to be with him after everything he did to you?" I turn around and make my way to the closed sitting room door, not that I need to be any closer to hear what's been said with how loud she's shouting, but I want to hear Zara's response.

"Mum, I lied. Jack never did any of those things I told you. I was the one who walked out on him, not the other way around, and he never laid a finger on me. Will you please just play along, and I'll tell you everything when he isn't here. Please," she begs. Anger bubbles up inside me and I'm more confused than ever. Her words replay over and over in my head, and I can't comprehend what she's saying. She left me and told her parents I'd hit her? What the fuck is going on? I want to storm in there and confront her, but I want the truth, and after all the lies she's told me, this might be the only time I get to hear it.

"You lied?" her mum says, quieter this time. "Why?"

"I never wanted a baby. I missed my old life, so I left. But it's true what people say. You don't know what you have 'til it's too late, and I want Jack."

"Why do we have to lie to the poor man?" a man's voice asks.

"It's a long story. He had an accident and lost his memory. He doesn't remember we split up. I contacted him before the accident, and he was visiting his sister in America. I decided to fly out and fight for him, but I realized I was too late. He was already in love with someone else. He'd moved on." I stumble at her words, grabbing on to the doorframe to steady myself. She's talking about Aria. She has to be. The now familiar feeling of dread settles in the pit of my stomach, and I know without a doubt I've hurt Aria. Why didn't she just tell me? It must have killed her to see me with Zara. I'm pulled from my thoughts when she carries on talking. "Then he had the accident and woke up missing the last three years of his life. He was in love with me again. He wanted me. I had to get him away from Aria. He was beginning to have feelings for her again and I couldn't let that happen. I told him Dad had a stroke to get him to come home with me."

"How could you do that to him, Zara?" her mum asks, and I can hear the disappointment in her voice.

Having heard enough, I push open the sitting room door,

my body humming with anger. All four people turn to face me, and I see the horror in Zara's eyes as she realizes I've heard everything.

"Please," I say, my voice calmer than I feel. "Answer the question. How could you do that to me, Zara?" Her mouth opens and closes, but no sound comes out. "What were you going to do when my memory came back? Surely you'd know I would *hate* you." I spit the word hate and her eyes widen. She still says nothing, so I continue. "Do you know the saddest part of all this? You didn't mention Jacob at all, only to say you never wanted a baby. He deserves so much better than that."

I turn to her parents. "Please may I use your phone?"

"Who are you calling?" Zara asks, finally finding her voice.

"A taxi. Not that it's any of your business."

"Where are you going?" Her voice sounds desperate, but I don't care.

"Away from you."

"No! Please!" she cries, rushing toward me.

I reach my arm out to stop her. "Don't touch me, or Jacob. I don't know how you can sleep at night knowing what you've done."

"But I love you." Tears are tracking down her face, but I don't care. They're crocodile tears. She's not capable of real emotion.

"You don't know what love is, Zara. You don't do that to someone you love. The only person you love is yourself." I look to her parents again. "The phone? Could I use it, please?"

"Yes, of course. I'll show you where it is," her mum says sadly. I follow her into the kitchen, and she gestures to the phone on the wall. "I'm so sorry, Jack. We had no idea. She told us lie after lie."

"I know. But please know I would never lay a finger on her. Not even now when I'm so angry I can't see straight." She nods, her eyes dropping to Jacob, whose head is on my shoulder.

"He's beautiful. I wish we could have seen him."

I sigh. "You can see him anytime, Mrs. Edwards. Just as long as Zara isn't here."

"Thank you, and please call me Ruth." I smile at her. It's not her fault Zara is crazy, and knowing she's missed out on Jacob's life when she wanted to see him makes me sad.

"Would you have a plaster? He's fallen on the driveway and cut open his knee." Her eyes drop to the blood on his jeans.

"Of course." She walks toward me and places her hand on Jacob's back. "You have been such a brave boy. Shall we get you a plaster while Daddy uses the phone?" Her eyes meet mine and I give her a small smile. She holds her arms out to him and he looks up to me for reassurance. When I nod, he cautiously leans forward for her to take him. She puts him on the counter and pulls up his jeans. "There's a local taxi number on the wall by the phone. I'm so sorry it's come to this, Jack."

"Me too."

I have to ask Ruth for the address when I order a taxi, and the woman on the phone promises me a car in around ten minutes. They feel like the longest ten minutes of my life, as I wait in the kitchen with Jacob. My mind swirls with a million questions, but I don't want to ask Zara and she makes no attempt to come and speak to us anyway, which I'm grateful for. I can't be held responsible for what I'd say to her if she did. I'll ask all my questions when I get to the ranch. At least I know the people there love me and I'll be getting the truth. When the car arrives, we say goodbye to Ruth and John, Zara's dad, who's joined us in the kitchen.

"Where will you go?" Ruth asks as she kisses Jacob goodbye.

"To a hotel to try and get a few hours' sleep, then back to the airport. I've unknowingly hurt someone I love, and I need to put that right."

"I'm so sorry this happened. Please come back and see us soon. We'd love to get to know you and Jacob better." I give her a small smile, and with Jacob in my arms, make for the front door. We've almost made it when Zara emerges from the sitting room, blocking the exit.

"Please don't go. I'm sorry. I never meant to hurt you."

John steps in front of me and ushers Zara out of the way. "It's over, Zara. Let them go."

"Thank you," I tell him as I pass them both and walk outside. I make quick work of switching Jacob's car seat over as well as our luggage, which is still in the boot of Dean's car, before strapping him securely into his seat. I'm just about to climb in myself when Zara comes running down the driveway.

"Wait!" she shouts, and I roll my eyes and take a deep breath before turning to face her. "I have your phone." My hands ball into fists at my sides and my jaw clenches. I don't trust myself to say anything, so I uncurl one of my fisted hands and hold it out. She hesitates for a second before placing the phone in my hand. I can't even bring myself to look at her, and I turn away, sliding into the car. Slamming the door, I feel a sense of relief as the car pulls away, leaving Zara and that fucked-up part of my life behind me.

I ask the driver to take us back to the airport, and to any

one of the hotels. I don't care which, I just need to sleep. I turn my phone on and wait for it to power up. When it does, the image on my home screen tells me exactly why Zara took my phone. Aria. Beautiful, perfect Aria. A picture of the two of us wrapped up in each other's arms fills the screen, and we look so happy. I touch the image, my fingers brushing over her cheek. I can't imagine what she must be feeling right now. I've spent the last week and a half thinking Zara was my girlfriend, when all the time, she was. No wonder I hadn't seen her around the house; I bet she couldn't stand to be there. Clicking into my photos, I see picture after picture of Aria, some with Jacob and some with me. She's smiling in all of them, and I suddenly realize I haven't seen a smile that genuine on her face since the day I woke up at hospital, only for it to be dashed when I asked for Zara. God, I've been an idiot.

"Ria!" Jacob shouts, and I jump, lost in my thoughts. Looking across at him, I smile when I see him looking at my screen. I can hear the excitement in his voice, and I know how much he loves her.

"Yeah, buddy. It's Aria. Shall we go back to the ranch and see her?"

"Yes!" he cries, kicking his legs in his car seat.

I lean forward. "Change of plan," I say to the driver. "Could you take us to departures?"

"Sure. Eager to get somewhere?" he asks.

"Yeah, you could say that."

Dragging my eyes off the images of Aria, I open Google and search for flights to Austin. There's one leaving in a few hours, and I book us two tickets. I can sleep on the plane. I'm too eager to get back to Aria. Even if I did book a hotel room, I doubt I'd sleep. When I've finished booking the tickets, I pull up her number, my fingers hovering over the call button. I want to speak to her desperately, but what I have to tell her will sound better in person. In less than twenty-four hours, she'll be in my arms, and hopefully this nightmare will be over.

CHAPTER 41

Aria

$\mathcal{A}$fter a fitful night's sleep, I drag my tired body into the bathroom. Gripping on to the vanity, I lift my head, wincing when I see my reflection. I look exhausted, and my eyes are red and puffy from all the crying. I hoped I'd go to sleep and wake up realizing this had been some horrible nightmare. When I opened my eyes this morning, reality had come crashing down on me, along with the crushing pain in my chest.

I brush my teeth before climbing into the shower. I don't wait for the water to warm up, but I barely feel the ice-cold water on my skin, my whole body numb. When the water does warm up, I tilt my head back and let it run over my face, washing my tears away.

I spend far too long under the water, my mind full of Jack and all the time we spent together. It hurts to remember now, but I know it won't always. I thought about what Savannah said yesterday. I thought about it all night, but I'm not going after him. I love him. I love him more than I ever thought possible, but despite what Savannah says, he doesn't feel the same. There might have been an attraction there for him after the accident, but nothing more.

When I'm finally dressed, I contemplate going downstairs. Emma, Libby, and Claire had all come to my room last night, but I'd sent them away, not wanting to talk. I know they mean well, but I just wanted to be on my own. Knowing I can't stay locked away forever, I head downstairs. I'm relieved when I find the house empty. I catch sight of the clock in the entryway, and it's later than I thought, 11:30 a.m. I'd either woken up late, or spent far longer in the shower than I thought.

Descending the porch steps, I round the house and make for the stables. I'm hoping Colt or Taylor will have seen to the horses this morning, and when I enter, I breathe a sigh of relief that the horses have been taken care of. They all have clean stalls and fresh food. Not knowing what to do, I wander aimlessly from stall to stall, stroking each horse. This is my safe place, the place I love, and right now I don't want to be anywhere else.

"I thought I might find you in here," Libby says, and I turn around to see her walking toward me with Annie in the stroller.

"A creature of habit, I guess," I say sadly, hugging her when she reaches me. I peek into Annie's stroller to see her fast asleep. "She's beautiful, Lib. Does she ever wake up? I don't think I've ever seen her awake," I ask, hoping to keep Libby from asking how I am.

She laughs. "Oh, yes. She's usually awake all night and asleep all day. She's a little upside down at the moment."

"She'll sort herself out. I guess it's all new to her."

"How are you, Aria?" Her eyes meet mine and I shrug.

"I'll be okay. What choice do I have?"

"Have you tried calling him?"

I shake my head. "I wouldn't know what to say." I fiddle with the hem of my tank, my eyes dropping to my fingers. "Have you heard from him? Did he land safely?"

"I don't know. He hasn't called. I've tried to call him, but it goes straight to voicemail. Maybe he hasn't had time to get a replacement phone yet."

"Maybe," I whisper. Or maybe he's just with Zara, and he doesn't have time to think about anyone else. I don't voice the last part; I don't want to upset Lib. I don't blame him. He doesn't remember what we shared. He remembers Zara.

"Shall we take a walk? You can push," she says, gesturing to the stroller. I smile and nod.

We walk in silence for a few minutes before Libby puts her hand on my arm, forcing me to stop. "I spoke to Savannah. Have you thought about what she said? About going after him?"

"I'm not going, Lib. Even if I went and told him everything, he's got to feel it and he doesn't, so what would be the point?"

"How do you know he doesn't?"

I gesture around us. "Do you see him here?"

"But—"

"No buts. It hurts. It hurts more than I ever thought possible, but maybe he's where he needs to be, and I'm where I need to be."

"I can't believe that, Aria. I just can't. You belong together. When he remembers—"

"He might never remember."

"He will," she insists. "Please don't give up on him."

"I wish I had your confidence," I tell her sadly. We've continued to walk, and I look up, seeing that we've ended up outside Savannah's.

"I thought some girl time might be in order. Quinn is here too."

I turn and pull her into a hug. "Thank you, Lib."

I set some ground rules once we're inside, the main one being that no one mentions Jack. I can see Savannah isn't happy, but I can't spend all day talking about what's happened. I'd go insane. She reluctantly agrees, and I can't love these women more for taking my mind off everything. I knew when I first got involved with Jack I'd end up losing my heart to him. I also knew if the worst happened and he left, these women would have my back, and I'd been right. They are my family, and I can't imagine being without them.

Savannah prepares what looks like a mountain of food for lunch, which we eat in the shade of the seating area outside. I use the word "eat" loosely, as I can't bring myself to eat much, my stomach churning every time Jack invades my thoughts, which is often. I know Sav, Quinn, and Lib notice, but they don't say anything, and I'm grateful for that. After we've eaten, I help Savannah clear the dishes, while Libby and Quinn see to Annie.

"Did you speak to Josh about the whole baby thing?" I ask

as I pass her the dirty plates to fill the dishwasher. Looking over her shoulder, she grins at me. "I'll take that as a yes! What happened?"

"Seems he knows me better than I give him credit for."

"What do you mean?"

"He brought it up before I did. He said he's seen me around Annie and wanted to know if there was any chance we could have a child together. He's been to see a fertility doctor in Austin!"

"Oh, wow, Savannah. What did the doctor say?"

"He's had a bunch of tests, and while the doctor told him it's almost impossible for me to get pregnant naturally, he said we could try IVF. Apparently, they can take a single sperm, inject it into one of my harvested eggs and watch it fertilize in a lab. Isn't that amazing? We have an appointment to discuss it all next week."

"That's incredible, Sav! Does anyone else know?"

She shakes her head. "No, not yet. We wanted to speak to the doctor together first. I'll need to have a few tests, and as long as everything is okay, then we'll be good to go."

"Your secret is safe with me. I am *so* happy for you." She smiles at me before pulling me in for a hug. I am happy for her. She's one of my best friends and I want nothing more than for her to be happy, but I can't help wondering when it's going to be my turn. I thought I'd found it with Jack, but it seems fate has other ideas, and now I'm alone again. Being left hurt and alone was my biggest worry when Jack and I first got together, but despite that, the old saying is true: it's better to have loved and lost than to never have loved at all. If I had to do it all over again, I would. It doesn't stop the heart-crushing pain I'm feeling right now though, but I'll never regret Jack walking into my life.

CHAPTER 42

Jack

I manage a few broken hours of sleep on the plane journey back to Austin. I'm exhausted, but the adrenaline and the thought of holding Aria in my arms again keeps me going. Jacob has been an absolute star. I'd been expecting tantrums and meltdowns with all the traveling and time differences, but he's surprised the hell out of me and slept for the majority of both plane journeys. I couldn't have asked for more.

We jump in a cab at arrivals and I give the ranch address to the driver. Once we're on the way, he makes small talk, and I'm grateful for the distraction. Despite that, my knee bounces up and down nervously, and I can't help the apprehension that builds in the pit of my stomach the closer we get to Marble Falls.

After what feels like forever, the driver turns off the main highway and up the driveway that leads to the house. It's falling dark by the time we arrive, and the lights from the cab illuminate the drive. Climbing out, I pull the luggage from the boot and get Jacob's car seat out. I pay the driver, then watch as he drives away, gravel and dirt spitting up behind him. Taking a deep breath, I take Jacob's hand and head up the porch steps. I leave the bags on the drive. They can wait until later, Aria can't.

I push open the front door and silently walk in. The house is quiet, and I wonder where everyone is. Glancing into the kitchen as we walk past, I see it's empty, so we continue along the hallway, coming to a stop outside the door to the den. I can hear voices and the hum of the TV playing behind the door. Opening it slowly, we walk in.

"Jack!" my mum exclaims, jumping up from the sofa and rushing toward us. "What are you doing here? Is everything okay?" She reaches down to Jacob and picks him up, showering kisses on his face like we've been gone for months rather than a couple of days. I glance around the room, my dad, Aunt Claire, and Uncle Ryan looking back at me. Aria isn't here though, and I wonder if she's in her room. "Well?" she asks when I don't answer her.

"I came back for Aria."

She gasps. "You remember?"

"No. It's a pretty long story, but Zara lied and I know everything. I need to find Aria. Do you know where she is?"

"Libby took her to Savannah's. I think she's still there,"

Aunt Claire says, a smile on her face. "I'm so glad you came back, Jack." I smile at her before looking at my mum.

"Can you watch Jacob? I need to go and find her."

"Yes! Of course. Go!" She takes my arm and propels me out into the hallway. "Good luck!"

I jog down the porch steps and run all the way to Savannah's, out of breath by the time the house comes into view. Waiting until I've caught my breath, I wipe my sweaty hands down my jeans before I knock on the door. It feels like a lifetime before the door swings open and I come face-to-face with Josh. The shock on his face tells me I was the last person he was expecting. I can't say I blame him after the way I left.

"Jack! Man, it's good to see you."

"You too, Josh. Is Aria here?"

He nods and smiles. "Your memory came back, and you've come to claim your woman, right?"

I chuckle. "No. My memory didn't come back." His eyes widen and I see the look of horror on his face when he realizes what he's said. "Don't worry. I know I'm meant to be with Aria. Turns out Zara's a lying bitch, and while I don't remember how me and Aria got together, I know we belong together."

"About fucking time. No offense," he says sheepishly.

"None taken. Now, can I come in and see my girl?"

"Absolutely. Everyone's out back."

He steps aside and I walk in, following him through the house and into the kitchen where the bi-folding doors lead onto the outdoor seating area. Libby and Mason sit on one sofa, with Brody and Quinn on the another. I can smell that Josh has the barbecue going, and Savannah is standing over it. My breath catches in my throat when I see Aria sitting on the chair, her legs curled up under her. I stop in my tracks, suddenly over-come with nerves. I've hurt her. What if she doesn't forgive me? What if she doesn't want to put her heart on the line again?

"You okay, man?" Josh asks, coming back to me when he realizes I'm not behind him.

"Yeah. I just need a minute."

"She loves you, Jack. She's going to be happy you're here."

"God, I hope so."

He slaps me on the shoulder and walks outside. "We have a visitor," he announces. Taking a deep breath, I follow him outside.

My eyes are fixed on Aria, and she doesn't look up at first. Her head is down as her fingers play with the stem of her wine-glass. She looks so sad, and I can see from her puffy red eyes she's been crying. My heart twists in my chest, knowing I'm the reason for her tears. I never want to be the reason she cries again. She finally looks up when Libby spots me and shouts my name.

"Jack! Oh my God! You came back." She rushes over to me, flinging her arms around my neck. I hug her back, my gaze fixed on Aria. Her eyes are wide, and I can see her chest moving up and down rapidly. "What happened? Is Jacob with you?" Libby asks, and I tear my eyes off Aria to look at her.

"Jacob's with Mum and Dad." My eyes flick to Aria again before coming back to Lib. "Can I speak to Aria first and then I'll explain?"

She smiles and nods. "I'm so glad you came back."

I drop my arms from around her waist and cross the small space to where Aria is sitting. "Hi," I say quietly. She looks so beautiful. I want to take her in my arms and kiss her, but I don't. Not yet.

"Hi." Her voice is barely above a whisper, but I can hear the tremble in it.

"Can we go for a walk?" I ask, holding my hand out to her. She nods and places her small hand in mine. Pulling her to her feet, I reach up and push a stray strand of her hair behind her ear. "Let's go." I turn around to see everyone watching us. "We'll be back," I tell them, leading Aria through the side gate.

We walk hand in hand toward the river, and when I don't say anything, she squeezes my hand. "You came back," she says softly. I stop and turn to face her, taking her other hand in mine.

"I'm so sorry I left."

"I understand. How is Zara's dad?"

I can't believe this woman. After everything Zara put her through, she's still concerned about how her dad is.

"You're pretty incredible, you know that?"

"What?" she asks, her eyes looking anywhere but at me.

"Look at me, Aria." I wait until she lifts her head. "I know what Zara did. I know how much she must have hurt you." I pause. "How much I must have hurt you."

"Jack—"

"Wait, let me finish." She nods and holds my gaze. "Zara's dad didn't have a stroke." She gasps, her eye wide. "She made it up to get me to leave."

Her eyebrows pull together in a frown. "How did she think she would get away with that?"

"She was hoping she could convince her parents to play along. Unfortunately for her, I overheard her, and everything came out."

"Everything?"

I nod. "I know I'm not with Zara and haven't been for months, and that I came here with Jacob and fell in love with you."

"You remember!" she gasps.

"No, baby." Her face falls and I pull her against me. "I don't need to remember. I can feel it. I can feel the pull between us. I haven't been able to stop thinking about you since the hospital. Zara must have seen that. She knew it was only a matter of time before I realized."

"Realized what?"

"That we're meant to be together." My eyes drop to her lips and her tongue darts out to lick them. "Can I kiss you now? I might go mad if I have to wait a minute longer." Her face erupts into a smile, and I chuckle. "What?"

"You said those exact words to me the first time we kissed."

"Did I?" She nods. "And what was your answer?"

"I said yes," she whispers.

I smile and cup her face with my hand, my fingers stroking her cheek. "Is it still a yes?"

"Yes."

I know I've kissed her before, but it's like the first time all over again for me, and nervous butterflies take flight in my stomach. Lowering my head, I gently brush my lips against hers. I move back a little, my eyes searching hers. She smiles before closing the distance and crashing her lips against mine. Her arms wind around my neck and I circle her waist, pulling her harder against me. I swipe my tongue against her bottom lip, seeking entrance. She opens up to me, her tongue colliding with mine. I can't get enough of her, my cock hardening in my jeans as she consumes me. How I could ever forget her and how she makes me feel, I'll never understand. She must be able to feel the effect she's having on me, and as much as I want to make love to her, I need to know what she's thinking.

I pull out of the kiss and we're both panting hard as I rest my forehead on her. "Fuck, Aria. Is it always like that?"

"Yeah." She chuckles. "Always." She pauses and lifts her head. "I've missed you so much, Jack. When your mom said you'd gone home, I thought I'd never see you again."

"Aria, you should know I was already having doubts about Zara. I was so unhappy. Nothing felt right unless I was with you. I couldn't explain it. I just knew I was drawn to you."

She bites down on her bottom lip, uncertainty etched on her face. "Can I ask you something?"

"You can ask me anything, Aria."

She takes a deep breath as if preparing herself. "Did you and Zara…" She stops and clears her throat. "Were you and Zara… *together?*"

"No, baby. I couldn't bring myself to. She tried, but…" Relief washes over her face before she lets out a breath. "It just didn't feel right," I say quietly.

"Thank you for telling me."

"I'm sorry you had to ask that. I can't imagine how hard it must have been for you. I'm so sorry I can't remember us."

"It's okay, Jack. You just get to experience everything for the first time again. I'm a little jealous," she jokes.

"You're not mad at me?"

She frowns. "Mad at you? Why would I be mad at you? I lo…" She trails off, and I know she's worried about saying those words. Worried I'm not there yet. She has nothing to worry about.

"Say it," I whisper, my forehead dropping back on hers.

"I love you."

"I love you too, baby." I lift my head to see silent tears running down her cheeks, and my heart stutters. "Hey, please don't cry. I swore I'd never be the reason for your tears again."

"They're happy tears, Jack. I promise."

Cupping her face, I wipe the tears away with my thumbs. "I know we have a lot to talk about, but we're good, right?"

"We're more than good."

"I want to make love to you."

She smiles and pulls my lips to hers. "I like the sound of that," she mutters against my mouth.

An image of making love to her in the rain flashes through my head, and I pull back sharply. Was that a memory or just wishful thinking?

"What's wrong?"

"Aria, did we ever make love in the rain?" I almost hold my breath as I wait for her answer.

"Yes," she whispers, excitement flicking across her eyes. "Do you remember?"

"I... I think so." I close my eyes. "At the river? Under the oak tree?"

"Yes!" she squeals, jumping up and down. "That was the first time we made love."

"And that's why you were quiet when I said I hadn't been there since the week of Lib and Mason's wedding?"

She nods and I pull her close. "Do you remember anything else?"

"Not yet, but if that was a memory, then hopefully it's just a matter of time. I can't wait to remember every second with you, Aria, and I can't wait for us to make even more memories."

"You asked me to go home with you, the day before the accident." Her voice is low and full of uncertainty. I can't remember asking her, but knowing how I feel about her, I'm not surprised I did.

"What did you say?"

"I said yes."

I smile. "And you still want to?"

"Yes, if you still want me to."

"Maybe we have two options now. Maybe me and Jacob could stay here?"

Her eyebrows rise in question. "Stay here? What about Zara?"

I shrug. "I don't care about Zara. She's not interested in Jacob. She never was. I don't want him around someone as poisonous as her. I'm pretty sure she won't question me if I tell her I'm moving here. Not after what she's done. If she kicks up a fuss, then we have other options. One thing I do know is I'm *never* being away from you again."

A beautiful smile erupts on her face. "Is this really happening?"

"You'd better believe it is. You are it for me, Aria. Not even a crazy ex, a fractured skull, or short-term memory loss can keep me away from you."

She giggles. "Kiss me again?"

Smiling, I drop my mouth to hers, losing myself in her again. I've no idea if my memory will come back, but I'm not worried about that anymore. I know without any hesitation how

I feel about Aria, how I will always feel about her. We'll make new memories, the three of us, and hopefully give Jacob a brother or sister one day, maybe both. If my memories do come back, then that's a bonus, but I know I don't need them. I know who I am, and I know who I'm meant to be with. It's Aria. It's always been Aria.

EPILOGUE

Aria – six months later

"I think that's all the boxes, baby," Jack calls from the driveway, and I beckon him inside, out of the cold. Summers in Marble Falls might be hot, but the winters are cold, and we'd unwittingly chosen to move on the coldest weekend of the year.

"Come inside. It's freezing," I shout, dancing around in the doorway to keep warm.

"Baby, trust me, it isn't that cold. You should live in the UK!" He walks in and wraps his arms around me. "How about I warm you up?"

"As good as that sounds, your whole family is in the living room, and I think they may wonder where we've gone if we sneak upstairs."

"Dammit! Why does my family have to be so helpful? They could have waited until we'd moved in and christened every room before visiting."

I smack him gently on his chest. "Shh, they'll hear you."

"I don't care. I want to make love to my fiancée."

I grin like an idiot, loving it when he calls me that. He proposed on New Year's Eve, under the stars down by the Colorado River, and I didn't hesitate to say yes. I love this man with everything I have. There was never any doubt I will spend the rest of my life with him.

"You'll have to wait until they're all gone," I tease.

"Would it be rude to ask them to leave?"

"Yes!" I laugh, tugging him out of the entryway and into the living room.

"We heard every word of that, you know!" Josh exclaims when we walk in. "You do know I shifted a load of boxes for you today, Davis!" His voice is full of humor, so I know he's joking.

Jack shrugs. "I still want you all to go."

"Jack," I hiss, thankful his parents are in the kitchen with Claire and Ryan and can't hear him. He wraps his arms around me and pulls me into his side.

"It's not my fault I can't keep my hands off you. You shouldn't be so hot." I roll my eyes at him and push his hands away.

"Does everyone want pizza?" I shout, turning and sticking my tongue out at Jack, who groans when he realizes no one will be leaving anytime soon.

"Yes!" Hope and Jacob shout in unison, and I laugh.

"I thought you two might say yes. Anyone else?"

After receiving a chorus of yeses, I make my way into the entryway, away from the noise to make the call. I place the order, giving over our new address, and take a seat on the stairs. The last six months have been some of the best months of my life, and I still have to pinch myself every day that I ever got so lucky. After Jack's first memory came back, everything else he'd forgotten slowly trickled through as well. It was great he'd begun to remember our relationship, but for me, the return of his memories with Jacob were what mattered the most. I know how he struggled not being able to remember the important milestones in his life, so when those memories started to return, I couldn't have been happier for him. It did cause a few issues though, as along with those memories came Zara, and what she did to him. He felt guilty about the time he spent with her after the accident, knowing how much she'd lied to him and how hurt I'd been. I assured him I didn't blame him, but it took some working through, and now we are even stronger.

As for Zara, Jack contacted a lawyer back in the UK and set the paperwork in motion for Zara to give up her parental rights to Jacob. She never fought us once, signing the paperwork as soon as she received it. As happy as that made us, it was bittersweet for Jacob, knowing one day he would have to know the truth. I love him like he's mine though, and he's even recently started calling me Mommy, which I love. He will know about Zara, but only when he's old enough to understand. I hope he feels enough love from me and Jack to never have to feel like he's missed out.

Jack and I have decided on a short engagement, and Quinn is going to help plan the wedding. We want to get married at the ranch where it all began, and I can't wait to be Mrs. Aria

Davis. I'll have to wait a couple of months for my wedding planner though, considering she's just given birth to twins. Asher and Sofia were born by C-section a few days ago. They came a little early at thirty-six weeks, but they were good weights. Asher weighed 4lb 8oz, and Sofia, a little smaller at 4lb 2oz. Both are absolutely perfect. They had to spend a couple of days in the NICU, but both are doing well and they're coming home from the hospital today. I can't wait to see them in person and get to hold them. Jack and I have talked babies and we've both said as soon as we're married, we're going to try. I know from Savannah and Josh's struggles that nothing is guaranteed. It took three rounds of IVF for Savannah to get pregnant, and although she's only eight weeks along, they've had a sonogram, and all looks good. I have everything crossed it all works out for them. I know if it doesn't happen for us, how lucky we are to have Jacob, but I can't say I don't long to carry Jack's baby.

"What are you doing out here, sweetheart?" Jack asks as he comes into the entryway, concern lacing his voice. "Is everything okay?" I look at him and my heart pounds out of my chest. I'm so in love with him. I never thought I could feel this way, and sometimes the intensity of my feelings scares me. I don't worry though. I know Jack will always be there to catch me if I fall.

"Everything is perfect. Do you know how happy I am?"

He smiles. "I think so. About as happy as I am?"

"Happier," I tell him, standing up and throwing my arms around him.

"I doubt that," he whispers into my hair as he holds me close.

"I love you."

"I love you too, Aria."

He kisses me, and I get lost in him like I always do when he kisses me. My body comes alive, and it's now me wishing we didn't have a houseful of guests. I love how close everyone is though, and I know they will always be there for us, just like we will always be there for them. We might have taken the long way, but I know for sure we're finally home.

THE END

ALSO BY LAURA FARR

Healing Hearts Series

Taking Chances (Healing Hearts book 1)

Defying Gravity (Healing Hearts book 2)

Whatever it Takes (Healing Hearts book 3)

The Long Way Home (Healing Hearts book 4)

Christmas at the Cabin (Healing Hearts short story)

Standalones

Pieces of Me

Crossing the Line

Sweet Montana Kisses

The Paris Pact

The Hope Creek Series

Loving Paisley (Hope Creek book 1)

SOCIAL MEDIA LINKS

Facebook Profile: https://www.facebook.com/laura.farr.547

Facebook Page: https://www.facebook.com/Laura-Farr-Author-191769224641474/

Instagram: https://www.instagram.com/laurafarr_author/

Twitter: @laurafarr4

TikTok: @laurafarrauthor

Printed in Great Britain
by Amazon

81567565R00203